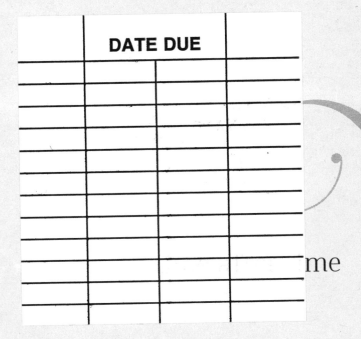

	DATE DUE		

me

time
after
time

TAMARA IRELAND STONE

SCHOLASTIC INC.

ISBN 978-0-545-80062-4

12 11 10 9 8 7 6 5 4 3 2 1   14 15 16 17 18 19/0

Printed in the U.S.A.   40

First Scholastic printing, September 2014

Interior design by Abby Kuperstock

For Aidan and Lauren, siblings and best friends.
Carriers of my heart.

Time will explain.

JANE AUSTEN

time after time

august 2012

1

san francisco, california

Nothing's changed. I was gone for three months, I've been home for three more, and still, everything here is exactly the same as it was before I left.

"You guys going to Megan's party next week?" Sam asks.

My gaze travels around the circle as everyone nods. Of course they're going. Summer is almost over and Megan's parents are loaded and never home, a combination that pretty much guarantees copious opportunities to drink and hook up.

"What about you?" Sam points at me with his chin. "You in, Coop?"

"Can't," I say, avoiding his eyes. "I'll be out of town." I tip my head back and down my Gatorade. The eight of us have been skating around Lafayette Park for the last hour and I'm parched.

"Again?" He reaches in for a handful of Doritos and then passes the bag around. "You missed her last party, and that was epic." Everyone nods again. Ryan parrots Sam with a "Seriously epic."

I look away as I shrug it off. "I hate to miss it, but I promised my mom I'd go see my grandmother before school starts." I feel a little guilty about these back-to-back lies: I probably wouldn't go to Megan's party, even if I was sticking around, and my mom has no idea that I'm going to see my grandmother.

Sam clears his throat and looks around the circle. "Who's got the chips?" Drew takes a big handful and everyone keeps the bag moving until it eventually makes its way back to Sam. "You sure there isn't another reason you're leaving town?" he asks. The crunching stops as all the guys turn and look at us, waiting for me to reply.

I lean back on my skateboard. "Like what?" My heart starts racing, but I force myself to stay still. To look cool and unfazed. I push Anna out of my mind, hoping that will make me look more convincing.

A smile tugs at the corners of Sam's mouth. I can feel the rest of the guys shifting in place around us. Sam suddenly reaches into the bag and chucks a chip at my head, and I duck out of the way as it flies past me. "I'm just giving you shit," he says, and everyone laughs as the crunching sounds return.

Ryan pulls his phone from his pocket and checks the screen. "Break's over." He stands up, pops his board into his hand, and takes off for the flat cement area surrounded by NO SKATE-BOARDING signs. He's right. We've probably got another ten minutes before one of the neighbors calls the cops.

Everyone else takes off, but Sam and I hang behind. I hold the chip bag out to him, and just as he's about to take it, I tip my head back and shake the rest of the crumbs into my mouth.

"Here." I hand it to him.

"You suck," he says, but he's smiling as he takes the empty bag from me and stuffs it into his backpack. I can see him staring at me out of the corner of my eye, but then he shakes his head hard and looks away. "So," he says, intentionally making his voice sound lighter. "Lindsey and I ran into her at the movies the other night."

"Her?" I wipe the grease and chip dust from my mouth with my shirtsleeve. "*Her* who?"

He looks at me like he can't believe I'd ask. "Megan." Then he adds, "*Hot* Megan."

"The one who throws all the parties?"

"Yes, that Megan. How many *hot* Megans do you know?"

I shrug. "I don't know. At least"—I count on my fingers—"four." He rolls his eyes.

"Well, I don't know about the other three, but this one asked about you. Again. She told me to make sure I bring you to her party this time." He looks at me expectantly, as if I should leap up off the ground and hurry home to rearrange my flight. Instead, I stand up slowly and reach for my board.

"Sorry, I would, but—"

"I know," he says. "Your grandma. In Illinois. Who's sick."

"Exactly."

Sam stands up too, and steps hard on the end of his board so it flips into his hand. "Look, you've managed to avoid her all summer, but when school starts next week, you won't have a choice. The way I see it, there is only one reason you wouldn't ask Megan out."

"Because she's kind of . . . vacuous?" She's a junior, a year younger than all of us, and I haven't spoken to her long enough to know if this is true or not. But I feel compelled to steer Sam away from his "one reason."

He looks back at me. "If you really don't like her, I get it. But she's Lindsey's friend, you know? The four of us could go out sometime. It might be fun." My mind flashes on an image of Anna, Emma, Justin, and me, walking into a movie theater, my arm draped over Anna's shoulder and Emma's arm threaded through Justin's. I already have a "four of us." Or at least, I did.

I run my hand through my hair. "I'll think about it, okay?" I won't, but hopefully I put enough sincerity in my voice to make him think I will.

"Don't think about it. Just ask her out. Because, seriously, she's nice and really cool and, in my humble opinion, not at all vacuous. And Lindsey likes her," he adds, knowing that could be a selling point.

The rest of the guys come back to grab their stuff and I'm relieved. They mutter good-byes and start down the path that leads to the bottom of the hill. Sam follows them, but then stops and looks back at me. "You coming?"

"I'm going to grab a coffee," I say, gesturing toward the Fillmore Street shops in the opposite direction. He gives me a quick "See ya" and takes off with everyone else as I head the other way.

When they're out of sight, I double back to the bench overlooking the bay and watch the sailboats skim across the water.

Nothing's changed, but everything's different now. Because Anna sat here once, right next to me, and handed me a letter that told me I'd meet her someday. I wish she'd warned me that once I had, I wouldn't quite know how to be here without her.

2

When I reach our house at the top of the hill, I open the front door and toss my skateboard and backpack on the floor in the foyer next to the giant houseplant. I'm heading upstairs to my room when I hear something strange coming from the kitchen. It sounds like chopping. And . . . singing.

Dad shouldn't be home from work yet and Mom had a planning meeting for one of her fund-raisers tonight. I turn around and head for the kitchen, and that's where I find my sister, Brooke. Her hair is pulled back in a ponytail and she's standing at the island, surrounded by vegetables.

She's now humming under her breath as she brings her knife down hard and slides it through a bundle of asparagus.

"What on earth are you doing?" I ask, and she looks up wearing a smile and gives me a little wave with the knife. She goes back to chopping as I walk around the kitchen, staring at the mountain of fresh produce, assessing the situation.

"I thought I'd make stir fry for dinner," she says proudly.

I stand next to her, leaning back against the counter. "Since when do you know how to make stir fry?"

She shrugs and continues chopping. "I don't. I'm practicing for my new dorm-food-free life. Caroline texted me earlier and right this minute, as we speak, she is lugging boxes from her Prius into our new apartment. Shona will be there tomorrow." She looks over at me. "One of us is going to need to know how to cook."

Brooke sets the knife on the cutting board, then gathers up the asparagus and drops it into a bowl. Then she brushes her hands together. "In a few more days I'll be back in Boulder, done with the dorms forever and settling into my new room." She looks right into my eyes. "And I'll be living with people I actually like again. Cool roommates. Like I had in Chicago."

Brooke and I have spent most of our summer talking about the three months I spent in 1995 Evanston while she was stuck in 1994 Chicago. She told me about the two roommates she found through the *Sun-Times* and the loft they shared in Wrigleyville. How she spent her days waiting tables at a local restaurant and her evenings watching live music at the local clubs. Her roommates liked everything, from jazz to punk, and they saw it all. Even folk night every Tuesday, where a heavyset woman sat on a wooden stool with her acoustic guitar, playing old songs like "American Pie" and "Leaving on a Jet Plane" to a packed house that sang along. As I suspected she would, Brooke settled in just fine. And like me, she would have been happy to stay where she was a lot longer.

But one Sunday afternoon, she and her roommates were hanging out on the rooftop deck, enjoying the sun and reading the paper, when one of them spotted a story about the city's plans to demolish the Chicago Stadium. Brooke's ears perked up. She hadn't been back in over two months—not since the night the two of us lost each other.

That afternoon she took an El train and two buses to the stadium. It was closed, but she walked around, peeking through the windows, trying to get a better view, and remembering how she watched me disappear before her eyes while Pearl Jam played on stage.

She made it all the way to the back entrance before she felt the stabbing pain in her stomach, and less than a minute later she was doubled over, screaming and squeezing her eyes shut. When she opened them again, she was crouched down in the same position, but the Chicago Stadium was gone, her Chicago roommates were gone, and she was alone in my room in San Francisco in the exact spot we originally left from.

"So . . ." Brooke reaches for the broccoli and goes back to chopping. "Are you still going to see Anna?"

There's no one else home, but I still take a paranoid glance around the kitchen before I answer. "Yeah. She gets back from her exchange on Saturday. I thought I'd go on Wednesday. Give her a few days to see her friends and get settled post-Mexico."

"And what are you going to tell Mom?"

I shrug. "I already told her: I'm going on a climbing trip with Sam."

Now it's Brooke's turn to scan the room and verify that we're still alone. "You know," she says quietly, "you'd make things a lot easier on yourself if you'd just go to Evanston and return back here as if you never left."

I stare at her but she doesn't look up. "And do three whole days over again? If *I* do those days over, I'm pretty sure that means *you* do, too. You really want to do over three entire days of your life?"

"That depends," she says. "If I got another speeding ticket, that'd be a plus. But if I met some amazing guy and you wiped him out, I'd never forgive you." Brooke glances up and shoots me a grin. "Not that I'd remember any of this."

"Well, I have no idea what I'd wipe out the second time around. So, if it's all the same to you, I'm going to stick with the climbing thing."

Brooke clears her throat. "Of course, you could also make it easier on yourself by just telling Mom and Dad where you're going."

"You know I can't do that."

Brooke knows everything, but I've said very little to my parents about my time in Evanston. Surprisingly, they barely asked any questions, not even about my grandmother, Maggie. They just sat me down in the living room and told me that the traveling needed to stop immediately. That it's far too dangerous, and I don't have control over it. And that it's time I started "living in the present," as Mom put it. "Like a normal person." I don't think Dad agreed completely, but he sat by her side and nodded anyway.

~~~~~~

That was three months ago. I don't even want to think about how furious Mom would be if she found out about all the concerts Brooke and I have traveled to this summer. Or that I went to 1995 La Paz last week. Or that, say, Anna Greene exists.

"I have an idea." Brooke elbows me and says, "Take me with you," like it's no big deal.

I laugh.

"No way, Brooke." She gives me a pleading look, as if that will have an impact on my decision.

"No," I repeat, this time with a little more weight in my voice. "Besides, you'd blow my cover. Climbing trips require *camping*." I raise my eyebrows and stare at her. "Mom and Dad would never believe you'd go camping."

"I can camp!" She crosses her arms, tapping her manicured fingernails against her skin. "I can camp," she repeats. I look at her sideways.

Then she brings her hands to her hips and looks me straight on. "Look, I'm your sister," she says, her tone serious, "and she's your girlfriend, and it's not like you can bring her here, you know . . . *ever*. And you're definitely not going to bring Mom and Dad there. So you might as well have the whole 'meet the parents' moment with me."

"No. Way."

"Please . . ." She presses her palms together in front of her. "You know she wants to meet *me*." She looks at me out of the corner of her eye and shoots me the look she reserves for moments when she knows she's right. And she is. When I brought Anna to present-day San Francisco, she got knocked back right away. She would love to know the people in my world the same way I know the ones in hers, but she never will.

I take off for the refrigerator but I can feel Brooke's eyes boring into my back. Eventually she gives up and heads for the stove, and the room fills with the sound of sizzling oil. "Brooke?" I say, and she takes a quick look over her shoulder at me. She doesn't say anything, but I know she's listening. "If anything comes up, will you cover for me?"

"Again?" she asks.

"Yes," I say. "Again."

I see her nod. "Of course." Things get quiet for a while, and then she adds, "What are you going to do with the Jeep?"

"What do you mean?"

"You can't leave it in the garage if they think you're going camping. They know Sam doesn't have a car."

"Hmm. Good point." If I park the Jeep on a random street or in a parking lot somewhere, it will definitely get towed. I can't leave it at Sam's house without coming up with some complicated excuse. I can't believe that the Jeep didn't even occur to me.

"You know my friend Kathryn?" Brooke asks.

"Yeah."

"She didn't need her car at school, and her parents didn't

want it taking up room in the driveway, so they rented a garage." There's a long pause. "They found it on Craigslist."

"Thanks," I say, making a mental note to hit the website after dinner.

"See? You kind of need me." Brooke doesn't turn around, but I think I hear smug satisfaction in her voice. Until she looks over her shoulder wearing a disheartened half smile, and there isn't a trace of smugness in her expression. She just looks sad.

"Hey, what were you humming earlier?"

She thinks about it for half a second. "Coldplay."

I pull my phone out of my pocket and do some speedy research. "Munich? In two thousand two? Looks like a small club."

Her head whips around and she lets out a squeal. "Really?" she asks. Her hands are clenched into fists by her sides, and when I nod, she dances back and forth in place. She turns the dial on the stove so the blue flame disappears underneath the burner and looks around the kitchen. "Mom and Dad are going to be so pissed when they come home to this mess."

"Yeah, but they'll never remember it." *This* we'll do over. Messing with multiple days feels dangerous. Going back a few hours in time so we don't have to tell Mom and Dad we were in Munich for a Coldplay concert feels like a perk I should capitalize on. "When we get back, you can pick right up where you left off. We'll have dinner and pretend we're a happy family."

"We are a happy family."

"Trust me," I say as I navigate over to the club's website, "That's only because they're so glad you're back home, they've temporarily forgotten that they're furious at me for losing you in the first place. As soon as you're back at school, the three of us will be our usual bickering selves again." I click around until I find an interior view, and I pan and zoom on the best photo I can find. I have no way of knowing if it looked like this back in 2002, but chances are, even if they've done a remodel or two, the bathrooms are still in the same spot.

"Okay, we're set." I steal a glance at the clock on the microwave and by the time I turn around again, Brooke's standing in front of me, arms extended.

She looks down, assessing her outfit. "Am I good?" she asks, referring to her jeans, a plain-looking shirt, and a pair of flip-flops. I'm not so sure about flip-flops in March, but I don't want to waste time waiting for her to pick something else.

"Yeah. You're good." As soon as I take her hands, she grips mine hard and gives her arms a nervous shake like she always does. Then she squeezes her eyes shut.

I close mine, and we're gone.

On Wednesday afternoon, I pack up the Jeep with all my camping and climbing equipment, and then do one last check of the stuff that actually matters. The white plastic container is sitting on the front seat, and inside I've stored everything I'll need when I return: a dozen plastic bottles of water, a Starbucks Doubleshot, and a Red Bull six-pack.

The music's on loud and I'm so lost in my thoughts, I jump when I feel a tap on my shoulder. I slam the cover closed and flip around to find Mom with her hand over her mouth, looking amused. "Sorry!" She yells so she can be heard over the music. "I didn't mean to scare you."

"It's okay. Hold on." I lean in through the open window to turn down the volume.

"How's the packing going?" She glances from the hood of the car to the back cargo area, now filled to the brim with camping gear and colorful ropes. The soft top is already off and secured in place.

"Fine. I think I have everything."

"Good . . . that's good." She stands there, nodding and smiling, like she's gathering the nerve to say something else. She distributes her weight onto both feet and roots herself in place.

"What?" The tone of my voice makes it pretty clear that I don't really want to know.

"Is there any chance I can get you to change your mind about this camping trip?" She folds her arms across her chest. "It's just that . . . Brooke is going back to Boulder this weekend and then you'll be starting your senior year, and these are the last few days we have together as a family."

I want to tell her that we've had a whole summer and we haven't done anything "together as a family" with a single second of it. I'm not sure what makes her think this is the week to start, other than the fact that I'm leaving town and she doesn't want me to.

"It'll be fine, Mom. I want to go climbing with my friends,"

I say, smashing my sleeping bag deep into the back of the Jeep so it won't blow away when I start driving. "It's only for a few days. I'll be back by Friday." That part's true, so I turn around when I say it.

"You won't have *any* cell phone coverage?"

"Probably not. You know how it is out there. You can try, but it's really spotty." Yeah. Mainly because my cell phone will be in the glove compartment of the Jeep, locked in a clown-car-sized garage I found on Craigslist yesterday.

"Bennett?"

"Yeah?"

"You're not traveling, are you?" she asks, her forehead creased.

I freeze, then force my expression to look relaxed. "You told me *not* to travel."

"Yes. I did."

I shrug and look straight into her eyes. "And that's why I'm packing up my car to go camping." Is that a lie? Technically it's not, but I'm pretty sure Mom wouldn't see it the same way. She stares at me and I wait. I don't know if I just said the right thing or the wrong thing, or something so in between the two that she can't quite figure out what to do with it.

She looks worried and, God, I wish she wouldn't be. If only she'd relax and trust that I have this whole thing under control, I could tell her *everything*—about Maggie and Anna and the Greenes. And then she'd know exactly where I'm going and when I'll be back and what's inside the box on the passenger seat that she keeps eyeing but hasn't asked about.

"Be careful, okay?"

"I always am." I kiss her on the cheek. "You worry too much, Mom." I want to say more, but I don't.

I can tell from the look on her face that she has a lot more to say too, but instead, she just gives me a somber-looking smile and says, "You make it pretty hard not to, sweetie," and leaves it at that.

august 1995

3

evanston, illinois

When I push the door open, the little cluster of bells bangs against the glass and a guy standing over at the New in Paperback table turns around and gives me a quick glance. I step inside and look around. I've never seen the bookstore so crowded.

I walk down the main aisle, looking for Anna between the bookshelves. I'm halfway through the store when I see her behind the counter. She's ringing up a customer, so I keep a bit of a distance and wait, and try to ignore my heart smacking against my rib cage.

Her hair is longer than I remember it, and it occurs to me that every time I saw her in La Paz over the summer she was wearing it up in a clip or a ponytail. It's even curlier now, and I feel the familiar urge to pull on one of those strands so I can watch it spring back into place. What's different about her?

She looks tanned and happy and . . . somehow even more beautiful than before.

She's making small talk with the customer, fingers flying as she punches numbers into the register, and then she takes his credit card and runs it through some loud contraption and hands his card back to him. And that's when she sees me.

I just smile. I watch as her expression changes, morphing into this perfect mix of surprise and relief.

Anna looks back at the customer and pushes the overstuffed bag in his direction. "Here you go," she says with giddiness that the moment doesn't call for. Her eyes keep darting in my direction.

"Thanks," he says.

"Any time. Have a good quarter."

Instead of reaching for the bag, he rests one hip against the counter and watches her, like he's expecting her to say something else. I wonder if he thinks that smile is for him. He is standing right in front of her, after all. But I can tell from this vantage point that she's not looking *at* him, she's looking *past* him. Anna has lots of different smiles, but the one she's wearing right now is one she reserves for me.

"Bye," she says, pushing the bag across the counter again, this time with more force, and he must get the message because he grabs it with both hands and heads for the front door.

She starts heading in my direction. "Shoot," the guy says, "I almost forgot." He turns around and struts back to the counter, and Anna returns to her spot behind the register, looking official again.

I watch her, picturing that surprised look she wore on her face just a moment ago. I think about how nice it would be to see it one more time.

No one's ever in the Travel section, so I take a chance. Ducking back behind the shelves, I hide from her view and close my eyes. I picture the row on the opposite side of the store, and when I open them, I'm standing in it. I take my backpack off and set it down by my feet.

I can still hear her voice at the counter but now I'm too far away to make out what she's saying. I stare down at the shelf marked with the word MEXICO, remembering the night I came in here last April.

I should have been studying, but couldn't stop thinking about her. All day, I'd been looking for a chance to get her alone so I could tell her the second part of my secret, but I never found one. So before I could change my mind, I fed my arms into the sleeves of my jacket and walked to the bookstore.

Her face completely lit up when she saw me walk in, and all I wanted to do was kiss her. Instead, I told her I was there to pick up a book on Mexico. She led me over here to the Travel section.

At first, we talked about our assignment, but then she stopped me in midsentence and said, "I want to hear the rest of the second thing." When I looked in her eyes, I knew she meant it. And so I told her everything. That I was born in 1995. That I'm seventeen in 2012. That I wasn't supposed to be here. That I could visit, but I couldn't stay.

And then, against my better judgment, I finally did what

I'd wanted to do since the day I met her. I came up on my knees and I kissed her, no longer caring about my rules or where and when I was supposed to be. Just as I was about to pull away like I knew I should, I felt her hands on my back, drawing me in until we were pressed against the bookcase and there was nowhere else for us to go but closer to each other. I kissed her harder.

The bells on the door jingle, snapping me back to reality.

"Bennett?" I hear Anna call from across the room.

I duck around the corner and press my chest into the end of the shelving unit, keeping my eyes fixed on the aisle and waiting for her to walk by. I don't see or hear her, so I stay silent as I listen for breathing and wait for her to come into view.

I'm just about to take a step forward when I feel her hands grip my sides. I jump.

"Gotcha," she whispers in my ear. Her forehead falls against the back of my neck and her arms wrap around me. I can feel her breathing.

"That's an understatement," I say, bringing her hands to my face, kissing her fingers.

"I didn't see where you went," she says.

"Yeah." I let out a small laugh. "Remember? I do that."

"Just to mess with me." I can hear the eye roll in her voice.

"Just to mess with you."

"Maybe you should start thinking about doing more with this little talent of yours than surprising your girlfriend."

"Say that last part again."

She laughs. Squeezes me harder. "Surprising your *girlfriend*."

I smile. "I like the way that sounds." I loosen her grip on my waist and turn around. Her whole face is lit up so bright, I swear we could turn off all the lights in the bookstore and still see each other perfectly.

"Hi." I twist a strand of her curls around my finger.

"Hi." She reaches up and musses my hair. "You're here," she says, but something in her voice makes her sound unsure.

"I'm here." I bring my hands to her cheeks. "I've missed you like crazy." She presses her lips together and gives me the slightest nod, and before she can say anything I tip her head back and kiss her, softly, slowly, savoring the feeling of being here in this room with her again. I kiss her harder. And just like that first night, she kisses me back, pulling me into her, like she still wants me here and still trusts me with her heart, even though she probably knows by now that she shouldn't.

4

When the clock reads 9:02, Anna walks the perimeter of the store, shutting off lights and adjusting books as she goes. I flip the sign on the door from OPEN to CLOSED, and we step outside. She presses some buttons on the keypad by the door to set the alarm, and clicks the deadbolt in place behind us.

I reach for her hand and we walk in silence toward the end of the block. The familiar sounds from the coffeehouse grow louder with each step, and I take a big whiff of the air, inhaling the scent. We're about to pass the entrance when Anna stops. "Do you want to go in and get something? We could hang out for a bit."

I peer through the window. It's not nearly as busy as it is when bands play on Sunday nights, but it's still pretty crowded. All of the couches are taken and the only option I see is a high table in the middle of the room. I've hardly been alone with her all summer, and I really don't feel like sharing her with anyone else tonight. "I was hoping for something a bit quieter."

She pivots so she's facing me and reaches for my other hand. "In that case, you have two choices: my room or yours. Who do you want to face first, my parents or Maggie?"

I make the sound of a game-show buzzer. "I don't like either of those. What's my third choice?"

She laughs and shakes her head slightly at me. "There's no third choice."

"Sure there is."

Anna raises her eyebrows and stares at me.

"We'll bypass the parents and just sneak up to your bedroom. No one needs to know I'm in town yet."

"Too late. I already told them you were coming tonight."

I snap my fingers and laugh under my breath. "Damn." Anna shakes her head at me again while I think about my options. "I'm not ready for Maggie yet," I say, and Anna gives me an understanding nod and drops my other hand. We continue walking toward her house.

"So, how did they take it?" I ask.

"My parents?" She shrugs. "Pretty well, I guess. Mom was cooler about you being back than Dad was, which kind of surprised me. Actually, he wasn't too upset until I mentioned that you came to visit me in La Paz. He wasn't at all pleased about that." Her head spins toward mine. "Oh, and I said you visited twice, not four times, so stick to that if he asks, okay?"

I silently hope he won't ask. I'm also silently disappointed that she's started lying to her parents. She didn't do that before I showed up.

"I can't tell what they really think," she says. "The other night, my mom came into my room to tell me that she likes you, and that she's glad we'll get to spend our senior year together. She actually looked giddy when she started talking about homecoming and prom and stuff." I feel the lump rise in my throat and I swallow it back down. "But then she and my dad must have talked about it again, because last night at dinner, they laid it on thick. I got this big lecture about making sure I continue to focus on my running and not let my grades slip because of you."

"Because of me?"

"I know, right?" She winks at me. "As if."

I raise one eyebrow. "As *if*?"

She shrugs again. "Come on, you're not *that* big a deal."

"Nah. Of course I'm not," I say, suppressing a grin.

She squeezes my hand. "You are, you know?"

I squeeze hers back. "You are too."

We pass the hedge that lines her neighbor's yard, and Anna's house comes into view. It looks exactly the same as it did when I left last May, with its wraparound porch and overgrown shrubs. There's a soft light glowing from the kitchen window like it always does at night.

Once we're inside, Anna leads me toward the sound coming from the living room. We turn the corner and I spot her parents. Mrs. Greene has her feet curled up underneath her and she's resting her head on Mr. Greene's shoulder. They're watching some old TV show. Which, I instantly remind myself, probably isn't old at all.

Anna stops at my side and grips my arm with both hands. The movement must catch her dad's attention, because he suddenly looks up and sees us. His eyes grow wide and he gives Mrs. Greene a little nudge that makes her sit up straight. "Hi. We didn't hear you come in." He aims the remote at the TV and mutes the sound.

Mr. Greene stands up, extending his hand, and even though it feels overly formal for him—for us—I reach out and shake it politely. Anna's mom gives me a halfhearted wave from her spot on the couch. "It's nice to have you back," she says, but her voice sounds hollow and insincere. Then she adds the word "Finally." It's not an afterthought; it's more like it was the one word she was trying *not* to say, but couldn't quite keep from slipping out.

"It's good to see you both too," I say. Then I stand there, nodding and waiting for one of them to say more and feeling my stomach sink. I should probably be happy they aren't outwardly furious with me. After all, not only did I disappear on their daughter in the middle of a date, I disappeared from all of their lives in the middle of, well, *everything.* I know it would be too much to expect a motherly hug or a fatherly back-pat, and I was hardly expecting tears of joy at the sight of my face in their living room. But I was sort of hoping we wouldn't be starting from scratch. Or, as it appears to be, less than scratch.

Anna gives my arm a squeeze and I look over at her. Unlike her mom's blank stare, her expression speaks volumes. She's beaming at me, her eyes full of joy and wonder, like she can't believe I'm actually standing here. Without even thinking about it, I let out a relieved sigh and kiss her on the forehead; and she tightens her grip on my arm again and lifts herself up on her toes. She bounces in place a few times.

When I look over at her parents again, their eyes are locked on Anna. But then Mrs. Greene's gaze slowly travels over to me and the corners of her mouth turn up in a half smile, almost as if she can't help herself. I give her a grateful nod.

"How's your sister doing?" Mr. Greene's voice takes me by surprise and my head snaps in his direction.

"Um . . . She's good." I quickly come up with a way to phrase the rest of my response to give him as little information as possible. "It was touch and go for a while there, but she's back home now." I leave it at that and hope that he doesn't press me for more information, because if he does, I'll have to lie to him and I'd really like to stop doing that.

"All great to hear." He waits for a moment, and then it looks like he's about to say something else. "Ah, never mind, you probably don't want to talk about it."

"Not really," I say.

The cagey thing probably isn't winning me any points, but now that I think about it, that could be a good thing. If I'm starting at the bottom, I won't have as far to fall once they learn the truth.

"We're going to go upstairs," Anna says, jumping in with

a rescue. Before her parents can say anything else, she leads me out of the room. We've only climbed the first two stairs when we hear her mom yell, "Leave your door open." Anna stops, gripping the banister with one hand and hiding her face behind the other.

She shakes it off. "Follow me. I'm dying to show you something."

Not much has changed since the last time I was in this room. Anna's impressive CD collection takes up every bit of shelf space, broken up only by the dozens of racing trophies that hold the alphabetized jewel cases in place. The walls are plastered with paper race numbers that were once pinned to her jersey and photos of her breaking through finish-line tape.

The bulletin board over her desk still holds the same lonely Pearl Jam concert stub from March 1994, but next to it I spot something new: a framed photo of Anna, Emma, and Justin. Emma's mouth is open wide, like she's squealing. She's standing behind Justin with her arms wrapped loosely around his neck, and Anna's on his right, her head resting on his shoulder. The picture must have been taken last June, after I left town but before Anna took off for La Paz. They look happy.

"How's Emma?"

"Eh, not so good. I went over to her house right after I got home and she told me that she and Justin broke up over the summer."

"Really? Why?"

Anna turns her back to me, runs her finger along the jewel cases, and selects one. "I don't know *why* exactly, because I haven't heard Justin's side of the story yet—I stopped by the record store the other day and he was too busy to talk—but according to Emma, he doesn't think they have enough in common . . . that they're better as friends."

She drops the disc in her CD player, and when the music begins, it sounds familiar, but I can't place the song. But then the lyrics begin and I instantly recognize Alanis Morissette's voice. I'm trying to recall which album this is when Anna says, "Have you heard this before?" She waves the case for *Jagged Little Pill* in the air, and I nod. "I love her. I've been running to this CD all summer." I wish I could tell Anna that she has a lot more Alanis to look forward to, but I keep it to myself. Instead I tell her that I'll look up the tour schedule and take her to a concert.

I spot the map that takes up the largest wall in her room. I walk over to it and stand there, counting the number of little red pins Anna uses to mark her travels. Nine, including the new one at the bottom of the Baja peninsula. Five more than the first time I stood here, admiring Anna's intense desire to see the world and enjoying the idea that I could give her a small piece of it.

I turn around and find her standing next to me. "Here." She hands me a small bag and I peek inside. My Westlake student ID. A blank postcard from Ko Tao. The postcard Anna wrote to me in Vernazza Square. A stubby yellow pencil. A carabiner.

One of her pins. "You left them in your desk at Maggie's. She thought I should hold on to them for you."

"Thanks." I remove the postcard from Vernazza, shooting her a glance as I run my finger across the edge. Anna's watching me as I read it, and I feel myself suck in a breath when I get to the last line, *wherever you are in this world, that's where I want to be,* and a wave of guilt washes over me. My chest feels heavy as I drop the card back in the bag and then toss the whole thing on the floor next to the door along with my backpack. "Is that what you wanted to show me?"

Anna's eyes light up. "Nope." She turns on her heel and crosses the room. She crouches down low, wrestling with something underneath her bed.

"Close your eyes," she calls over her shoulder.

Less than a minute later, I feel her behind me, her hands on my waist, pushing me forward. "Keep 'em closed. A few more steps. Okay, stop." I feel her next to me. "You can open them now."

It takes a moment for my eyes to adjust, and I'm not exactly sure where I'm supposed to be looking. But then I see something lying flat on top of her bedspread, and I take a few steps closer.

It's a photograph, printed on a huge sheet of thick-looking paper. I recognize the tall rocks and jagged cliffs immediately. "Is that our beach?" I ask, but I already know it is. That's the spot where I found her in La Paz. The same place I've arrived off and on all summer to surprise her during her morning runs. I lean in close to get a better look. "This is incredible. How did you find a print of the *exact* spot?"

"It's not a print," she says as she rests her hands on her hips. "I took it."

I know nothing about photography, but it looks pretty impressive to me. I can see every tiny crack in the rock face, and the tall cliff is perfectly mirrored in the water below. "You took this?"

"Señora Moreno helped me." I remember her telling me that her host mom in La Paz was also a local photographer. "I thought you could hang it on your bedroom wall." She doesn't clarify which bedroom and I decide not to ask.

"But wait . . . get this," she says, holding up a finger. Anna undoes the Velcro on a black canvas bag and removes a 35-millimeter camera. Her thumb glides along the back and over the buttons. "Look what she gave me. I guess it's pretty old, but I don't care." It looks ancient. I watch her twist the long lens, remove it from the body, and replace it with a fatter, stubbier one. She brings the camera to her face, and I can't see anything but her mouth. I hear the shutter snap and a weird, motorized sound.

Throwing the strap over her shoulder, she reaches under the bed again and returns holding a large envelope. She plops down on the floor and motions for me to join her. We sit close together, our hips touching, and she shakes a pile of images onto the shag rug and tells me the backstory on each one. There are lots of beaches and rocks and vista point views, but my eye goes straight to a close-up photo of a man with dark, wrinkled skin, holding a guitar and wearing the warmest smile.

"These are really good," I tell her. "*Really* good." I watch the flush creep into her cheeks.

"They have this darkroom in their basement. I spent hours in there with Señora Moreno and her daughter, learning how to develop film. It was incredible." She shrugs. "When I told Dad, he said he might be able to build one for me in that old shed in the backyard." She reaches for her camera and aims it at my face. "Until then, it's one-hour photo. Smile. I don't have a single picture of you."

I reach around her waist and pull her down onto the rug next to me. "There's no reason for a picture of me if you're not in it."

She laughs as she extends her arm as high in the air as she can and aims the lens at us. *Click*. She kisses me on the cheek. *Click*. She sticks out her tongue and I crack up. *Click*. And then, in one fluid series of motions, I take the camera out of her hands, set it on the floor, and roll over on top of her, kissing her like I've wanted to all night.

But the longer we kiss, the guiltier I feel. I promised I wouldn't keep secrets from her any longer. "Anna," I say. "There's something I need to tell you."

The knock is soft, but startling enough to send us scampering in opposite directions. The door was ajar as instructed and we didn't have much time, but we move so quickly that by the time Mrs. Greene's head pops in, Anna and I are already sitting up, a generous amount of shag rug between the two of us.

"Your dad and I are going to bed," she says.

"Okay. Good night," Anna says brightly.

Her mom clears her throat. "That means that Bennett needs to leave now."

"Mom—" Anna huffs.

"It's okay." I stand up quickly and cross the room toward my backpack. "I'll see you tomorrow," I say to Anna. I squeeze past Mrs. Greene and into the hallway, heading for the front door.

I'm just about to turn the knob when I hear Anna's voice behind me. "Wait a sec!" I turn around and find her halfway down the stairs. "Where are you going?" she whispers.

I shrug. "I don't know. I'll probably just go home and come back in the morning."

She looks around to be sure her dad's out of earshot. "What, like, home-home? San Francisco *home*?" She doesn't add *2012 home*, but I know that's what she means.

"Yeah, it's too late to go to Maggie's now. Don't worry. I'll be back tomorrow. I'll go over to her house and then we can go do something together."

She shakes her head hard. "No. I mean, you're here. You can't just . . . *leave*."

I don't want to leave, but I picture the look on Mrs. Greene's face a minute ago and think it's probably better not to push my luck tonight. I go could back to San Francisco, to the tiny garage, and crash in the Jeep. Or I could go back to my room and hope my parents don't walk in and find me. Come to think of it, maybe Anna's right. I might be better off staying put. I could always sleep on the couch in the back room of the bookstore.

Anna holds up a finger. "Don't move. I'll be right back." Before I can say another word, she's gone, flying back up the stairs.

I stand in the foyer and look around. On my left, I see the built-in bench, and on the wall above it, a row of empty coat hooks. It reminds me of the first time I came to this house. Anna had stayed home from school, and when I showed up, she took my jacket and hung it there. Then I told her my secret, showed her what I could do. Took her somewhere warm and far away. I consider doing it again tonight.

I hear her bare feet padding down the stairs. She's holding an armful of bedding. "You're sleeping on the couch."

My eyes dart to her parents' bedroom door at the top of the stairs. "No way." I rub my forehead hard with my fingertips and think about the idea. "Your parents actually said I could sleep on your couch?"

Anna nods. "Just for tonight. They agreed that it was too late for you to walk home in the dark. I told them you'd call Maggie and tell her not to expect you until tomorrow."

"I can't call Maggie," I whisper in her ear.

"I know. Just pretend to do it." She gestures toward the kitchen and I see the phone hanging on the wall next to the microwave. I cover my face with my hand. I wish I'd just said

good night, gone outside, and *poof,* appeared back in her bedroom ten minutes later like I originally planned to.

"You can change in the downstairs bathroom." She points
to a door I've never noticed before. "I'll go get you set up."

5

I fluff up the pillow and twist around in the blankets. For possibly the tenth time in the last hour, I sit up, resting my hands on my knees and staring out the sliding glass door and into the Greenes' backyard. According to the clock on the mantel, it's a quarter after midnight.

The last time I sat on this couch, Anna and I were wrapped up in this exact corner while Justin and Emma curled up on the opposite side. We watched a movie and took turns reaching into an enormous bowl of buttered popcorn that her mom made for us.

I throw my feet onto the floor and stand up. I walk through the kitchen and into the hallway, stopping at the bottom of the stairs. Her parents' door is open a crack. Anna's is completely shut. I'm about to close my eyes and bring myself to her bedroom, when I think of the look on her parents' faces tonight. Sure, if they caught me in their daughter's room, I could just go back five minutes, ten minutes, and do it all over. But going up there at all feels like a violation of their trust and I'm already on thin ice here.

There's no reason to rush things. I have plenty of time to see her tomorrow, the next day. I turn around, shuffle back to the couch, and collapse with my head in my hands. After a while, I settle into the pillow again and close my eyes, attempting to empty my mind. I finally feel like I'm about to drift off when I hear something that sounds like breathing.

I crack my eyes open, lift my head up, and see a silhouette in the doorway. "Oh, God. I'm sorry," Anna whispers. "I didn't mean to wake you."

"It's okay. . . . I wasn't sleeping." I sit up a little bit and gesture for her to come closer. She sits across from me on the coffee table. The sight of her, the sound of her voice in this room, fills me with relief. "What are you doing down here? What about your parents?"

"I checked. They're asleep. Trust me, once they're out, they're out."

She sweeps her hair away from her face and twists it around a finger, holding it against the back of her neck. "I couldn't sleep either. I've just been lying in bed, staring at my map, and thinking that, for the last few months, we've had all this distance between the two of us, you know?" She lets her hair fall, and then pushes it behind her ears. "And it suddenly dawned on me that tonight—finally—there was nothing between us but a door and a staircase, and it seemed"—she blinks fast—"silly."

I nod. "That's definitely silly." Even though the room is dark, lit only by the porch light on the back patio, I can see her blush. "I'm glad you remedied that." I say.

"Yeah, me too."

"But there's still more, you know?"

Her eyebrows lower and pinch together. "What do you mean 'more'?" she asks.

I stretch my arm out in her direction, angling it so my fingertip comes within a centimeter of her knee. "There's this distance here—a whole arm's length—which is really quite a lot if you think about it. This is, like, seventh-grade-dance kind of distance."

She laughs quietly. "That's not even silly. That's just . . . unacceptable."

"Right? And then there's this," I say, pinching a corner of the wool blanket she covered me with a little earlier. "What do you make of this?"

She reaches out, rubbing the fabric between her thumb and her forefinger. "Yeah, that's definitely a problem."

"Exactly what I was thinking."

I start to pull the blanket back, but before I can, Anna moves from the coffee table to the couch, sealing the opening shut with her weight. "What did you want to tell me earlier?" Her dark eyes fix on mine and I feel a sudden chill that hits my core. I wasn't expecting this turn in the conversation, and I'm trying to decide how to start, but she doesn't give me time.

"You aren't staying this year, are you?"

I shake my head no.

She rolls her shoulders back and looks up at the ceiling. "I knew it. Every time I've mentioned something about school, you've looked away and changed the subject." Her gaze ping-pongs around the room. Now she won't look at me. "Why not?"

"I can't."

"Can't or won't?"

"Can't." I sit up so I can face her straight on. "Look, I've been experimenting with this all summer. I even told every-one I was going on a two-week climbing trip and took off by myself. I pitched a tent where no one would find it and went to London. I wandered around, enjoyed the sights—missing you the whole time, by the way—but after three days, I was knocked back to the tent. The migraine was excruciating, but just like I did when I first got to Evanston, I immediately closed my eyes and brought myself back. It worked. I stayed another day, almost two. But then I got knocked back to the tent again. I kept bringing myself back, but each time . . ." I trail off, shaking my head, remembering migraines so debili-tating I could barely open my eyes for nearly an hour. "The side effects got worse, not better. After a week, I closed my eyes and nothing happened."

"Why could you stay last time?"

I shake my head. "I don't know. I think it's because Brooke wasn't where she was supposed to be, you know? Like . . . things were off and once they were righted again . . ." Anna just stares at me, and I look at her, trying to figure out what she's thinking. "The two must be connected, because once she got back, I couldn't return here. And now it looks like my ability to stay here has changed too."

She still won't look at me and she clearly doesn't know what to say. She brings her hands to her forehead and rubs hard, like that will help the information sink in or something. "So, what? This is how it's going to be?" she asks.

"I don't know. This is the way it is right now."

I feel horrible. Back in the beginning, I prepared her for the fact that I couldn't stay here with her. I never should have let her believe that I could. I never should have let *myself* believe that I could.

"But I want to come back. A lot. I figure I can't visit too frequently or your parents will get suspicious, you know, but we can come up with, like, a schedule or something."

She doesn't say anything.

"If you think about it, this is how we always thought it was going to be, right up until Vernazza. Remember?" I stop one step short of saying what I'm really thinking: *You already agreed to be part of the most screwed-up long-distance relationship on the planet.*

She wrings her hands while she weighs the pros and cons of everything I've just said. We'll be together, but not every day, like we were before, and not on either of our terms. We won't go to the same school or hang out with the same people and, at least while we're both still living at home with our parents, we'll spend most of our days seventeen years away from each other. So many people take proximity for granted. We just want to be in the same place at the same time.

Her eyes are fixed on the carpet. "I can handle a lot, you know? I can handle everything about you and what you can do, but what happened last time . . . I can't let that happen to me again." She lifts her head and looks right at me. "I know you didn't *want* it to happen, and I realize you didn't do it on purpose, but you were here and then you were just *gone*, and when you didn't come back, I . . ."

She grabs a strand of hair and twists it around her finger. I'm just about to speak when she opens her mouth and looks me straight in the eye again. "Here's the thing. When you left, I sort of . . . fell apart." Her shoulders hunch forward and she starts breathing faster. "I mean, I *completely* fell apart," she repeats. "I don't fall apart, Bennett, and I don't want to *be* someone who falls apart and . . ." She inhales deeply and wraps her arms around her waist. "I can't let that happen again."

I look at her, bracing myself for what she's about to say. What she *should* say. She wants me to leave. She doesn't want me to come back here again.

"I need to think about it," she says.

The words aren't as bad as the ones I was expecting, but they still take me by surprise. "Yeah." It takes effort to keep my voice steady. "Of course you do."

She presses her lips together, hard, like she's holding something in, and I realize she's trying not to cry. But I wish she would. I wish she would just sit here and fall apart, like she apparently did when I left, because unlike last time, I could actually be there for her now. I could tell her everything I would have said then: That we'll be okay. That this whole thing is weird and twisted and unfair to both of us, but especially unfair to her, because it's always harder to be the one who's left behind than the one who leaves. And I'd tell her that I love her, and that I'll do anything to be with her, any way I can be.

"When are you leaving?"

I swallow hard. "Friday. I promised my mom I'd be home for the weekend. Brooke's heading back to college on Sunday." I start to tell her about our plans to take the boat out on the bay but I decide against it. "Then I start school on Monday."

She gives me a sad smile. "Me too."

We're both silent for a long time. She scoots back to her spot on the coffee table, and I think she's about to say good night and head back upstairs, but she doesn't move. I can tell she's contemplating what to do next, and I should probably stay silent and not say anything that might sway her decision to stay, but I can't help myself.

"I'm here now," I say quietly.

She looks up from under her lashes. Then her expression softens and a smile spreads across her face. "I'm glad." She reaches over, grabs the edge of the wool blanket, and rubs it between her thumb and her forefinger again. "There's still the matter of this, you know?"

My heart starts racing and I laugh, happy to follow her lead. "Is that *still* there?" I lift up the edge of the blanket and Anna climbs underneath, stretching out next to me. Her arms wrap around my waist and she wedges one of her legs between mine.

"Much better," she says, sliding her hands under my T-shirt, up my back, kissing me. In a matter of minutes, we both seem to forget about the complications around this whole crazy thing we're doing. For the rest of the night, it doesn't seem complicated at all.

6

I wake to the faint sound of water running. I try to lift my head off the pillow to take a better look, but my movement is restricted by the weight of Anna's head, buried in the crook of my neck.

I kiss her cheek. "Anna," I whisper. "Wake up." She tightens her grip on my shoulder and, without opening her eyes, settles into my chest and lets out a happy sigh.

The water sound stops and it's almost instantly replaced by a light plinking noise. I'm trying to place it when I hear the unmistakable—and extremely loud—whir of a coffee grinder.

Anna jumps and her lids pop open. The second she sees me, she lets out a gasp. She lifts her head and scans the living room.

"It's okay. We just fell asleep."

"My *dad's* in there," she whispers, her eyes darting back and forth between the kitchen and me.

"I know. It's okay," I repeat, thinking she didn't hear me the first time.

Her eyes grow even wider. "It's not *okay*! He can't find us like this. He'll never—" She comes closer, within an inch of my face. "I'm dead."

"Come on . . . just tell him we were talking and we fell asleep." I try to look at the scene from her father's point of view. Anna's shirt is back where it belongs but I have no idea where mine is.

"He'll never believe that."

I start to speak but she covers my mouth with her hand. "*Shhh.*" The coffee grinder comes to a stop. She looks at me, wide-eyed. *Do something*, she mouths. *Please.*

It takes a second or two for understanding to kick in, possibly because I'm still a little groggy and she's whisper-shouting at me in the near dark. "You sure?" I mouth back, and she answers my question with a quick, panicky nod.

I find the clock immediately—God knows I stared at it enough last night—and check the time. A little after six thirty. I slide my hands under the blankets, feeling for hers, and when I find them I grip them tight.

Her eyes are already shut.

I kick the blanket onto the floor and squeeze my eyes closed as I picture her room. When I open them, we're on her bed, wrapped up in the exact same position we were on the couch— Anna curled up into my chest, our hands clenched together, our legs intertwined. I really don't want to move, but I have to twist away from her so I can read the clock on her nightstand. Six o'clock on the dot.

Minutes pass as we lie side by side, silent and unmoving. Then Anna bends her knees to her chest and starts quietly cracking up.

"See why you need to keep me around," I whisper, still looking up at the ceiling.

She stretches out and throws her arm over her forehead. Her head falls to one side and she looks at me. "There are lots of other reasons to keep you around."

I roll over on top of her, my legs straddling her hips, my face only inches away from hers. "So will you?" I kiss her. "Keep me around?"

She inhales sharply. "I'm still thinking about it."

"Good." I kiss her again. "How are you feeling?"

She crinkles her nose. "A little . . . twisty. But I don't feel sick or anything." She pushes my hair off my face but it just flops back down again. "How about you? How's your head?"

"It's good. But you know, I only feel the side effects on the return trip and only if I change time zones. I'm just popping back downstairs." I look over at the clock and kiss her again. "Unless you keep me here too long."

Anna glances at the time. "You should probably go. It's already ten after."

I plant a kiss on her cheek and then hop off the bed. I give her a little wave. She waves back. "See you downstairs," I say, closing my eyes and picturing her living room.

My eyelids pop open and I'm standing next to the couch, staring at the jumble of blankets we left behind. I see my shirt on the floor and pull it over my head. Then I crawl back under the covers, where I belong.

Twenty minutes later, Anna's dad peeks around the corner. He sees that I'm already awake and gives me a wave. I wave back and wonder if he checked in here last time and saw something quite different.

I hear the water running. The coffee beans tumble into the grinder. The whirring sound starts and stops. I wait for a few more minutes and then head toward the kitchen, where I'm greeted by the sounds of dripping and percolating and an unmistakable aroma that makes my mouth water. Anna's dad is wrapping the cord around the grinder and returning it to its home in the cupboard when he sees me out of the corner of his eye.

"Good morning."

I lift my chin in his direction. "Good morning, Mr. Greene."

He leans back against the counter. "How'd you sleep?" He crosses his arms and stares at me, and I feel the adrenaline start racing through my veins.

I rest my hip against the counter opposite him, hoping I appear calm and not at all guilty. I look at him straight on. "Great," I say. "Thanks for letting me stay last night."

He stares at me for what feels like a full minute. I hold my breath and try not to move.

Finally he uncrosses his arms and says, "No problem. Glad

we could help." His tone is friendly, and when he turns his back to me, I silently exhale.

He reaches into a high cabinet and pulls out two mugs. "Do you drink coffee, Bennett?"

"Yes, sir," I say, and he reaches into the cabinet again and grabs a third.

7

Two cups of coffee, three tall glasses of water, a bowl of cereal, and a couple of hours later, I leave the Greenes' and walk the four familiar blocks to Maggie's house. My heart is beating hard in my chest by the time I reach the porch, and speeds into a whole new gear when I pick up the lion's-head door knocker.

Sweat drips down the back of my neck and my shirt sticks to my skin. Today the weather may be different, but I'm just as nervous as I was when I stood in this same spot last March, bending the corners of an index card back and forth while I waited for her to answer the door.

I'd just come from the Northwestern student housing office. I had no way of recognizing the penmanship, but as I stood in front of the giant bulletin board, one card stood out, its letters carefully drawn and perfectly slanted, as if someone who cared how it looked had written it. I pulled out the thumbtack and turned it over to verify what I already knew. Then I went straight to the address.

When my grandmother opened the door, I introduced myself as a Northwestern student and asked her if her room was still available to rent. She wore a guarded expression, but nodded, and when I handed her enough cash for the remainder of the quarter—even though I had no intention of staying that long—she invited me in for tea and showed me my new room. But two months later I disappeared without saying a word, leaving behind a closet full of clothes, a brand-new SUV, and a bunch of questions Anna had to do her best to answer for me.

I hear the floorboards creak on the other side of the door. Maggie peeks through the curtains, takes one look at me, and disappears again. Everything's quiet. No floorboards creaking as she walks away, but no deadbolt snapping either.

Finally, the door opens. She's wearing a loose-fitting dress that hangs almost to the ground and, as usual, there's a brightly colored scarf draped around her neck. I look up at her face and when I see her eyes, I lock on to them. They're blue-gray and striking, but that's not the reason I can't stop staring at them. It's because I know them well. Her eyes are exactly the same color as my mother's. Exactly the same color as mine. I can't help wondering if she's thinking the same thing.

"Hi, Maggie," I say. For something to do, I shift my backpack from one shoulder to the other.

"Hi." She stares at me for an uncomfortably long time. But then her forehead wrinkles and her eyes light up and she actually looks happy to see me. "Anna told me you'd come by this week, but she didn't know when, exactly." She stands a bit straighter, bracing herself against the side of the door. "Do you want to come in?"

I step into the foyer and follow her to the living room. Sunlight streams in through the floor-to-ceiling windows that look out onto the street. I set my backpack on the floor and sit on the couch.

It's impossible to ignore the images around me. On every wall and every surface in Maggie's living room, I see framed photos of my family. Me as an infant in my mother's arms. Brooke as a little girl, with her long dark hair and her bangs cut straight across her forehead. My mom and dad on their wedding day. We're everywhere, decorating my grandmother's home, even though she doesn't appear in a single photo. I can practically hear the words my mother said every time Brooke or I asked about her: "She only met you once." Then Mom would show Brooke and me a photograph of the three of us at the zoo. When we'd press her for more information, she'd say that she and her mother had a falling out and that she didn't want to talk about it.

Maggie catches me staring at the pictures and crosses the room to pick up a silver frame. "Here. You'll like this one. It's new," she says as she hands it to me.

Maggie has a tiny infant me folded up in one arm, and

Brooke is by her side, holding Maggie's other hand. I stare at her. She looks happy. And then I notice the giraffes in the background.

"We went to the zoo," she says.

I squint at the photo, realizing that it's the same picture we have back home.

She taps her fingernail against the glass. "I hadn't met the baby before. You remember that you two have the same name, right?" She shakes her head in disbelief like she always does when she thinks about it.

Maggie settles in to her usual chair and leans forward, like she wants to get a closer look at me, and I feel myself move away from her, my back sinking further into the couch cushions. Something's not right about this. "You went to San Francisco?"

She adjusts her scarf around her shoulders. "Anna was actually the one who encouraged me to go," she says, and my stomach drops. "But it might not have been a good idea. My daughter and I got into a fight while I was there and . . ." Her eyes lock on mine and she looks at me wearing a sad smile. "Let's just say I'm not so sure when I'll be going back again."

I take a deep breath and try not to look panicked about what she just said. The only reason Brooke and I have a picture of the two of us at the zoo with our grandmother—the only reason we ever *met* Maggie—is that Anna told her to visit?

"So." She leans back into her chair. "I hear you left town so quickly because of a family emergency. Is everything okay?"

I nod vacantly.

"Good. So are you back here for school, then?" Her word choice is deliberate, and the generic reference to "school" isn't lost on me. Anna told me over the summer that Maggie found out I was really going to Westlake the whole time.

I avoid the school thing entirely. "I need to go back to San Francisco," I say, intentionally avoiding this perfect opportunity to come clean. "But I'm planning to come back. To visit." That is, if Anna wants me to.

Maggie doesn't say another word, but she doesn't take her eyes off me, either. She's waiting me out, and I know I'm supposed to tell her everything because Anna promised her I would when I returned. I check out the photographs again and feel sick to my stomach. Does she have any idea who I am?

I take a deep breath and open my mouth to speak. "There's—" I start to say, at the same time that she says, "Well—" We both stop in midsentence.

"Were you going to say something?" she asks.

"It's okay. You go first."

I wait for her to talk. To tell me she found my red notebook in its hiding place upstairs and pieced everything together. To call me out with such direct questions, I won't have a choice but to tell her everything. It will come out sloppy and rushed, possibly as a single run-on sentence with very few breaths in between, but the words will be out there and I won't be able to take them back. And my grandmother will become the fifth person in the world to know who I am and what I can do.

"I was just going to ask if you needed a place to stay when you visit. Your room is still available. If you want it."

I suck in some air, feeling disappointment that I didn't expect. "Yeah. Sure," I say. "That'd be great."

"Good. I haven't rented it out yet. I'd certainly prefer it to go to . . ." She pauses. *Say the words. Say, "my grandson." Tell me you know who I am.* Instead she finishes her sentence with "someone I already know."

She stands up and I do the same. I comb my hair off my forehead and cast my eyes down at the ground. *Tell her.*

"Maggie . . ." I say.

Her head springs up. "Yes?"

"I'm . . ." I can't do it. I can't say it. If she already knew about me, that would be one thing. But she doesn't. At least, I don't think she does. "I'm not supposed to be here."

And there it is, that warm smile I remember so well. "And yet, you came back," she says as she reaches over and grips my arm high up by my shoulder and gives it a reassuring squeeze. Maybe that's her way of giving me permission to *not* tell her. Or maybe I'm just looking to be let off the hook.

"I'm going to go get some sheets for your bed," she says. "All of your clothes are boxed up in the attic. You can put everything back where it belongs."

She starts to leave the room, and for some reason I start talking about logistics. "I'll pay you the same amount, of course. Even though I won't be here as often."

She's walking away, but I can hear her clearly. "It's your room, Bennett. Come as often as you like and stay as long as you want to." Then she stops and turns around. "You should decorate it a bit too. Hang up some posters or something. Make it your own."

Three hours later, I've reassembled my bedroom at Maggie's so it looks exactly the way I left it, a process which has left me soaked in sweat from hauling boxes from a 120-degree attic into a 105-degree bedroom. How can she not have air-conditioning?

As I suspected, my clothing options here are limited to long-sleeved flannels, concert tees, and an assortment of thick sweaters. I dig around in my backpack for a clean shirt and a pair of underwear, and then shuffle across the hallway.

While I was unpacking, Maggie must have been stocking the bathroom with me in mind. Fresh towels hang from the racks, there's a new bar of soap on the counter, and on the shelf next to the tub I spot a bottle of all-in-one shampoo and conditioner. I turn on the water and toss my sweat-drenched clothes on the floor.

After I'm showered and dressed again, I return to my room and crouch down in front of the giant mahogany armoire that dominates this room. I feel around on the bottom for the lock, and inside I find everything I left behind last time: big stacks of cash, all minted pre-1995, and the red notebook I've used to calculate my travels for the last year or so. I pick it up, give the rubber band that holds it together a little snap, and return it to the cabinet.

The twenties in my wallet are from home, so I take them out and stuff them into the opposite corner of the compartment where they won't get mixed up. Then I count out five hundred dollars in safe bills, fold them into my wallet, and shove all of it into the back pocket of my jeans. I put everything back the way it was.

Downstairs, I find Maggie standing in front of the narrow desk in the foyer with her purse wide open. She fishes out her car keys and then stuffs a bunch of envelopes inside. She looks up and sees me. "Are you all settled up there?"

"Yeah. And thanks for the shampoo and stuff." She gives me a dismissive flick of her wrist as if it were no big deal.

"I have a doctor's appointment, but I'll be back in a few hours." She gives her keys a little jingle but then stops cold. "Oh . . . Did you need your car today?" She gives me a confused stare. "I've been using it while you were gone."

When I walked into the dealership last March, I paid cash for the '95 Jeep Grand Cherokee and figured I'd leave it for Maggie when it was time for me to go home. Which is why I put the title in her name. It's also why I chose the color blue. "That's okay. I hoped you would."

She gives me a funny look, and I'm pretty sure she's about to start asking questions I don't want to answer.

"I've got to run. I'm meeting Anna in town. Drive the car as much as you want. I'll just tell you if I need it, okay?" I step onto the porch and pull the door closed behind me.

8

Anna and I spend the rest of the afternoon wandering around downtown Evanston shopping for clothes. Anna's dad gave her money to buy some new running shoes, so we start there. Then we start looking for clothes for me. Plaid Bermuda shorts appear to be in style, but I can't seem to bring myself to even try them on. Instead, I grab another pair of jeans.

Anna picks out a button-down shirt and holds it up to me for size.

"What do you think?"

I don't even look at it. I just grab her by the shoulders and pull her into me, and she looks down and laughs when she sees the shirt she picked out smashed in between our chests. "It's perfect," I say, and I kiss her, right in the middle of the Gap.

An hour and four stores later, I have a new pair of Chuck

Taylors and enough mid-90s fashion to get me through the next few months.

We head over to the deli and order huge subs to eat in the park. We hang out for a long time, talking about everything *but* the upcoming school year. I ask her about concerts she wants to see, and quiz her about the places she wants me to take her next. She asks me questions about San Francisco, and I tell her how I've spent most of my summer skateboarding around the city, climbing on an indoor rock wall, and missing her. I realize how pathetic I sound, but Anna must not hear it that way, because she scoots in closer and hooks her arms around the back of my neck.

She kisses me. When she pulls away, I look straight into her eyes. "What was that for?"

She shrugs. "I just love you."

"Good. I just love you too."

She kisses me again. Then she stands up, brushes the dirt off her shorts, and offers her hand to help me up. "Time to get you some music."

Justin is busy ringing up a customer, but he waves when he sees us come in. Anna waves back, and then leads me down one of the narrow aisles. I twist my head as we walk by the wooden bins, trying to get a better glimpse of the CDs.

We're near the back of the store looking through the Hot Summer Sounds kiosk when Justin comes up behind us. "You're back. How was the world?"

Anna flips around. "I don't know about the world, but

Mexico was really, really good," she says, throwing her arms around him. When Justin hugs her, he closes his eyes. But it must click that I'm standing here watching, because they suddenly spring open and lock on mine. I smile at him as his arms fall to his sides. He takes a big step back.

"Well, I'm glad you're home," he says to her.

"Me too."

He lifts his chin in my direction. "What's up?" He raises his hand in the air and I start to give him a fist bump, but then I realize that his palm is open. I correct quickly, giving him a high five instead. "So, you're back." The inflection in his voice makes it more of a question than a statement.

"Yeah. For now."

Anna shoots me a sideways glance and changes the subject. "What's this?" she asks, pointing up to the ceiling.

"Latest from Blind Melon." He gives a disappointed shake of his head. "Nowhere near as good as the last one. I think they're done." When Justin turns his back, Anna gives me a questioning look and I return it with a shrug. I've never heard of them, so I can only assume he's right.

"You two catch up, I'm going to go look around." I'm happy to leave them alone. This place is far too fascinating to spend another second talking when I could be thumbing through the bins.

Hand drawn signs hang from the ceiling and identify each section—R&B, Jazz, Rock. I wander around the record store, picking up CDs and turning them over to read the track lists, adding to my mental list of concerts I want to check out. I'm heading to the Ska section when I spot the poster rack in the far corner.

This proves to be even more entertaining. I stand there for a long time, flipping through the posters, wondering who half of these musicians are, and laughing out loud at the impressive collection of 90s boy bands.

I flip a few more frames and stop. "That one," I hear Anna say from behind me. I didn't even know she was standing there. She slides in front of me and taps on Billy Corgan's chest. "Please tell me you know these guys."

"Yeah." I nod, staring at the Smashing Pumpkins, marveling at the ridiculous amount of eyeliner they're each wearing.

"Have you seen them?" she asks.

I glance around to be sure Justin's nowhere near us. "Three times," I say. I rest my chin on Anna's shoulder and whisper in her ear, "Miami in '97, Dublin in 2000, Sydney in 2010."

She tilts her head toward me. I can tell from the look on her face that she's surprised to hear me share even the slightest hint of future information. "Good," she says with a satisfied grin. "They're from Chicago."

"I know."

Then I tell her what Maggie said about decorating my room and making it my own. "I could hang this one next to the window. Or maybe on the wall by the closet." I shrug. "Of course, it's kind of pointless to put posters on the walls if I won't be coming back here to visit."

She bites her lip and stares at me. Then she reaches down into the bin, grabs a rolled-up poster, and hands it to me.

When I take it, she turns on her heel and walks away. I'm smiling as I pick out a second one.

⌒

By late Friday afternoon, my room at Maggie's is starting to come together. Anna's photograph of our beach in La Paz is in a new frame and hanging above my bed. The closet is filled with enough new clothes to take me through the rest of the summer and well into fall, and I already had plenty of stuff to keep me warm this winter. I thumbtacked the postcards that used to be hidden in my top drawer onto the wall above my desk, and I hung a 1995 wall calendar there too, so I wouldn't forget *when* I am.

We hung the Weezer poster on the left side of the window and we're almost done hanging the Smashing Pumpkins on the right. "Down just a bit," Anna says. "There. Stop."

"It's good?" I raise an eyebrow and look over my shoulder at her. When she nods, I tape the corner in place and then take a few steps back to check out the result. "Better?" I ask.

She flops down on the edge of my bed and folds her legs underneath her. Reclining back on her hands, she slowly scans the room. "It's starting to look like you," she says. I take my own glance around. She's right: it does look more like me, but that wasn't my only intention. I wanted it to look more permanent, partially for me, but also for her.

"What are you going to do if I tell you I don't want you to keep coming back?" she asks.

I walk toward her, shaking my head. "I don't know. . . . Show up in a few weeks, I guess. Say good-bye to you and Maggie. Haul all this stuff up to the attic as slowly as possible, hoping the entire time that you'll change your mind."

"You seriously want to keep coming back here?"

I plant both palms on the bed, right next to her hips, and lean over her. "I told you before. I'll keep coming back until you're sick of me." Her lower lip quivers, like she's trying not to smile. "I don't know. Something tells me you're not sick of me yet."

She stares at me but doesn't speak for the longest time. "No," she finally says. "I'm not sick of you yet."

I brush my lips lightly against hers. "Good," I whisper.

"So," she begins, never breaking eye contact, "how would this work, exactly, you . . . visiting but not . . . staying?"

"I'll be here for anything that's important to you—races, dances, parties, whatever. We'll plan it all out, down to the minute. You'll never be surprised." She fakes a pout. "Well, not in a bad way, that is." That gets the slightest hint of a smile before her expression turns serious again.

"I'll know when you're leaving?"

"Every time."

"And when you're coming back again?"

"Every. Time," I repeat, this time with more emphasis on each word. "I promise."

"How can you be so certain you won't get knocked back?" I think about what she said the other night. How she fell apart after I left.

"I'll never stay longer than a few days. I'll be in control the whole time. If I ever feel like I'm losing control, I'll tell you right away."

She licks her lips and considers me for a moment. I think she's about to say something, but instead she slides one hand up my arm and around the back of my neck.

"Okay," she says.

"Okay?"

She nods and I feel a smile spread across my face. "Yes," she says as she hooks her finger into my belt loop and scoots back, giving me a little tug. I climb up and settle in next to her. "But I have a condition."

I kiss her. "Let's hear it."

"You need to tell Maggie who you are." I pull away from her. My first instinct is to shake my head no, but when I see the look on her face, I decide against it. I bite my tongue and let her finish her thought. "You could come and go without having to hide anything. Besides, don't you think she deserves to know?

"Also—and this is totally selfish, I realize—but when you left last time, Maggie was the only person I could really talk to. And now you're going to leave again. And again. And when you do, it would be nice to have one person in my life that I can talk to about you—one person I don't have to keep your secret from."

I rake my hands through my hair while I consider her request. I was all ready to tell Maggie the other night, but only because I thought she already knew who I was. I didn't think I had a choice. But she seems content with the way things are. I certainly am.

I decide to stall. "Do I have to tell her before I leave tonight?" I ask.

She shakes her head no and I blow out a breath. "Just . . . whenever . . ."

Whenever. My mind starts racing with all the ways I could tell Maggie who I am, and each time, my stomach knots up. But then Anna wipes the whole thing from my mind when she scoots in closer and kisses me hard, her hands on my skin and her hair everywhere, reminding me of all the reasons I'm here and all the reasons I have to keep coming back and the fact that I'll do anything to make her happy. When she pulls away, she smiles and says, "Emma's eighteenth birthday is in three weeks and her parents are throwing her a party. It'll be embarrassingly over the top."

"Then I'll be here."

"I have a few cross-country races you could come to. And homecoming's in October. Wait, we need to write this down." She hops up off the bed and comes back holding a pen and the wall calendar, and over the next fifteen minutes, the rest of our schedule falls into place. Homecoming. Cross Country State Finals. Thanksgiving. Christmas. We have plans to see each other every two or three weeks, but I can already tell that won't be enough. I'm not sure how to do it yet, but I'm already concocting ways to squeeze in more time with her without making her parents suspicious or running the risk of getting knocked back.

Anna closes the calendar and tosses it on the floor. "When are you leaving?" she asks.

"Soon," I say as I play with her curls. "Maggie will be home in a few hours. I should take off before she gets back; otherwise I'll have to stage some elaborate cab ride to the airport or something."

She reaches up and brushes my hair off my forehead. "I want to be here when you go."

I can't imagine how that's going to make this whole thing easier, but she looks pretty determined. "Are you sure?" I ask.

She nods and says, "Positive. In fact, do you mind if I stick around for a little while . . . afterward?" Her nose crinkles up. "Or is that just weird?"

I smile as I picture Anna and Maggie, hanging out in the kitchen drinking tea. "Stay as long as you want to. I bet Maggie would like the company. You can even come over when I'm gone."

She rolls her eyes before she covers her face with her hand. "I did that last time you left. I moped around in here for hours." She looks at me and says, "I even put on your coat," and then hides her face again. She lets out a sigh and shakes her head, like she can't believe she's admitting this to me. But I like the idea of her wearing my coat. I like the idea that this room might help us feel some kind of connection to each other, even when we're apart. I pull her hand away from her face and knit her fingers together with mine.

Before I can say anything, she changes the subject. "You should probably leave Maggie a note before you go."

"Good idea," I say. I come up on my knees and pin her hands

above her head. I kiss her neck and she squirms underneath me. "I'll be right back. Don't move."

Downstairs on the narrow desk in the hallway, I spot the Post-its right away. I write a note telling Maggie I'll be here in three weeks, and stick it on the shelf next to the basket where she always drops her keys.

Then I stare at it. I picture Anna, sitting in my room after I've left, alone and wishing she weren't. I picture myself doing the same thing in a different room two thousand miles and seventeen years away. I don't want to leave. But at least I'm here now.

I race back up the stairs and open the door.

And she's right where I left her.

august 2012

9

san francisco, california

I shut my eyes tight and lift my forehead off the steering wheel. My neck goes slack and I fall back into the seat, gripping the sides of my head and trying to piece together where I am. There's a faint bit of light streaming in through the cracks on each side of the garage door, and I strain to read the clock on the dashboard: 6:03 P.M.

I rip into the box of supplies on the passenger seat, blindly groping for one of the water bottles. I down the first one without stopping and reach for another. My eyelids are still half closed when I pop the top on the Starbucks Doubleshot, and I let them fall shut completely as I tip my head back, letting the coffee slide down my throat. My whole body is shaking, and there's sweat dripping down my face even though I'm freezing.

It takes a good twenty minutes for the pounding to turn into more of a dull throbbing, and when it does, I reach into the glove compartment for the car keys and my phone. The screen shows two missed calls from Mom back on Wednesday night, and four texts from Brooke over the last two days. I open the texts first and read them in order:

> Ugh. Too quiet without you here. Having fun?

> Seeing a show @ the Bottom of the Hill tonight. In real time. Like normal person I am. Borrring . . .

> Worried about you. Reply when you're back, okay?

> No "mom" jokes in reply to last text, pls. Miss ya.

I squint at the screen, hit reply, and type out my message:

> No jokes. Back home now. C U soon.

My mouth is still dry and my limbs feel weak, so I reach for another bottle of water and recline back in the seat, looking around the garage. In his e-mail, the owner had mentioned that it was "on the small side," but that turned out to be a major understatement. When I first opened the door, I stood in the alley for the longest time trying to figure out if the Jeep would even fit.

It proved to be as challenging as it looked, but I folded the side mirrors flat against the frame, backed in slowly, and pressed the button on the electronic garage door opener, hoping for the best. I was a little surprised when it actually closed. I press that button again and the garage door jolts to life, squeaking and rattling and eventually settling into place over my head.

In the alley, I leave the Jeep running and hop out. There's not much back here other than trash cans and rusting garden equipment. I grab a water bottle and throw my backpack over my shoulder, heading toward an abandoned pile of old flower-pots, and then I take a handful of dirt, dump some water over the top, and work the mud into the grooves of the shiny cara-biners that hang from the external straps of my backpack.

But my cover-up efforts turn out to be unnecessary. When I get home, there's a note from Mom on the counter saying that Brooke's out on a date, Dad's at a dinner meeting, and she's going to the movies with friends. So much for family night.

I make myself something to eat and flop down on the couch. For the rest of the evening, I flip through channels, stare at the empty space next to me, and wonder how Anna and I are going to pull this off. She should be here right now. Or I should be there. But we shouldn't be *this*.

I must eventually drift off because when I open my eyes again, the room is pitch-black, the television is off, and I'm covered with a blanket. I haul myself up to my room and fall into bed, still wearing the same clothes I had on when I left Evanston.

⟋⟍⟋⟍○

The voices coming from the TV in the kitchen are low but audible, and when I turn the corner, I find Dad with his hip against the counter, spooning yogurt into his mouth and watching the news. He looks up when I walk in.

"Hey. Welcome home. How was your trip?"

I'm grateful that he asked the question the way he did so that I don't need to lie when I answer. "The trip was great. A lot of fun."

Dad takes his glasses off and cleans them with the edge of his shirt. He puts them back in place and looks at me over the top of the frames. "The nights must have been cold."

It takes me a second or two to think about how to phrase this one. None of the nights in Maggie's house were even remotely chilly. "No, the nights were actually really warm," I say. Too warm, in fact.

Dad finishes his yogurt and pours himself a glass of orange juice. Once I start in on my cereal there's a lot of crunching, but the only voices in the room are coming from the television. He glances up at me a few times, as if he's trying to think of something to fill the uncomfortable silence. But then something on the screen gets his attention, and he's off the hook.

He reaches for the remote, turning up the volume, and pivoting to face the screen. "Breaking news this morning," the anchorwoman says. A red and blue graphic that reads TRAGEDY IN THE TENDERLOIN flies in from the side of the screen and stops in the center—large and ominous, for effect—before it shrinks and settles at the bottom where it can't interfere with the video footage of a building ablaze against the backdrop of the early-morning sky.

> *An apartment fire in the Tenderloin district claimed the lives of two young children in the early hours this morning. Five-year-old Rebecca Walker and her three-year-old brother, Robert, were asleep when a fire broke out in the bedroom they share on the third floor of an apartment complex on Ellis Street. The parents were rushed to the hospital for smoke inhalation. Firefighters were unable to rescue the two children.*

I take a big bite of cereal and walk over to the counter to pour myself a cup of coffee, listening as the anchorwoman passes the story to the on-the-scene reporter. I'm only half paying attention, but I catch the gist. The parents were unable to get to the children, there was no smoke detector, and an investigation is underway to determine the cause. I peek at the screen when the downstairs neighbor describes hearing screams through the ceiling and calling 911. After one more shot of the high-drama burning-building footage, they move back to the studio and the anchorwoman wraps up the story and moves along to a new one about a fender bender that's currently being cleared from the Bay Bridge.

"That's horrible," Dad says, staring at the screen. I'm pretty sure he's referring to the previous news item about the fire and not the minor car accident. "Those poor parents. They must feel so guilty." He's tips his head back, downing his juice, and brings his glass to the sink. He won't look at me, but he doesn't have to. I can feel it. The space around us is already filling up with all the things he wants so badly to say right now.

Until recently, I bolted from any room that contained both Dad and news. I'd learned my lesson. If some horrible tragedy took place and I stayed silent, he'd shoot me this contemptuous look and say something like, "Doesn't this even *bother* you?" On the flip side, if I made a comment that expressed even the slightest bit of remorse for the situation, he'd whip out a pen and paper and start plotting out all the ways I could go back and stop the plane crash/bus crash/shooting/stabbing/explosion/carjacking/terrorist attack/etc. Either way, my response to him would be the same. I don't change things. It's not my place to change things, just because I can. And yes, of course it bothers me. All the time. I'm not heartless.

Losing my sister in a previous decade came with its share of complications, but as it turns out, there were also a few silver linings. Meeting Anna was one. No longer having these excruciating conversations with my dad was another.

Brooke nearly spills my coffee when she throws her arms around my neck. "You're home!" After a quick hug, she bounces over to Dad and gives him a peck on the cheek. She stops suddenly, and her gaze darts back and forth between the two of us. "Uh-oh," she says, wiggling her fingers in the air. "There's tension . . ." Brooke slips into her usual role, using humor to restore peace to our somewhat dysfunctional family. She slaps Dad's arm with the back of her hand. "So, what'd he do this time?" She looks over at me and gives me a wink.

"Nothing," Dad says. "Nothing at all."

The double meaning isn't lost on me.

He cleans his glasses again, this time with a dishcloth, looking out the window the entire time. "It's going to be a gorgeous day." His voice is higher that usual and that enthusiastic tone sounds forced. "Let's get that boat on the bay, shall we?" He checks his watch. "I want to leave in a half hour. Can you two be ready?"

Brooke and I nod.

"Good. I'd better go see if your mom needs help."

As soon as he's out of earshot, I turn to Brooke. "Family day," I say flatly. "Super."

She raises an eyebrow at me. "Come on. They're not that bad, you know?"

"Easy for you to say. *You're* not a huge source of disappointment to one and a constant worry to the other."

"And neither are you, but whatever . . ." She lifts herself onto the kitchen counter and points to the half-empty coffee mug I'm holding. "Hurry up, we only have a few minutes. Top off your coffee, pour me a cup, and tell me *everything*."

So I do. In hushed tones I speed through the details, telling her all about Maggie and the reason there's a photo of the three of us at the zoo. Brooke's eyes grow wide, and she asks for more details about the stuff I try to breeze past, like Emma and Justin's breakup and how the Greenes let me crash on their couch the first night. She sips her coffee, hanging on every word, and after I've given her a play-by-play of practically the entire trip, I shake my head and tell her how Anna decided—once again, and for reasons I honestly can't fathom—that she'd rather put up with the oddities of this bizarre relationship than tell me to stay where I belong. I tell Brooke how hard it was to leave, and with every word, I'm more relieved to have one person here who understands. The thought makes me remember Anna's request for a confidante of her own. I wish I hadn't left town without giving her one.

Mom and Dad walk back into the kitchen carrying bags over their shoulders and jackets in their arms. Dad heads straight for the garage, but Mom takes a detour to give me a peck on the cheek and tell me she's happy I'm home. Then she asks me to carry the cooler out to the car.

As I'm picking it up, Brooke leans in close and nudges me with her elbow. "I'm glad you're home too," she says.

It feels so strange to lie to Brooke, but I do it anyway. "So am I," I say.

10

People keep walking by, but so far no one seems to have noticed that I'm sitting here alone in the Jeep, staring at the door that leads to my locker. The warning bell sounded thirty seconds ago, but I can't bring myself to leave this spot.

It would be so easy to close my eyes right now, disappear from this car, and open them in a secluded corner of Westlake Academy. I'd go straight to the office and tell Ms. Dawson at the front desk that my family's plans have changed, I am back in town for my senior year after all, and, if possible, I'd like a class schedule. Then I'd walk the hallway until I found Anna. We'd eat lunch with Emma and Danielle like we always did. That night, while we were sprawled out on her bedroom floor studying together, I'd surprise her by grabbing her hands and transporting her to a quiet spot far away, like a beach in Bora-Bora.

The final bell rings. I reach down for my backpack, throw it over my shoulder, and slam the Jeep door. As I cross the student parking lot, I look down at my jeans and T-shirt. I never thought I'd actually miss the Westlake uniform.

I don't pass a single person as I climb the staircase that leads to my locker on the third floor, and when I pull up on the latch, the click echoes in the empty hall. Inside, there's nothing but empty water bottles, a few granola-bar wrappers, and a bunch of loose papers that someone fed through the slats while I was gone. Collectively, they represent everything I missed last spring. There's a prom court voting ballot, a sign-up sheet for the annual senior class Olympics, and a flyer for the spring musical. I push them back in my locker and shut the door.

I printed out my class schedule this morning, but I barely even glanced at it before I shoved it into the front pocket of my jeans. I haven't the slightest clue where I'm supposed to be right now, so I dig it out and open it. First period: AP World Civilizations with Mrs. McGibney. Building C, the one farthest from my locker, clear on the other side of the quad. I check the time on my phone. I'm already five minutes late.

It takes me another five minutes to reach the classroom door, and when I open it, a roomful of faces I haven't thought about in months turns to look at me. I take a few tentative steps inside, and the next time I look around I see Cameron in the back row. He lifts his hand and gives me a nod.

"You must be my missing student." McGibney doesn't look up or stop writing on the whiteboard as she addresses me. "Are you Mr. Cooper?" she asks, but she keeps talking and doesn't wait for me to answer. "I was just going over the rules of this class. The first one is that I expect my students to be sitting in their seats when the bell rings."

"Sorry," I mumble under my breath.

"I give one freebie, and you just used it." She still hasn't looked away from the board. I have no idea how she can talk to me and write at the same time, but I'm a little bit impressed. She's already written the words "First Civilizations" and started a bulleted list below: "agriculture," "significant cities," "writing systems." "Are you going to sit down and join us, Mr. Cooper, or would you prefer to stand by the door for the rest of my class?" She adds a bullet and the words "formal states" as she speaks.

The only empty seat is in the first row, directly in front of her desk, and I can feel every eye watching me as I shuffle across the room and settle in. Trying not to move too quickly, too slowly, or too loudly, I unzip my backpack and remove my notebook and a pencil.

A pencil. I run it back and forth between my fingers as I picture Anna piling her curls on top of her head and using my pencil to hold them in place.

"Hi." The voice jolts me from my thoughts, and I look to my left. Megan Jenks is leaning over her desk, writing in her notebook, and looking at me from behind a veil of blond hair.

"Hi," I say under my breath.

She smiles before she turns back to her notes. I return to mine, madly copying the words on the whiteboard into my composition book, as if the exercise alone will give them some kind of meaning. McGibney asks a question but I only half hear it. Not that it matters since I have no idea how to answer.

Megan's hand shoots up next to me. "Miss Jenks," McGibney says, pointing at her.

"The Neolithic Revolution."

"Yes. Good." McGibney returns to the whiteboard and writes something under the word "agriculture" as Megan looks over and sends another quick smile my way. I give her a nod, turn to my notebook, and write "Neolithic Revolution." It's the first day of school, and I'm already wondering if I missed some required reading or something, because I have absolutely no idea what they're talking about.

<hr />

The day moves at a painfully slow pace, and I muddle through Statistics, Spanish, and Physics until it's finally time for lunch. I make small talk with the people in line. When they ask me how I am, I tell them I'm fine. When they ask me where I've been, I give them one of several answers: Traveling around. Seeing the world. And, I'd prefer not to talk about it.

Everything happened so quickly last spring. When I lost Brooke in 1994, Mom insisted I get as close to her as I could, and it was my idea to stay with my grandmother in 1995 Evanston. It wasn't 1994 Chicago, but it was close enough. Against my better judgment, I left it to Mom to come up with an excuse to explain why I was missing school here.

She panicked. At first she told them I was "Away, sorting

out a few things." But when a week turned into two, she had no other choice but to expand upon her story, and suddenly I was "sorting things out" at a treatment center for troubled teens on the east coast. They had no idea when I'd be home. That was up to the doctors.

At least word didn't get out to my friends, who seem to believe my version of events: I tapped into some latent rebellious streak and took off to backpack around Europe.

I grab a sandwich and a huge bottle of water, head into the cafeteria, and immediately spot the guys on the other side of the double glass doors. They're sitting outside on the deck at the long table that overlooks the quad.

When I arrive, Adam scoots over and I slide my tray next to his. He has a mouthful of food, but after he finishes chewing and washes it down with his water, he looks at me like I'm the new kid or something. "Hey. I almost forgot you were back here."

I glare at him like I'm offended. "Thanks . . . missed you too."

Cameron has been talking nonstop all summer about his new girlfriend, but since I've barely seen him outside the park, I haven't met her yet. Now she's watching me with a curious expression, but he's too fixated on his pasta to notice.

I reach across the table. "Hi," I say. "I don't think we've met. I'm Bennett."

She brings her hand to her chest and says, "Sophie," before she extends it in my direction. Cameron looks up and attempts a smile even though his mouth is full of noodles and sauce. He gestures back and forth between the two of us and then sticks his thumb up.

Another tray slides across the table, and Sam slaps me on the shoulder as he sits down. "Hey. How's the first day going?"

He looks different. It's only been a few days since I saw him last, but his hair is cropped closer to his head than I've ever seen it, and it doesn't look like he has shaved in the last day or two. He looks older or something.

I shrug and say, "Good, I guess," as I look around campus. "Just . . . different." I've always found the glass walls and metal railings interesting, but today they serve as a reminder that everything about this place and its modern architecture is in such stark contrast with the refined look of Westlake Academy. I can't imagine what Anna would think of these buildings. I'm pretty sure she'd have no idea what to make of the solar panels next to the living roof above the art studio.

"What do you have after lunch?" Sam asks as he bites into his burger.

I lean back, digging into the front pocket of my jeans for my schedule. I unfold it and look for the fifth-period box. "English. With Wilson."

Sam wipes his mouth with the back of his hand and says, "Hey, me too. Good." Just as he says the last word, someone lets out a gasp from behind us and we both turn our heads. "Hey, Linds," Sam says, sliding down the bench to make room for her between us.

"*What* did you do to your hair?" Lindsey puts her food on

the table and stares at his nearly bald head in wonder. She reaches out like she's going to touch it, but then pulls her hand back again.

"I cut it."

"With what?"

Sam laughs as he rubs his hand back and forth over the top of his head. "I love it. It feels cool. Here," he says, leaning over in her direction. "Touch it."

"No." She smacks his shoulder with the back of her hand but laughs along with him. Then she plants her palms on the sides of his face and kisses him on the forehead. "I just saw you yesterday. You couldn't have warned me?" Lindsey's shaking her head as she sits down.

He shrugs. "It was spontaneous."

She stares at me pointedly. I resist the urge to laugh. And to touch my own hair. "See, Coop, this is the kind of stuff that happened last year when you weren't around to keep him in line. Where were you during yesterday's head-shaving debacle?"

I hold my hands up in front of me, palms out. "Not my night to watch him." Lindsey rolls her eyes and takes a long draw of soda from her straw. She's still shaking her head as she digs into her pasta.

Sam runs his hand over his head wearing a wide grin. "I like it."

Lindsey and Sam have been together since the beginning of our junior year. She's a full inch taller than any of us, including Sam, and dominates on the volleyball court. We'd always been friends with her, but at some point during our sopho-more year, she started eating lunch at our table. I don't even remember it being weird. She just sat down.

I think she had a falling out with her friends. I once asked her about it, and she admitted that, aside from her teammates, she didn't have a lot of close girlfriends. *I like to know where I stand with people*, I remember her saying. *None of this today we're friends, tomorrow . . . poof.* She had pinched her fingers together and made them explode apart. *Guys are so much easier.* A long pause. *That's a compliment, by the way.*

Maybe we're more complicated than you think, I'd said, keeping a straight face. *What if we don't like you at all and we just don't know how to tell you?*

She'd looked at me right in the eyes. *Do you guys like me, Coop?*

I couldn't help but smile. *Yeah. We do.*

She had shrugged. *See.*

Months later, a bunch of us were hanging out at the beach. Sam was on one side of the bonfire telling one of his *remember that time* stories, complete with animated facial expressions and exaggerated gestures, when Lindsey wrapped her hand around my arm and rested her chin on my shoulder. "I think I like him," she admitted, and I stared at her in disbelief. "Sam?" I asked, and she shrugged and said, "Look at him. He's kind of adorable."

I looked at him. I didn't find him adorable. But then I looked back at her and saw that she meant every word. Sam caught her looking his way and shot her a smile that made her turn red and bury her face in my shoulder, and just so he wouldn't get the wrong idea, I subtly motioned back and forth between the two of them. Two weeks later, they were Sam and Lindsey. I gave her endless amounts of grief for blushing so hard that night.

She twists her pasta around her fork and looks at me out of the corner of her eye. "So tell me everything. I barely got to see you this summer. How was it? What did you do?"

"It was fine." I can't think of anything interesting to tell her outside of the concerts I went to with Brooke or my trips to visit Anna in La Paz, so I leave it at that and ask her what she did. She tells me she spent most of the summer driving back and forth to beach volleyball tournaments in Southern California.

It reminds me that it's been a long time since I saw her play. "When's your first game?" I ask.

"A week from Saturday," she says. "You should come. Sam will be there." She elbows him and gives him a half smile. "He'll be the one wearing a hat."

Sam ignores her comment and leans forward on the table, resting his chin in his hand. "What are you doing after school today?" he asks me.

"Homework." I think about the mountain of assignments that have been doled out over the last four classes, and the sad fact that I still have three more to go.

"That's it?" Lindsey asks.

"I don't know. I guess I was thinking about heading over to the climbing gym." I look at Sam. "Want to come?"

"Sure. But it'll have to be on the late side. I'm tutoring tonight."

Since when does Sam tutor? "You're tutoring?"

He shrugs. "I must've told you. I started at the end of last year, but this year I'm running the sixth grade math program, so it's a lot more intense." He takes a big sip of his drink. "It's fun. You should do it. It'll look good on your college apps."

I haven't even thought about college applications. "Are the kids cool?"

Sam shakes his head. "Hell, no. They're a bunch of spoiled brats with some serious entitlement issues."

I laugh. "Way to sell it."

"I'm kidding. There are, like, two cool ones. But seriously, you'd be good at it," he says to me. "You're good with kids and stuff."

"Yeah," I say sarcastically, "I'm super patient. Especially with the spoiled ones with entitlement issues." I give him a wide smile and two overly enthusiastic thumbs-up.

I reach for my water, suddenly realizing what Lindsey meant by her *That's it?* question. Everyone's afternoons are filled with sports, clubs, and community service projects that look good to a college admissions staff. I haven't even thought about what I'm doing next year, let alone boosting my application.

The bell rings and everyone dumps their trash in the bins before taking off in their separate directions. Lindsey gives Sam one more eye roll before she pushes his head in my direction. "Watch him," she says with a wink. I laugh, thinking how much Lindsey and Anna would like each other. The four of *us* would have fun together.

I'm glad Sam and I are going the same way, because I didn't even look at the room number before I stuffed my schedule back into my pocket. As we walk through the halls toward our lockers, my mind drifts back to Anna again, and I start piecing together her schedule, wondering what she'd be doing back in 1995 Evanston. Would she still be in class, or out on the track? Would it be her day to work at the bookstore? Did she, Emma, and Danielle talk about me over lunch? Did Anna tell them that I'm coming back? Did Emma lose it when she found out?

Sam comes to a stop.

"What?"

He points at a row of lockers. "Don't you need your stuff?"

"Huh? Oh, yeah. . . ." It suddenly dawns on me that we're standing in front of *my* locker.

Sam shakes his head and gives me a pitying look. "I swear, man, it's like you're back but you're not."

I avoid his eyes as I spin the combination dial.

I couldn't have said it better myself.

11

After an hour at the climbing gym with Sam and a rushed dinner with my parents, I head upstairs to start on my homework. I navigate to the school website and check this week's assignments. I have a couple of hours of reading for Chemistry, a paper due in two weeks on the rise of the Tigris-Euphrates civilization, and an essay I'm supposed to begin writing for English.

I lean back with my arms folded behind my head, staring up at the ceiling. Until recently, I'd never really thought much about my bedroom. Mom had it professionally decorated when we moved in four years ago, and I don't recall picking out a single thing.

Unlike Anna's room, there are no posters on my walls, no maps of the world, no bookshelves filled with trophies and CD cases. It's just really white. White walls. White ceiling. White rug. White comforter. The desk is glass and metal, but that does very little to break up the monotony. The only color in the room comes from the huge canvas painting my mom bought at an art auction a couple of years ago, and the red glass bowl— overflowing with ticket stubs from every live concert I've ever seen—that's perched on the nightstand next to my bed. Aside from that bowl, this room could belong to anyone.

Anna was only in my bedroom for a matter of minutes, but in that short amount of time, she must have seen it for what it is: a room that looks like it's staged for an upcoming sale.

I should start on homework, but instead I reach for my phone. It's a little after nine o'clock here and an hour later in Boulder. I type out a message to Brooke:

> U there?

I wait for her to reply, and finally the phone chirps.

> Yup. Studying.

> How was your first day back?

I type in one word:

> Sucked.

Brooke's reply appears quickly.

> Sorry. :(

I stare at the screen, thinking about what to say. Finally I type:

> I miss her.

I look at the words before I hit send. A few minutes pass before Brooke replies.

> I know. Go do something to take your mind off it.

That's what the climbing was for, but it just made me wish I were outside on real rocks and reminded me of my first date with Anna.

> Like what?

I picture Brooke letting out an exasperated huff when she reads my message. She comes back with three rapid-fire responses:

> IDK.

> Something fun.

> Something good.

I go back to my computer, where I find myself drifting off into thoughts about college admissions and catching up with everyone else on extracurricular activities. I search for volunteer opportunities and find hundreds in San Francisco alone, ranging from part-time jobs that support senior citizens to working with kids in the city's poorer neighborhoods.

This one site catches my eye, and the reason isn't entirely lost on me. I click on it, check out the programs, and watch the video. Then I navigate back to the map. The building is in the heart of the Tenderloin, only a block away from where last Saturday's fire took place.

It's not as if I've forgotten about it. It's been hanging out in the back of my mind for the last three days. But now that this map is filling the screen, I can't block it out of my mind anymore. Without even thinking about what I'm about to do, I move the cursor to the search field and type the words "Tenderloin fire."

There's a long list of links and I click on the most recent one. It basically says the same thing the TV news story reported last Saturday morning: an apartment fire on the third floor killed two children, a five-year-old girl and a three-year-old boy. Neighbors called 911. Source of fire remains unknown. Investigation underway.

I scroll down to the bottom of the screen and find an update to the story: investigators are still trying to determine the cause. The parents aren't speaking to the media.

When I click the corner of the window, the browser closes and the story disappears. I push my chair away from my desk and reach for the enormous English book I was given today during class. I flop down on my bed and start reading. I'm only a couple of paragraphs into the homework assignment when my mind starts wandering again.

I stand up and return to my desk. I open the bottom drawer and dig deep, shuffling through a collection of postcards I've bought to give to Anna, little scraps of paper I've saved for no particular reason, and climbing maps folded haphazardly and stuffed inside. At the bottom, I feel the red notebook I hid when I got back from Evanston last weekend. I open it to a dog-eared page near the back.

The calculations are especially messy, stretching across the binding and continuing down the sides. Even the pencil marks themselves have a bit of a manic look to them, but with complete clarity, I remember writing them and know precisely what they mean.

I barely knew Emma at the time, but I stayed up all night calculating and weighing the risks of altering an entire day to prevent an accident and possibly save her life. Sure, I'd gone back before—five minutes here, ten minutes there, each time changing totally minor, completely insignificant events. But I'd never gone back that far or deliberately changed *that* many minor things. I didn't even know if it would be possible. And even though it was, I decided I would never do it again.

But looking at the dates and calculations reminds me how I felt when it was all over and I saw the look of pure relief on Anna's face. She practically skipped down the driveway after seeing Emma that Saturday morning—all of her various internal organs intact and the skin on her face scratch-free and perfect—and as I stared at her through the windshield, this feeling of intense pride washed over me. *I* had done that. *I* made that happen. It was the first time I'd ever felt that maybe I had been wrong about this gift of mine. It was the first time I'd wondered if maybe Dad was right.

Now I run my finger along the pages, thinking about the look on his face as we stood in the kitchen last week, watching the news on the screen. He wanted to say something, but he knew I wasn't supposed to travel anymore. Besides, I'd told him so many times that he probably knew it was senseless to bring it up again: I don't change things.

I wonder what he'd say if he knew that I once did.

For Emma, I'd gone back fifty-two hours. Could I go back even further?

I turn to a clean page and start scribbling some new calculations. I know I'll never be able to answer the big ethical questions with any certainty, but a few minutes later, I've figured out the math. I'll need to go back about sixty-four hours. Two and a half . . . almost *three* days. I'd have to stay back there, just like I did with Emma, and repeat those three days again to be sure that the do-over stuck, that nothing unintentional got altered along the way. I slam the notebook shut, bury it deep in my drawer again, and go back to my homework.

~~~

This is officially insane.

I'm standing in my room, zipping up my backpack. It's

heavy, filled to bursting with water bottles, Doubleshots, Red Bulls, a wad of cash, a flashlight, a smoke detector, and a fire extinguisher. I look around the room and shake my head. What am I doing?

Before I can give it another thought, I close my eyes and visualize my destination. When I open them, I'm in the alley I found on Google Maps, just one block south of the apartment complex. I've never been here before and already I hope I won't have to come back again.

To describe this neighborhood as sketchy would be a massive understatement. It's only a little after five A.M., but there are pockets of activity everywhere. A group of guys are hanging in front of a liquor store on the corner, and the doorways are filled with homeless people curled up in sleeping bags. There's an eerie buzz around me, and I feel my guard go up as I walk down the street toward the address. I keep my eyes up, my feet moving.

I'm relieved to find the apartment and somehow feel a little bit safer as I slip into the entryway. I scan the directory on the wall, reading the last names next to each of the little black buttons until I find Walker. I check to be sure no one's watching me.

I close my eyes and when I open them again, I'm on the other side of the main entrance. There are no lights on the lower floor and the staircase is barely visible. I reach into my backpack for my flashlight, and I shine it on the stairs as I climb the three flights that lead to 3c. Closing my eyes, I visualize the other side of the door.

In the apartment, I sneak down the hallway with my flashlight. School pictures line the walls, and for the first time tonight, I don't question whether or not this will work, I just hope it does.

I creep around the corner, past the living room and toward the bedrooms. After I pass the bathroom, I stand frozen, facing two closed doors. I have no idea which one belongs to the kids, so I think back to the video footage of the building on fire and make the educated guess that it's the door on the right; the one closest to the street. I twist the handle and the door creaks open.

On the far side of the room, two twin beds bookend a large window that looks out over the street below. A thin stream of light is coming in from between the curtains, casting a soft glow on the dingy carpet.

The kids are breathing, low and soft, and neither one of them moves as I remove my backpack and cross the room. I crouch down, remove the brand-new smoke detector I found buried in a box out in our garage marked HOME IMPROVEMENT, and position it as high on the wall as I can reach. Back in the hall, I grab the small fire extinguisher I snagged from under our kitchen sink and prop it against the short wall between the two bedrooms.

I close my eyes and visualize the exact same spot I was in before the fire broke out last Saturday in the early-morning hours. My bedroom.

By the time I open my eyes, the other me has already disappeared, sent back to who knows where and when, and I'm free to take his place.

The last time I was here, I had just hauled myself up from the couch downstairs. My head was still aching and my mouth was uncomfortably dry. But right now my heart is racing in a good way, and I'm so full of adrenaline I'm about to burst out of my own skin. I don't know if I was successful or not, and I won't know until the news comes on in a few hours, but somehow, I have a feeling it worked. This wasn't what Brooke meant when she said I should do "something good," but I'm pretty sure I just did.

12

The first time around, I had climbed into bed with my clothes on and fallen back into a deep sleep. But there's no way I could have fallen asleep tonight. I've been sitting here for the last hour waiting to see the first signs of daylight, and thinking about what I just did.

Suddenly it dawns on me. In fact, it's odd that I didn't think of it until now, or factor it into my decision process as I sat in my bedroom on the Monday night I just wiped away. I'd been three days closer to returning to Anna. Now I have to do those days all over again, like I just rolled the dice and landed on the square that reads, *Go back three spaces*. I don't know if this do-over will work, but one thing's certain: it may actually be the most unselfish thing I've ever done in my life.

The TV is the first thing I hear, and when I turn the corner I find Dad in the exact same place he was the first time:

leaning against the counter, spooning yogurt into his mouth, watching the news.

The expression on my face must look different this time, because he takes one look at me and breaks into a grin. "Well, someone's in a good mood," he says. "Nice trip?" My heart starts beating fast and I force myself to keep a straight face.

It's a completely unfounded superstition, but I still feel the intense need to keep things exactly the same—at least until I know if the do-over was a success. So even though I'm not at all hungry, I head for the pantry and emerge with the same box of cereal. "The trip was great."

"The nights must have been cold."

It takes me a second to remember what I said last time. "No, the nights were actually really warm."

Dad finishes his yogurt and pours his juice while I force down a spoonful of cereal. There's the same uncomfortable silence. The only voices in the room are coming from the television. Three. Two. One.

"Breaking news," the anchorwoman says. I set my bowl on the counter and my head flips around. There's no fancy TRAGEDY IN THE TENDERLOIN graphic today. Instead, the first thing I see is similar-looking video footage of the apartment building ablaze against the backdrop of a dark night sky.

An apartment fire broke out in the Tenderloin district in the early hours this morning. Neighbors say they were awoken by a smoke alarm and helped all four

residents of the apartment escape before the flames
engulfed the building. Two children, their parents, and
a neighbor are currently being treated at San Francisco
General for smoke inhalation. All five are expected to
be released later today.

I look over at Dad. He's glanced up at the newscast here and there, but this time, he doesn't set his yogurt container down or reach for the remote to turn up the volume. On screen, the anchorwoman never breaks to an on-the-scene reporter, because there is no on-the-scene reporter. Instead, the camera goes to a wide shot of the studio, and she turns to her coanchor, who flashes her most concerned expression. "A good reminder to check those batteries in your smoke detectors."

The newscast moves to the fender bender that's currently being cleared from the Bay Bridge. Dad doesn't notice me staring at him, unable to speak or move or take in a good deep breath.

I did that.

"Do you remember that apartment we lived in when you were born?" Dad asks. "It was way out on the edge of the city. We moved to a different building when you were four, but when you were really little, your mom and I lived on the third floor of an apartment complex."

I actually did that.

Now that I know the do-over was a success, I no longer feel the urge to keep every element of our conversation exactly the same as it was the first time around. Which is good, since I'm frozen in place, staring at him while I try to force my jaw back where it belongs.

"Your mom hated living on such a high floor. We had this rickety old fire escape, and I thought it was kind of cool, but she was always afraid of a fire breaking out and all of us having to use it. She's still terribly paranoid about fires. Have you seen all the smoke detectors we have in this house?" He laughs. "She even makes me keep spare ones in the garage. Are you okay, Bennett?"

I have to speak. Now.

"I did that." My voice shakes.

"Did what?"

"That," I say, pointing lamely at the TV.

He turns and looks at it. "Oh? Really? I didn't know that. I always thought that looked a bit dangerous."

The newscast has moved on to a story about this Friday's Critical Mass bike ride through downtown. "No. Not that," I say, and Dad looks back at me quizzically.

I'd better talk quickly. If everything goes roughly the same way it did last time, I have about three more minutes before Brooke arrives. I want Dad to be the first to know what happened. I want to tell him while we're alone.

I keep my voice low and strong. "Dad, listen to me. I did that over. The fire in the Tenderloin." I gesture to the TV again, but he doesn't look away from me this time. His eyes are locked on mine, hanging on every word. "We've been here before, and that story was different then. Those kids didn't make it out of the fire. They died."

My heart was already racing, but now that I've said the word "died," it kicks into a whole new gear. My legs are shaking, so I rest a hand on the counter to steady myself. Dad looks at the TV, then back at me, then back at the TV. "What?" he asks.

"Those kids died. But I went back and changed what happened."

Dad's staring at me like I told a joke and he doesn't get the punch line.

I give the kitchen a paranoid glance to be sure we're still alone before I blurt it all out. "I came downstairs—just like I did ten minutes ago—and when I walked into the kitchen there was a news story about a fire in the Tenderloin that killed two kids. You didn't say anything, but I knew you wanted to. And you probably thought I didn't care, but I did."

Dad pulls his glasses low on his nose and watches me over the top of them. "Later, we went sailing, and the next day we drove Brooke to the airport, and then I started school on Monday and, frankly, it was kind of a shitty day and I couldn't stop thinking about those kids anyway so I thought . . . why not try it? I wanted to see if I could fix it. I wanted to know if I could stop it from happening the way it did."

Dad opens his mouth to speak, but he stops. He looks at me for a full minute, his face contorting into new expressions the whole time. I'm waiting, watching him, holding my breath and trying to figure out what he's thinking. Finally, his whole face relaxes. His eyes shine. I can tell he's proud of me.

"Hey! You're home!" I startle as Brooke wraps her arms around my neck and whispers, "God, it sucks here without you." She takes two steps back and looks from me to Dad. "What's up? You okay?" She rises to her tiptoes and pecks him on the cheek.

"Yeah, I'm okay." Dad gives her a small smile, but he doesn't look at me at all.

Brooke bounces over to the refrigerator and opens the door. She stands in the chill while she tries to decide what to eat.

Dad looks a little unstable. "We should get going soon. I'm just . . ." He trails off as he looks around the kitchen. "I'll go see if your mom needs help."

Brooke pours herself a bowl of cereal and lifts herself up to sit on the kitchen counter. "Okay, we only have a few minutes. Tell me *everything*."

Exactly like last time, I speak in hushed tones, telling her all about Maggie and the reason there's a photo of the three of us at the zoo, Emma and Justin's breakup, and how the Greenes let me crash on their couch the first night. She sips her coffee, hanging on every word, and after I've given her a play-by-play of practically the entire trip, I lower my head and say, "There's more."

I tell her about two kids who were killed in a fire in the Tenderloin.

And then I tell her how they weren't.

13

My second first day of school starts off differently. I don't sit in the car, listening as the bell rings in the distance and wishing I could close my eyes and open them at Westlake. Instead, my car is one of the first ones in the student lot, and I'm one the first people in the building.

I head straight to my locker, drag the recycling can over and park it underneath the door, and scoop all the papers and granola bar wrappers into the bin. I give my locker one more sweep with my hand and I look inside. With the exception of the VANS sticker I put on the inside of the door freshman year, it's as empty at my locker at Westlake was.

When the first bell rings, I'm already more than halfway across the quad. I open the door to my World Civilizations classroom and discover that it's still empty, so I take a seat in the row closest to the window about halfway down the aisle, nowhere near McGibney's desk.

I grab my notebook and a pencil from my backpack, and as I'm doodling, she walks through the door. She crosses the room and sets her briefcase down next to her chair. "Punctual," McGibney says, and I look up at her.

"Excuse me?"

"You're punctual," she says plainly. "What's your name?"

"Bennett Cooper." I hold my hand up and she nods.

"Ah," she says, and I can practically see the wheels turning, my mom's ridiculous story clicking into place in her mind. "Welcome back, Mr. Cooper. I hear you have some catching up to do." She says the words plainly and without a trace of the sympathetic stare I know I'll be getting from the rest of the teachers today.

"Yeah," I say. "I do."

"Well let me know how I can help, okay?"

People come into the room, look around for a desk, and settle in. Cameron spots me, and as he walks down the aisle, we give each other a fist bump. He takes the seat behind me, just as Megan steps in and looks around. I turn to talk with Cameron and I can't say I'm surprised when I see her take the seat on my left.

"Hey, Bennett," she says.

"Hi," I say. I'm feeling good. Chatty. Full of adrenaline, like I could run a marathon and still have energy left to burn. "How was your summer?"

"It was good. Thanks. How was yours?"

"Good," I say, and Megan nods, like she's encouraging me to continue. And I would, but the bell rings and McGibney immediately launches into detail about the year's syllabus.

She goes over the rules of class, putting extensive emphasis on the importance of being on time and in one's seat at least a full minute before the bell rings. After she looks around the room and declares that everyone's present, she gestures toward the whiteboard in one big, dramatic movement.

"Now. Let's get right into it. We'll be talking about early civilizations for the next two weeks." She writes the words "First civilizations" and draws a line underneath, then begins adding bullet points. I remember this part, and now I start to predict what she's going to write next. "Significant cities," I guess accurately. Next, "writing systems". . . . She ends with the words "formal states."

She turns around and addresses the class. "Does anyone know the term we use to describe the transition from hunting and gathering to more formal agricultural systems?"

My hand shoots up and so does Megan's. McGibney calls on her, but I'm a little puffed up because this time, I knew the answer. Even though I cheated.

~───⌐

It takes more effort than I anticipated, but for the next three weeks, I "live in the present" as the bumper sticker wisdom says. I try *not* to think about my past with Anna, or even speculate about what my next visit with her will bring. I go to school during the day, make small talk with my parents at night, and do my best to fill my time on the weekends. I stay fixed in place on the timeline, avoiding concerts and news, and extinguishing any thoughts that creep in about do-overs.

I try to live like I'm normal. I force myself not to think about Anna every time I meet my friends for coffee, or skate at the park overlooking the bay, or pass a gift shop that sells San Francisco souvenirs and postcards. As hard as it is, I try not to think about the fact that she can't come here and meet my family and friends. I ignore the reality that I can take her anywhere in the world, but I can't show her the city I love more than any place I've ever been. And for the most part, I'm successful. But every few days, I find myself autopiloting over to the garage, where I pull the Jeep inside its rank-smelling walls and listen to music for a while.

september 1995

14

evanston, illinois

Before I even open my eyes, a cold breeze slaps me in the face. I'm expecting clouds and fog, but when I look up at the sky, I find it bright blue and cloudless. I peek out from behind the side of Maggie's house and see the sun is shining bright on her tomato garden.

I've been stumped about how and *where* to return. It was one thing when I was living here, coming and going every day, but now it feels weird to show up and just let myself in the front door as if this were my home, even though Maggie gave me a key and told me to use it. I'm not looking forward to telling her who I am and what I can do, but it would sure be nice to come back here without having to worry about my arrival giving my grandmother a heart attack.

There's no answer when I knock on the door. After a full minute, I let myself in.

"Maggie?" I call out from the foyer. I walk through the

house, checking the kitchen and the living room for signs of her, but there's nothing. She might be in her bedroom, but I'm not about to check there, so I head straight for mine.

My new posters are up on one wall and Anna's photograph of our beach in La Paz hangs above the bed. I drop my backpack on the chair by the door and head for the closet.

My new T-shirts are folded and stacked on a shelf and the new dress shirt Anna helped me pick out hangs in front. Smashed in the back of the closet are all of the winter clothes I bought during my first visit here. It's hard to imagine that next month I'll need those wool button-ups and long-sleeved T-shirts again.

My backpack is full of stuff I need but can't buy here: more cash, even though the hidden compartment is still sufficiently stocked. The fake State of Illinois driver's license I paid some guy to make for me, perfectly mimicking the photocopy I gave him of Maggie's, but with my photo and my birthday stated as March 6, 1978, rather than March 6, 1995. I open the top drawer to stick everything inside and spot a note:

Go look inside the cabinet.
Love,
Anna

I cover my mouth with my hand, hiding the smile that spreads across my face when I see the boom box. Resting against the handle is a postcard with a shot of downtown Evanston. I pick it up and flip it over:

Welcome back. I thought you might want to <u>play</u> those
CDs you bought last time you were here. ☺

I have to help Emma set up. I'll see you at her house
at 7:00.

The boom box is heavier than I expected it to be. I set it on top of the desk and sit down so I can study the vintage buttons and knobs, check out the dual tape deck and the radio dial, and press the button marked with the words "Mega Bass." When I press one of the buttons on top, a door slowly opens. Inside, I find one of the CDs we bought last time I was here.

I barely stifled a laugh when Justin pushed this CD into my hands. I already considered *The Bends* a classic, but around here they refer to it as the second album from a new band called Radiohead. I press play and the room fills with music—a steady guitar lick and soft drums, then voices and melodies—and I close my eyes, taking it in, feeling a smile spread across my face. I look around the room at the posters, realizing why they helped but felt a little insufficient. Music. That's what this room needed.

When I'm dressed and ready to go, I head to the kitchen to find something to eat. As I walk down the stairs I can't shake the feeling that I'm being watched by photos of my mother, now in reverse-chronological order starting with her wedding at the top and ending with her kindergarten photo near the foyer at the bottom.

Maggie still doesn't seem to be home. On the desk in the

hallway, there's a stack of bills underneath a Post-it cube, and I sit down and write three notes telling Maggie I'm here. I leave one on the kitchen table, another on the end table where she always sets her tea, and I stick the last one on the end of the banister, just in case she makes it to the stairs without spotting the other two.

—◦—

I'm still a good six or seven houses away from the Atkinses' when I hear the music drifting through the neighborhood, but it's not until I'm standing in front of the house that I begin to understand what Anna meant when she described Emma's birthday party as "over the top."

A long line of alternating dark-pink and white balloons line the driveway, creating a colorful path from the sidewalk to the side entrance of the enormous brick Tudor-style mansion. I look around. I think I'm supposed to walk through it.

At the end, I see a woman with short blond hair wearing a bright pink dress. She's standing next to a small table under a comically large balloon arch.

"Welcome!" she says, beaming. I'm not sure who she is until she asks, "Can I start you off with something to drink?" in a British accent so thick that she must be Emma's mom. She hands me a glass of pink lemonade and I take it and thank her politely. "Everyone's in the backyard," she says.

She turns her attention to the big group coming in behind me. "Welcome!" I hear her say as I turn the corner and walk into the "backyard." Which is really more like a small park.

Bright pink and purple flowers are bursting out from behind short hedges, and the grass is so green I feel the impulse to reach down and touch it to be sure it's real. The walkway takes me past smaller patios and hidden sitting areas until it ends at a huge lawn. There's a DJ parked on the far end.

I look around for Anna. Right in front of the DJ, I spot Alex and Courtney dancing. He's grabbing her by the hips and pulling her toward him while she shoots him fake smiles and pushes him away. I keep scanning the yard, and finally Danielle pops her head up from the crowd, gives me a wave, and starts walking toward me.

"She's going to be so happy to see you," she says, pulling me into a hug. "You're all she's talked about for the last few weeks."

I'm not sure what I'm supposed to say to that, but I'm glad to hear that she's been thinking about me as much as I've been thinking about her. "Where is she?" I take a quick sip of lemonade and I feel my whole face pucker up. I set my glass down on a small table next to a rosebush.

Danielle rises up on her toes but it doesn't give her much of an advantage. "I saw her earlier, but—oh, wait . . . there she is." She points off toward the edge of the garden and I follow her finger but still don't see Anna. "She's over by that big tree, talking with Justin."

I finally spot her. Justin's leaning against the tree and Anna's standing in front of him. She's wearing a short skirt that looks a lot more like something Emma would wear, and I'm pretty sure that means that Anna let Emma dress her for the occasion. Her hair is up on the sides, held in the back by a clip, but the rest of it is long. She's twirling her curls around her finger.

Justin sees me before she does and I hear him say, "He's here."

Anna turns around, and before I can take another step she throws both arms around my neck. Justin glances around the yard like he's looking for an excuse to leave.

"I'm going to grab a drink," he says, and then tells me where to find the beer they stashed in the bushes.

"Thanks." I don't tell him that I don't drink. I tried once, at a party my sophomore year, and it was a disaster. After two beers, all I had to do was *think* about needing to take a leak and I'd wind up back home in my bathroom.

Anna gives me another squeeze. "Did you get my present?"

I nod. "Thank you. It's perfect. Exactly what the room needed." I step back and take a closer look at her. "You look amazing."

Anna looks down at her outfit and shakes her head. "Emma's doing, of course." The shirt is lower cut than anything I've ever seen on her, but I don't want to make her self-conscious, so I don't say anything.

"How was your trip?" she asks, raising her eyebrows jokingly.

"Very short."

"No little bags of peanuts on board?"

I run my thumb along her cheek. "Nope. No peanuts."

She fake-pouts. "Bummer. I liked the peanuts."

"Can you stop talking now so I can kiss you?" I start to move in closer to her but she pulls away, glancing over my shoulder at the party in full swing behind me, and reaches for my hand.

"Not here." She gives me a peck on the cheek instead. "I have an idea. Follow me."

She leads me to the other side of the lawn, past the DJ and to the edge of the garden. We're not exactly out of sight, but this is a little more private.

I think I'm finally going to kiss her, but then she ducks down low and pulls me into a small grove of fruit trees. We push branches and leaves out of our way and when we're able to stand up straight again, we're standing at the edge of a hill. A tall, wrought-iron gate hugs the slope, and Anna feels around in the dark for the opening. She finds the latch and the gate swings toward us with a squeak.

It's dark back here, but the narrow path is illuminated by a series of lights hidden in the surrounding ferns and grasses. Tiny rocks crunch under our feet as we follow the path to a wooden bridge, and once we're across, I see a cement bench next to a giant Buddha statue. I can still hear the music, but it's muffled.

Anna stops in front of the bench and steps in close to me, resting her hands on my waist. "So . . . you were saying some-thing about peanuts," she says with a smile.

"No, I was saying something about kissing you." And before

she can say another word, my hands settle on the small of her back and I close what's left of the distance between us. I feel her hands on the back of my neck, her fingers traveling into my hair, pulling me into her, kissing me.

When we stop, she doesn't open her eyes or move away. I can feel her breath as she speaks. "I missed you." She runs her thumb along my jawbone and my pulse races. "Tell me about the last few weeks. I want to know everything."

Everything. I take a deep breath, preparing to launch in. I've been waiting for three weeks to tell Anna *everything.* How many times did I stare at my cell phone, wishing I could call and tell her about the fire, and two kids that are alive today but shouldn't be, and the look on my dad's face when I told him what I'd done? Finally, here she is, staring at me with this sweet, expectant look on her face, and my mind is totally blank.

I'm not ready to go there yet, so I decide to warm up with a few basics. I sit down, straddling the bench, and Anna sits right in front of me. When I talk, she leans in close, as if my class schedule is especially interesting, and when I tell her about my friends and how weird it is to be back with all of them, she scoots forward and takes my hand, lightly tracing the lines in my palm with her fingertip as she listens.

When I'm finished, I ask her about life at Westlake. She tells me about Argotta's class and how she has a new conversation partner, and that every time she turns around and looks at my old desk, it makes her happy to think that I sat there once but also makes her sad that I no longer do. Last weekend, she got the top time in her cross-country meet.

We're both quiet for a few minutes and I see my opening. I take a deep breath, preparing to tell her about the fire, but before I can, she squeezes my hand and says, "I have something to tell you."

I smile at her. "I have something to tell you, too."

"You first," she says.

"Yeah? You sure?" I ask, but I'm secretly glad I don't have to wait any longer. I was nervous at first, but now that we're all warmed up, I can't wait to see the look on her face when I tell her what I did.

Anna nods.

I shake my head, looking for the right words to kick off my bizarre story. It's still kind of hard to believe, let alone say out loud. "I did something really crazy. Or stupid. Or awesome. . . . I don't know. It's sort of hard to categorize."

She looks at me quizzically.

"My dad and I were watching the news one morning, and there was this story about two kids who were killed in an apartment fire. For the next few days, I—I—" I start stammering, and rake my fingers through my hair as I search for the right words. "I just couldn't get the image out of my mind."

I'm careful about what I say next, purposely withholding the future-specific things I can't tell her about, like the online news article and Google Maps. "It started as pure curiosity. I sat there, scratching equations and time conversions into my notebook, trying to figure out if it would even be possible, but before I knew it, I was combing the house for a fire extinguisher and a smoke detector."

"No way. . . ." Her eyes light up and a smile spreads across her face. "You stopped it?"

I shake my head. "I didn't stop it. I just . . . readjusted a few things."

"You . . . readjusted a few things?"

I tell her how I crept through the dark apartment. I describe the wall of school photos, and I explain how I worked quickly to mount the smoke detector without waking the kids.

"I went back and did nearly *three days* over again. Until Emma, I'd never gone back more than five or ten minutes, you know? I didn't even know it was possible. But it worked. When I went into the kitchen that morning, the news story on TV was about a fire that took out an apartment complex, not a fire that killed two kids. And when I told my dad what I did . . ." My words hang in the air. I look down at a cluster of plants and Anna rests her hands on my hips.

"You changed it."

I nod slowly. And then I can't help it. I break into a huge smile. "I don't know if it was right or not. It doesn't matter now, it was a one-time thing. Or, I guess, counting Emma, a two-time thing. I just wanted to see if I could do it again."

"And you did."

"Yeah."

Anna brings her hands to my face and kisses me. She pulls away and stares at me for what feels like a really long time, and I assume that she's trying to think of something to say. Finally I remember that she had something to tell me too.

"Hey, you said you had news too? What did you want to tell me?"

She checks her watch.

"Nothing. It can wait." She stands up and holds out her hand. "We've been gone a long time. Emma is probably starting to look for me."

I realize that tonight's supposed to be about Emma, but I'm not ready to go back out there and share Anna with the rest of her friends yet. I wish I knew when we'd get to be alone again.

Before I can say anything, she shrugs and says, "Really. It's no big deal. I'll tell you later."

We wind back up the path and reemerge from the trees. I spot Emma right away, but that's not saying much. She's pretty hard to miss, dancing with a big group of girls in her short skirt, tight half-shirt, and a huge fabric hat in the shape of a birthday cake.

When Emma sees us, she bounces over and gives me a big hug. I wish her a happy birthday and she grabs each of us by the arm and leads us back out to the patch of grass that's become a dance floor. I try not to think about the fact that I'm the only guy out here.

We've been dancing for about five minutes, and I'm thinking that's more than sufficient. I'm just about to leave when Emma throws her arm over my shoulder and pulls me in close to her. "I've missed you, *Shaggy*." She musses my hair and I can't help smiling. No one's called me that in months.

"I've missed you too, Em."

Then she stands up on her tiptoes and gets right in my face. "I hear you've turned my sweet little Anna into a big fat liar," she says, shaking her head.

That's the last thing I'd want to do. I look at her, genuinely confused. "How so?"

She stares at me like I should know what she's talking about. "Tonight?" she says, raising her eyebrows, waiting for it to sink in.

I'm starting to feel a little dense because I'm still not sure where she's going with this. "I have no idea what you're talking about."

She pulls away and studies my expression, and I guess she comes to the conclusion that I'm telling the truth. "She didn't tell you?" she asks, and I shake my head no. Resting a hand on my shoulder, she whispers in my ear, "Her parents don't know you're in town."

When she pulls away, I just look at her. I'm still not getting it.

"She told them she's spending the night here, at my house. She brought an overnight bag and everything." She winks.

I turn and look over my shoulder at Anna. She's dancing with a big group, but she keeps looking over at Emma and me.

"Really?" I say without taking my eyes off Anna.

"Yes, really." Emma musses my hair again. "I believe somebody owes me one," she sings.

We have a whole night together. We've never had a whole *planned* night together, and I know exactly what I'm going to do with it. But right now, I just need to get off this dance floor. I spot Justin over by the tree, talking with a couple of guys I don't know. "What if I go chat with your ex and see what I can do about getting you two back together again?"

She huffs. "What makes you think I want to get back together with him?"

"The way you've been looking over there the entire time I've been talking to you." The corners of her mouth twitch, like she's fighting back a smile.

She pokes me in the chest four times as she spits out each word: "We. Are. Just. Friends."

But you're not supposed to be, I want to say. *You're supposed to be together. You might still be if I hadn't wiped out the first four hours of your first date.* I flash back to the Saturday that Anna and I went back and changed. How we basically created two versions of the same day, one that ended with a horrible accident that left Emma in the ICU and another that ended with Anna, Emma, Justin, and me at the movies together. The first one ended with Justin telling Anna how he and Emma had this incredible morning hanging out at her house, bonding over a conversation that left him surprised and unquestionably interested in her. The second one ended with them breaking up a few months later.

It would be nice not to feel so responsible for the second version, but I *am*. "So, you don't want me to talk to him?" I ask.

She looks over at Justin and back at me. I wait her out. "Okay," she finally says with a heavy sigh. "If you want to."

I give Anna a small wave, thrilled to be honorably

discharged from the dance floor, and squeeze through the crowd toward Justin. On my way, I grab a Coke from a bucket of ice and pop the top.

He introduces me to his friends, two guys he works with at the radio station, and we spend the next ten minutes talking about music. Eventually they take off to find the hidden beer, and I'm standing alone with Justin.

"So," I say. I take a sip of my drink. "Can I ask you a question?" Justin nods.

"What happened with you and Emma over the summer?"

He looks in her direction. Emma and Anna are buried somewhere in the crowd of people jumping up and down because the song is telling them to.

"I don't know," he says without looking away from the dance floor. He stares into his red Solo cup, like he might find the answer he's looking for somewhere at the bottom. "At first, I thought we were a good match, you know? But after a while, it seemed like we were both trying too hard or something. Or . . . maybe I just was."

We both look back at the dance floor again. The song ends and we see Emma emerge, one arm hooked through Danielle's and the other around Anna's shoulders. She's leading both of them away from the dance floor toward the big bucket of drinks in the corner. She grabs three sodas, passes them around, and pops the top of her own.

"Don't get me wrong," Justin says. "She's funny and gorgeous and I'm sure everyone here thinks I'm crazy for breaking up with her. But honestly, I don't think I ever really got used to the idea of the two of us together."

"Maybe you didn't give her enough of a chance."

He laughs. "Now you sound like Anna." He looks away when he says her name, and there's something in his expression I can't read.

I think about how many times I sat in San Francisco, remembering the months I spent in this town, and not only missing Anna, but Justin and Emma too. "I know you broke up, but would it be too much to ask for the four of us to go out while I'm in town this weekend?"

"Sure. We still hang out. We're good friends."

"But that's it?" I ask. When I look over at Anna, I see the three of them heading our way.

Justin sees them too, and when he does, he looks down at the grass, suddenly bashful. "Yeah, that's it. But I like her. A lot," he says. "I always have."

I watch as his gaze travels toward them, and for a second I wonder if he's still talking about Emma.

⌒

Emma's mom sidles up next to Anna and asks her if she'll come inside and help with the cake, and I finally see my chance to get away from the party. Tracing the route Anna showed me earlier, I sneak past the food table and out toward the edge of the garden, under the fruit trees, through the wrought-iron gate, and deep into the backyard.

I follow the winding path that leads to the cement bench at the bottom and make my way over to the tiny gardening shed I noticed earlier. It's angled into the corner and, while the squeeze is tighter than I expected, it works well enough. I close my eyes. When I open them, I'm back in my room at Maggie's.

I work quickly. My red backpack is leaning up against my desk, and I fill it with a couple of shirts, a sweater, and a huge stack of cash from the cabinet. I check to be sure that my Illinois ID is in my wallet, and I add a few more bills in there for backup. I find the cardboard box I stuffed deep into the closet and remove the rest of the things Anna and I need: four plastic bottles of water, two bottles of Starbucks Frappuccino, and an unopened sleeve of saltines.

In the bathroom, I find that Maggie has now filled the drawers with me in mind. There's a new tube of toothpaste, still in its box. Three toothbrushes in sealed plastic packages. A six-pack of disposable razors.

I head downstairs and call out to Maggie a few times, but there's no reply, so I go to the desk, quickly scratch out new notes, and replace the ones I left earlier. I'm standing in the hallway, about to return to the party, when I have an idea. It's a huge risk but I'm assuming that by now, everyone's busy singing "Happy Birthday," so I close my eyes and open them in a quiet corner of Emma's bedroom. Right away, I spot Anna's overnight bag on the floor by the bed. There's plenty of room in my backpack, so I stuff the whole thing inside.

I close my eyes again picturing the tiny spot behind the

shed in Emma's backyard, and when I open them, I'm standing there. I drop my backpack, peek around the corner, and
sneak back to the party.

"Cake?" Anna asks when I return to her side. My face still
feels hot and my hands are shaking with nervous energy as I
take the plate from her hand, but she doesn't seem to notice.
She sees a group of her cross-country friends and pulls me in
their direction, saying that she wants me to get to know them
better.

When the temperature begins to drop and the balloon arch
has started sagging, the DJ announces his last song. I watch
Emma leave the lawn, find Justin, and pull him out to the
makeshift dance floor with her. He says something and she
throws her head back as she laughs. She stands on her tiptoes,
kisses his cheek, and puts her birthday cake hat on his head.
He tries to give it back, but she keeps pulling it down over
his eyes.

I nudge Anna with my elbow and subtly gesture toward the
two of them. "That's interesting."

Anna follows my gaze and then looks back at me wearing a
huge smile. "Yes it is."

Now Justin is dancing. Like, actually dancing. He's jumping
up and down and grabbing Emma around the waist, and she's
smiling like this is the best birthday she's ever had.

When I look over at Anna, she's still watching her two best
friends, and I wonder if she's thinking about what we did that
day. I wonder if she looks at them the same way I do, knowing that they should be together and feeling responsible for

the fact that they aren't. But suddenly, Emma and Justin disappear from my thoughts, and now I'm looking at her and all I can think about is the backpack stuffed behind the gardening shed at the bottom of the hill. Without meaning to, I let a small laugh slip out under my breath.

That gets her attention. "What?" she asks. There's this lilt in her voice, like she wants to know but at the same time she's a little bit afraid to.

"You had something to tell me," I say, fighting a grin.

She presses her lips together and takes a sharp inhale. "I did, yeah, I—" She starts to finish her sentence but I cut her off.

I push her hair back from her face and plant a kiss on her forehead. "Go say good-bye to Emma and meet me in the garden in ten minutes . . . where we were earlier. Don't let anyone see you."

Anna looks puzzled at first, but as she watches me, her mouth turns up at the corners and she nods without asking any questions. I turn and walk away from her, and for the third time tonight I follow the path until I reach the bottom of the garden. I wrestle my backpack out from behind the shed.

I pace the ground. I sit on the bench and stand up again. I examine the Buddha statue. Finally I see Anna's face peek out from behind the trees. The latch on the wrought-iron gate clicks and I hear it squeak open and closed.

Her feet crunch on the gravel as she winds down the path, and she stops when she finds me in the shadows, leaning up against the shed.

"Why are we down here?" she asks, and without saying a word, I step forward, wrap my fingers around the back of her neck, and kiss her. I can feel her smiling as she lets go of all her questions, parts her lips, and kisses me back. She tastes like cake.

Her hands settle on my hips and as she kisses me harder; her fingers creep under my shirt and up my back. I'm starting to wonder if we'll ever be able to get out of here, when she whispers, "Why are you wearing your backpack?"

I kiss her again. "Give me your hands."

She's breathing hard. "Why?" she asks, but doesn't hesitate for even a second. I can already feel her fingers sliding back down to my waist, feeling for my arms, following the bend in my elbow until they find their home in my hands.

Hers are shaking with anticipation or nerves or a combination of the two, and I take them, the whole time never letting her lips leave mine. All I can think about right now is that I'm so grateful for this crazy gift I possess; that I can take her away with me, just for a little while, disappearing completely into a faraway place where there's no people or voices in the background, and no one looks even vaguely familiar to either one of us.

Her eyes are already closed. I pull her hands behind my back, our fingers still locked, still connecting us, and I keep her body pressed into mine as I picture our destination.

I close my eyes.

And we disappear.

15

I open my eyes in a secluded area I found a few years ago when Brooke and I came here for a U2 concert in '97. Anna's hands are still locked behind my back and she's smiling, lids tightly shut, waiting for me to speak.

"We're here," I say. "Open your eyes." As soon as I say the words, my heart starts pumping hard.

I take a look around, but there's not much to see yet. Until we get out from behind this shrub, we could be anywhere. I follow Anna's gaze as she takes in the chain-link fences and the back windows along a line of similar-looking houses. She runs her toe across the gravel underneath our feet, like she's trying hard to piece it all together. There's hardly any light back here, but I can still make out the baffled expression she's wearing as she turns slowly in place. And then she looks up, beyond the shrubs, and sees the tower, its iron beams lit up with so many lights it looks like it's made of gold. She covers her mouth with her hand and laughs.

"No way . . ."

"I told you. You needed to see Paris next."

She takes a few steps backward, stops when she hits my chest, and without turning around, feels for my hands and wraps them around her waist. She twists her neck so she can see me, and even though we're nowhere near Emma's backyard anymore, we pick up right where we left off two minutes ago.

We hop over the short fence that leads to the park. Once we're out in the open we can see the entire Eiffel Tower, base to top, gleaming in front of us. It's only nine o'clock and, surprisingly, there aren't many people back here. Anna and I walk toward the base with our fingers knit together. She keeps looking over at me, smiling and shaking her head.

She suddenly drops my hand. "Race you," she says, and she takes off. Her speed keeps her well in front of me at first, but she has to keep adjusting her skirt, and that slows her down. I pass her just before we turn the corner that leads under the structure, and that's where we find everyone. The crowd is thick and the lines are long.

"Come on," I say as I start walking toward the end of the shortest one, but Anna grabs me by the arm. She tips her head back and looks straight up. Then she looks back at me. "We're waiting in line?"

"Yep."

"Oh." She looks up to the top of the tower again, then back at me. "Why?"

I rest my hands on her shoulders and give her a quick kiss. "No cheating." In the time it's taken us to have this discussion, at least ten people have stepped into the line. I jump in at the end.

"Why is, you know . . . *that*"—she makes this weird gesture with her hand—"cheating?"

"Because it is. It's like rock climbing. You can't just magically find yourself on top of a mountain, staring out at an insane view. You've got to earn it. *Without* cheating." She presses her lips together, like she's trying not to smile. "Besides, there aren't a lot of discreet places up there." She shoots me a confused look and I step closer so I can't be overheard. "There's nowhere to arrive without being seen by a bunch of people."

"Oh."

"Which, you know, some might find shocking."

"Yeah, I suppose some might." She nods and tries to hold a serious expression, but I can see that smile still trying to peek through. "So we're taking the elevator?" It's a question, but she says it more like a statement.

"Nope. That's cheating too." She starts to say something, but I hold my finger up, and say, "Wait a sec."

I haven't exchanged my American dollars for French francs yet, so I've been subtly scanning the people in line for the perfect target and I just found him: older guy, jeans and tennis shoes, fanny pack with an American flag pinned to the belt.

When the line snakes around, I hold up three twenty-dollar bills and ask him if he'll buy us two tickets to the second deck via the stairs in exchange for them. He checks the prices on the board, calculates the profit, and happily takes the money from my hand.

"The stairs?" Anna asks.

I just grin.

"How many stairs?"

"I don't know. A lot. We can count them if you want to." She smacks me with the back of her hand. "Trust me, you'll love this. We can stop and look at the view on the way up." Fanny-pack Guy hands me our two tickets and we head to the entrance.

As it turns out, there are six hundred and seventy steps, and we don't even have to count them, because every tenth one is conveniently painted with a number. The higher we go, the more frequently Anna stops, saying she has to catch her breath. But I notice she's refusing to look around, and whenever I point out the sites, she just nods and keeps climbing. She looks relieved when we finally reach the second platform.

Down on the ground, it was already much colder here in Paris than it was in Evanston, but up on the tower, it feels like the middle of winter. Anna's trying to play it off like she isn't cold, but I can see her shivering as we stand here, leaning against the railing, staring out over the city. I suddenly remember that I brought my sweater, so I take it out of my backpack and hand it to her. She pulls it over her head. It hangs almost to the edge of her skirt and the sleeves go past her fingers and she looks completely adorable.

Someone taps me on the shoulder and I turn around to find a woman grinning wide and holding a camera out in my direction. She says something in a language that's not English or French as she gestures between herself and the man standing to her right. I take the camera from her and hand it to Anna.

"You're the photographer," I say, and Anna looks grateful as she brings the camera to her face. She snaps a few pictures and hands it back to them.

"I hope one of those pictures turns out," Anna says when they're out of earshot. "They probably won't have another night on the Eiffel Tower again." I'm about to tell her that they're probably checking the pictures right now when I remember that cameras don't work that way yet. Then I realize that Anna's staring out at the view and not talking. I wish I'd thought to go to her house and get her camera for her.

"Stay here," I say, and without giving her any time to reply, I double back toward the elevator bank, past the people in line, and into the crowded gift shop. Right behind the counter, I find what I'm looking for. I convince the cashier to accept an American twenty in exchange for a ten-franc item, and less than ten minutes later I'm heading back to Anna with a plastic bag swinging by my side.

But when I return to the spot where I left her, she's gone. I walk all the way around the deck, but she's nowhere to be found. I head back toward the center of the platform and see her there, pacing back and forth in front of the elevators.

"Hey." I come up behind her and grab her by the waist. She jumps. "You okay?"

She flips around, arms crossed, eyes narrowed. "You left me on the Eiffel Tower?"

"Just for a minute," I say, and her eyes grow wide. I'm clearly not supposed to find this amusing, but I can't help it. She's just standing there, looking small and pissed off and adorable in my sweater.

"You're laughing at me?" Her eyes grow even wider and I think she's going to start yelling at me or something, but instead she steps forward and takes my face in her hands. "What if something happened to you? What if you got knocked back?" She shakes her head. "I don't even know what date it is," she practically whispers.

I'm still finding this amusing, even though I'm clearly not supposed to. "I'm sorry. I didn't mean to scare you." I kiss her and I'm relieved when she lets me. "I'm not going to get knocked back. And besides, you know I never take you out of your time. Never. You're always a really awkward phone call and an outrageously expensive plane ride away from your parents, but that's it. Okay?"

She presses her lips together and nods.

"I just wanted to get you this." I hand her the plastic gift-shop bag, and she peeks inside. Her whole expression relaxes as the grin spreads across her face.

"You bought a disposable camera?"

I shrug. "You looked a little sad about taking that couple's picture." I guide her over to the railing. "Smile," I say, holding the camera out in front of us. I press the button and the shutter snaps, but when I press it again, nothing happens. I'm turning it around in my hands, looking at it from all angles and trying to figure out what to do next, when Anna takes it from me, chuckling as she runs her thumb along a little wheel that must advance the film. She holds her arm out and presses the button.

After she's taken four or five shots, she stops and looks at the camera. I can tell by the way she's staring at it, running her finger along its edges, that this small cardboard box contains so much more than a few images of the two of us on an undeveloped strip of film. It's not a memory or a postcard, it's more than she's ever had—tangible proof that we exist together, outside both her world and mine.

"Bennett?" she says, still looking down at the camera.

"Yeah."

"Are we going back home tonight?" When her eyes find mine, I shake my head no.

Her gaze travels up to the brightly lit iron beams above us, and a grin spreads across her face. "I never thought I'd be standing on the Eiffel Tower and saying this but . . . can we get out of here?"

16

Clouds are filtering the morning sun but it's still bright enough to stir me from sleep. I rub my eyes as I take in the unfamiliar room, remembering little by little where I am right now. In Paris. With Anna.

She's sitting in the window ledge, her bare legs bent and visible below the hem of one of my T-shirts. Her chin is resting on her knees and she's staring out the window at the city below.

I kick off the covers and cross the room. "What are you doing way over here?" I pull her hair to one side and kiss the back of her neck.

"I couldn't sleep." She's quiet for a few seconds, and then she says, "I keep having to remind myself that this is all happening. That I'm actually here."

"Then we should get going. We have a whole day in Paris and we still won't come close to seeing everything."

Anna turns her head and gives me the biggest smile. And then she sits up straighter and spins in place, wrapping her legs around my waist and her arms around my neck. "I didn't mean Paris. I meant here, with you."

We grab coffees at the café downstairs and make a game plan. We decide to skip the obvious sights, the museums and cathedrals and monuments, but agree that we can't miss the Seine, so we order our *pain au chocolat* to go and head toward the river. We find a place to sit on the bank, and Anna pops a chunk of bread into her mouth. She closes her eyes, letting the dough and chocolate melt on her tongue.

"God, that's incredible. Why can't we make bread that tastes like this?"

"You and me?" I joke and she stares at me.

"Americans."

"Oh. Because we aren't French," I say matter-of-factly.

She tears off another chunk of bread and pops it into my mouth, presumably to shut me up.

We spend the rest of the morning wandering around aimlessly, meandering down the smallest alleys we can find, popping into bakeries when they smell too good to simply walk past. Anna stops at a corner store that appears to sell everything from drinks to cheesy Parisian trinkets, and heads for the cooler. She grabs two bottles of water and tosses one to me.

The clerk is ringing us up when Anna sees a display on the counter. "Ah, here you go." She hands me a laminated map.

"This is what we need," she says, tapping the surface.

I take it from her hand and slip it back into the rack where it was. "We don't need a map."

"Why not?" She looks confused at first, but then her face falls. "How many times have you been to Paris?"

"Twice. Both times for concerts, and I barely even walked around the city." Anna waits patiently for a better explanation. "I just prefer to get lost."

She raises her eyebrows and stares at me. "You want to get lost? In Paris?"

"It'll be fun."

She looks unconvinced. She might also look a bit terrified. So I grab the map from the rack and set it down on the counter. "Fine. We'll get a map. But it's purely for backup."

The cashier gives us the total but I hold my hand up in the air and tell her to wait. "Stay here. I'll be right back." Anna cocks her head to the side, and gives me a *Haven't we already covered this?* expression, but I laugh under my breath and take off anyway.

I have to snake around a few aisles, but I finally find a small section of bike accessories, and that's where I find the padlocks. I return to the counter, using a little sleight of hand to keep it hidden from her view.

"Here," I say as I take my backpack off and hand it to Anna, along with the map. "Find an extremely inconvenient pocket for that, would you?" While she's busy with the zipper, I remove the padlock and its key from their packaging, and slip them into the front pocket of my jeans.

I look at her and say, "Now we have a destination."

"We do?"

"Yeah. I want to show you something."

"Do you need the map?" She smiles.

I look at her and shake my head. "No, I do not need the map."

⁓

I may need the map. We've been walking along the banks of the river for a good forty minutes, and we keep passing bridges, but so far, I haven't seen the sign that marks the one I need. I give myself one more bridge before I fold. Then I spot it: a dark green sign with white type that reads PONT DES ARTS.

The pedestrian-only footbridge is more crowded than I expected it to be. Couples are sitting on the benches in the center and people are clustered in groups along the railings. Everyone seems to be speaking French.

I find a spot against the railing and sit down. I lean back against a post and Anna sits between my legs. Just as she's reclining against my chest, a police siren blares by and fades away. "I love how even the most common sounds remind you that you're somewhere else," she says.

We're quiet for a long time, looking out over the water, until Anna twists her neck and looks up at me. "I've been dying to ask you something," she says. I must be wearing an affirmative expression because she suddenly spins around to face me and looks me right in the eye. "When you stopped the fire, did you feel the same way you did after we changed things with Emma?"

Her question catches me off guard and I react by dodging it. "I didn't stop the fire. I changed a few things leading up to the fire. Big difference." But Anna stares at me, not letting me off the hook.

I look at her, remembering how I sat in my room that night, picturing the look on Anna's face when she first saw Emma, unbroken. "Before, during, or after?" I ask.

"All of the above." She reaches out for the hem of my shirt and plays with it, running her finger back and forth along the edge.

I start to fall back on the things I say when I don't want to let people in: simple words like "fine" and "good" that slip so easily off my tongue. But instead, I feel myself lean in a little closer, like I'm ready to tell her everything.

"Before? Scared," I say flatly. "When you asked me to go back and help Emma, I honestly didn't think I could do over that many days, and even if I could, I had no idea if it would work. Anything could have happened. We could have been knocked back right away. Or we could have changed the sequence of events, but the car accident might have happened a few hours later regardless. The number of things that could have gone wrong were just . . ." I trail off, shaking my head.

"I thought Emma would be the first and last time I'd ever do anything like that. But when I heard what happened to those kids, I guess I just wanted to try it again. I mean, if could go back two days, why not three? And if it *did* work, if I could *change* it . . . Still, I'd be lying if I said I wasn't terrified the entire time."

Anna doesn't say anything, but she's tracing tiny circles in my palms again, just like she did in Emma's backyard last night. I think that means I'm supposed to keep talking.

"During, I didn't think about anything else. I just hoped it would work." I'm hit with a vision of the school pictures that lined the hallway of apartment 3C.

"And after . . ." I stop. I don't know what to say about the after. After I installed the smoke detector and came home, I waited to see the news, and discovered that the do-over had worked. My dad looked proud and shocked at the same time, like I'd hit that inexplicable home run in a tied game, bottom of the ninth.

"After," I repeat. "It was like being in one of those Choose Your Own Adventure books and I chose a different ending. Those two kids were alive and safe, and I knew they shouldn't have been. And that was . . . strange . . . to know that they died."

Anna brings my hand to her lips and kisses it. "And what about the side effects?"

"Nothing," I whisper. "No migraine. No dehydration. No side effects at all. I felt like I could have run around the block." Another tour boat goes by and we stop to listen to the guide rattle off the interesting facts about this bridge that we've heard twice now.

"Do you think—" Anna begins. She stops, waiting for a group of kids in matching soccer uniforms to walk past us.

"Do you think it's possible that do-overs aren't such a bad thing?"

I shake my head. "What do you mean? That I'm *supposed* to change things? No way. I did it once for you. I guess I did it this second time for my dad. But those were isolated incidents that I *chose* to do. It's not like I'm now on a mission to stop the world's tragedies. Besides, I still don't know if there are ramifications or not." I can't even say it aloud, but part of me is still wondering if the people whose lives I've altered are affected by their changed pasts. Does Emma know at some unconscious level that she was in a massive car accident? Will those two kids . . . I can't think about it. "Look, nothing's changed. I'm purely an observer. I'm not supposed to alter the future."

"I'm not saying you're *supposed* to, just that it felt good when you did. I mean, Emma and Justin are fine, right? Nothing horrible happened to them, they just . . . got a second chance. And because of you, so did those kids."

I look past her, staring out over the water. A second chance. I sort of like the idea of that. Not that it matters, since I'm not doing it again.

"Hey," I say, as I lean back and reach into my front pocket. "I almost forgot why I brought you here in the first place."

She looks at me with a curious grin. I open her hand and rest the brass padlock in her palm. She takes her eyes off me to look down at it. "Why am I holding a padlock?" The sunlight bounces off the surface as she twists it around, examining it from all sides as if that will enlighten her.

"I probably shouldn't tell you this—it involves a few future details—but I heard this story and thought it was cool." I shift in place and take a deep breath. "No one really knows when it started exactly, but by the end of two thousand nine, all of the railings on this bridge will be covered with padlocks. Couples who came to Paris from all over the world started writing their names on them, clipping them to this railing, and tossing the key into the river as a symbol . . ." Anna's wearing an expression I can't read, and I suddenly realize how lame I sound. ". . . of, like, their . . . Oh, never mind." I reach for the padlock, but she snaps her hand closed.

"Stop it. You're not taking our lock."

"Yes, I am." I reach for it again but she laughs and pulls her hand behind her back.

She looks me in the eyes. "Go on."

"No. I heard that story and thought it was kind of romantic, but now that I say it out loud it sounds so cheesy."

"No, it doesn't." I lean back against the post. Once she can tell I'm not going to try to take it away again, she brings her hand back to her lap and opens her palm. "I love it."

"Yeah?"

"Yeah." She turns the padlock over in her palm again, this time as if she's admiring it. "We don't have anything to write with."

I lean back and pull a black Sharpie from my jeans pocket. When I hand it to her, she laughs. "Typical. Here," she says, handing me the lock. "You should write it. It was your idea."

I shake my head. We're in 1995, in her world, and it seems

like something she's supposed to do. When I tell her this, she uncaps the pen and brings the felt tip to the metal.

"What should I say?"

"Whatever you want to say."

She thinks about it for a moment and writes ANNA ♥ BENNETT across the surface. "That's not very inspired, is it?" She stops and looks out over the water like she's trying to decide how to finish what she started. She brings the pen back to the lock and writes '95/'12. She stares at it.

"I like it," I say. "Now it's both cheesy *and* mysterious."

"Aww. Just like us."

"Nah, nothing like us," I say. "We're not at all mysterious."

I hand her the key and she slips it inside. The latch opens with a tiny click, and she threads the lock through the chain-link fence and snaps it closed. She runs her fingertip across the surface and lets out a little laugh. "Wouldn't it be funny if we're the ones that start the whole lock thing?"

"Maybe we do."

"I like that," she says.

I don't have the heart to tell her that in 2010, all the locks will be removed. Or that, in 2011, they'll start reappearing, and by 2012, there will be very few spaces left on the railing again. They can cut our lock off. We'll just come back here together—in 1998 and 2008 and 2018—and replace it every time it gets removed. I stare at the key in Anna's hand, wondering if it's realistic to think that we will still be together years from now, living this way.

I never even wished for her, but right now, all I want is for this person who gets me so completely to be part of my present and my future. As long as I don't think about the logistics, it seems possible.

Anna kisses me. Then we both kiss the key and she tosses it into the river.

17

Anna and I spend the rest of the afternoon wandering around. We don't have a destination in mind, so we turn when we feel like turning and stop when we feel like stopping and poke our heads into shops that look interesting. We pop into record stores so we can buy CD imports that would cost a fortune back in the States. We pick out postcards.

We stop at a bakery for a baguette, and then, without even discussing it, we head through a set of wrought iron gates and into a park. It's alive with activity, and as we meander down the path, people jog past us and in-line skaters roll by. Anna surprises me when she pulls me off the walkway and behind a dense cluster of trees to kiss me.

We spot a soccer game and sit on the grass to watch. The whole thing is nonstop action, but we both find it difficult to take our eyes off this one guy in a bright green shirt. He's the shortest one out there, and he's *so* quick, but it's more than that—he's just fun to watch. His face is completely serious until he takes a shot, but then he throws his hands up in the air in victory and lets out a yell, even when he misses.

A half hour later, we're still glued to the game, and it's now tied, two-two. Green-shirt Guy kicks the ball and takes off running toward the goal. Then he's open, waving his arms in the air, and the ball comes sailing back in his direction. But just as he's about to kick it, another player comes running at him from the opposite direction. The two of them collide hard, and Green-shirt Guy falls to the ground, clutching his leg. Everyone gathers around him, so it's impossible to see what's going on.

A few minutes later, he emerges from the crowd with his arms draped over two of his teammates' shoulders. His face is full of agony as he hops on one leg to the closest bench. He sits down and buries his face into his hands while they remove his shoe.

"I wonder if it's broken," Anna says.

All I can think to say is, "They hit hard."

"Bennett," she says quietly.

I look over at her. "Yeah?"

Her eyes are still glued to the guy in the green shirt and she's wearing the strangest expression. "What if you gave him a second chance?"

I shake my head. Hard.

She looks at me. "You could test yourself. See if the side effects kick in or not. And if they do, I can help you."

It's a ridiculous idea. I don't even know what time it is or how long we've been here, but I do know that we've been completely out in the open, in full view of everyone. We'd need a safe point we could return to without being seen, and we don't have one. But then I remember how Anna pulled me behind the bushes to kiss me.

"There was a clock in the bakery," she says. "It was 2:10. We got to the park and walked around and it was, what do you think, 2:30 when we sat down here?" She's talking fast, thinking too much, and getting way too excited about this. But before I can say anything, she stands up, heads back to the path, and returns less than a minute later. "It's 3:05 right now."

I look back over at the guy in the green shirt. His face is pinched and his leg is stretched out in front of him, and I still can't tell if it's broken or not, but he's definitely in a lot of pain. I think through the times Anna just rattled off to me and before I know it, I'm grabbing her hand and steering her back to that spot behind the bushes.

"This is crazy," I say.

When we arrive, she pivots to face me. When were we here last? 2:20? 2:23? I can't be sure, and I have to be sure, or the Anna and Bennett back on that part of the timeline will disappear into thin air in the middle of the street, or at the entrance to the park, or from the front of the bakery line.

I think through every step we made, and then I grab her hands and shut my eyes. When I open them, we're standing a few feet from where we started, back on the path, and in plain sight. We both speed back behind the bushes and hide there for a minute or two, until I'm certain that no one saw us.

We rush back to the soccer game in progress and sit in the

same spot, watching the same game. The guy in the bright green shirt is perfectly fine, speeding toward the ball, making solid kicks, and throwing his arms up in delight with every attempt. Anna's sitting closer to me this time, her legs folded in front of her and one leg resting on mine. She tightens her grip on my hand and we come up with a plan.

The score reaches two-two, and they're all lined up, about to make that last play. Before the ball gets thrown out, Anna looks at me, stands up, and races down the edge of the field near the goal. The play goes the same way. He kicks it and takes off running, but this time, just as he's about to throw his arms up, Anna yells, "Stop!" at the top of her lungs.

Most of the guys ignore her, but Green-shirt Guy turns around, just for a second, and looks at her. By the time he returns his attention to the game, it's too late. The other guy has the ball and he's taking it to the goal at the opposite end. He kicks it hard, scores, and the game is over. Green-shirt Guy throws his hands up in Anna's direction, and yells at her in French.

She takes off toward me, running and laughing, grabbing my hand as she speeds by. We spot a bench out of sight and collapse on it. My hands are shaking and my heart is pounding so hard I feel like it's about to burst out of my chest.

"I have no idea why I let you talk me into these things," I say, breathing fast. "You and Brooke." I shake my head. "You have far too much in common." I look over at her and she's sitting there, catching her breath, beaming and obviously quite proud of herself. "You look adorable when stopping tragedies, by the way."

She brings her hands to my face and kisses me, even though there are people everywhere.

I've spent all these years trying not to alter the slightest event, and now, in the seven months since I met Anna, I've purposely changed things four times. And none of them seems to have thrown the universe off-kilter or anything.

"How do you feel?" she asks as she pulls away.

"Good." I look at her and smile. "Really good."

By the time the sun starts to set, our legs are rubbery from climbing so many stairs and hills, and now we're standing in a secluded corner of a dead-end street, holding hands, smiling at each other and stalling.

"You ready?" I ask.

"No," she says. "Not even close."

But we can't stay away any longer. I tell her to close her eyes and she does, but before I do the same, I take a glance around this Parisian street one more time. Then I let my eyes fall shut.

When I open them, we're in the exact same position, back in my room at Maggie's, and it's Saturday morning. I check the clock. Ten A.M.

Almost instantly, Anna lets out a quiet groan and her hands find her stomach. She slumps down on the floor and pulls her knees to her chest. I slide down next to her, and even though my head is throbbing and my vision is blurry, I remove my backpack and grope around inside, searching for the sleeve of saltines. When I find them, I tear into the package and hand it to her. Anna mumbles a thank-you as she starts in on a corner of the cracker, and I search for the water bottles.

We sit like that for a good twenty minutes, me downing waters and Frappuccinos, Anna nibbling crackers and trying not to hurl. "Now *this* is romantic," she says, resting her head on my shoulder.

I let out a weak laugh and let my head fall against hers.

Anna finally declares herself strong enough to stand. But when I try to say, "I'll walk you home," my words slur, and when I stand up, my legs wobble. I lean on the bed, resting my hand on the surface for stability. I'm utterly exhausted. I can't remember the last time I felt this tired.

"Lie down," Anna insists as she pushes me gently toward the bed and lifts my feet off the floor. I hear her tell me to scoot up a little. I feel her adjust my pillow under my head. I think she takes off my shoes. "Close your eyes," I hear her say, quiet and soothing, as she sits on the edge of the bed and runs her thumbs back and forth along my forehead.

I don't remember anything after that.

18

The faint sound of knocking wakes me up from a deep sleep. I sit up in bed and rub my head with both hands. The next knock is louder.

"Come in." I feel like my eyes have been glued shut, but I force them open when the door creaks and Maggie pokes her head inside. She looks surprised to see me twisted and disheveled on top of my comforter.

"I'm sorry," she says. "I didn't realize you were sleeping. I just wanted to know if you were going to be here for dinner."

I press my fingertips into my temples and glance over at the clock radio on the nightstand. Is it really 6:12? Have I been out all afternoon? The last thing I remember was Anna helping me lie down. Was that really almost eight hours ago?

"I'm making a pot roast." Maggie smiles as she says it, like I might need convincing. But I don't. I take a big whiff of something that smells delicious. I'm just about to tell her that

I'll be down in a minute when she crosses her arms and her expression turns serious. "Are you okay, Bennett?"

I force myself to sit up and throw my feet to the floor. "I'm okay. Just really tired."

"Jet lag," she says plainly, and closes the door behind her. If only she knew that I've never been on a jet.

I pull on a clean pair of jeans and reach into the chest of drawers for a shirt. I still feel shaky and a bit cold, so I throw on a flannel.

Downstairs, I find Maggie setting the table for two. She glances up at me and returns to folding the cloth napkins into triangles. I slip right into my old role here, reaching into the cabinet for two glasses and filling them with milk.

Maggie and I politely take our seats like I'm a guest in her home. I try to come up with topics for small talk, but all I can think about is Anna and our day in Paris. I block it from my mind as I dig into the pot roast, I tell her all about Emma's party, right down to the details of the balloon arch and the DJ in the backyard. Maggie gives me encouraging laughs and asks a lot of questions about the people I know here. Then there's a pause in the discussion and she looks at me pointedly.

"It sounds like you made a lot of friends at Westlake," she says without looking at me. I start to respond, but I freeze instead. It's the first time she's acknowledged knowing that I lied to her about being a student at Northwestern last year, but she throws it out there and goes back to eating like it's no big deal. "My daughter loved it there too."

This would be a great time to apologize for lying to her. It would also be a great time to tell her that her daughter and my mom are the same person. While both are true, I feel a little bit sick the moment I have these two thoughts, so I ignore them and try to go back to my dinner as if Maggie's statement doesn't require a response. But then I hear Anna's words in my head: *It would be nice to have one person in my life that I can talk to about you—one person I don't have to keep your secret from.* That, I can't ignore.

My stomach is turning and what I really want to do right now is bolt out the back door, run past the tomato garden, and find an empty spot to disappear from. I could be back in San Francisco in less than a minute.

Before I let my feet dictate my next steps, I force out the words, "Maggie, I need to tell you something." And there it is. Now I don't have a choice. There's nothing else I need to tell her.

"Sure." I think she's trying not to look at me now. And I'm definitely trying not to look at her.

I'm pushing mashed potatoes around with my fork like the words I need to find are buried somewhere underneath. "I'm not quite sure how to explain this. Thre's something about me that's . . . unusual." I cringe as I hear the words come out of my mouth. She's looking at me, waiting for me to continue, and I suddenly wonder if it wouldn't be better to just show her. After all, it worked with Anna. I push my chair away from the table and stand over by the counter.

I blow out a breath. Here we go.

Maggie sets her fork down and wipes her face with her napkin.

"Watch," I say. And I close my eyes, but before I let myself disappear, I add the words "Please don't freak out."

Seconds after I picture my room upstairs, I'm standing in the center of it. Downstairs, I hear Maggie scream. I count to ten and close my eyes again, returning to the exact same spot in the kitchen. She's standing right in front of me and when she goes to move away, she smacks me hard on the shoulder. She mutters something that might be an apology and reaches for the counter to steady herself. Perhaps this wasn't the best way to break the news.

I reach forward and grip her arms. "It's okay. There's nothing to be afraid of."

She stares at me, her mouth hanging open and her eyes wide. I lead her over to the chair, and she sits down, forearms pressed into the Formica, staring at her half-eaten plate of food.

I sit down next to her. "I want you to know who I am, Maggie."

She doesn't look up at me but I see her head nod.

"There's a lot you already know about me. My name is Bennett. I live in San Francisco. I think you know I'm seventeen and that I never went to Northwestern, and I'm sorry I lied and told you that I did."

This whole thing sounded so much better in my head. It isn't coming out at all the way I wanted it to. Maggie gives me a slight nod, but I don't know if she's following me or if she just wants me to continue in hopes that I'll eventually get to the point. "There's also a lot you don't know about me. Like . . . that . . . my mom is your daughter. Her pictures are all over your house." My hands feel clammy so I rub them on my jeans and keep talking. I can't stop now. "There aren't many of your grandson because he's only seven months old right now. And . . ." I pause to take a deep breath, but it seems pointless. I should just spit it out. "This is going to sound really weird, but . . . that's the reason your grandson and I have the same name."

This time, her head doesn't move at all.

"I'm . . ." I stop. Breathe. Go again. "I'm your grandson and I'm seventeen"—I stammer—"in two thousand twelve. Not in nineteen ninety-five."

Still no response. I have no idea what to do, so I keep going even though I'm stumbling over every word.

"When I was ten, I sort of . . . accidentally . . . discovered that I could . . . travel. I can go back in time—five seconds, ten minutes, four months, several years . . . all the way back to the day I was born. March 6, 1995. That's as far back as I can go."

Maggie's shoulders rise and fall.

"I'd never tried to stay anywhere in the past before, not until the last time I was here. Do you remember when I arrived last March . . . how I was so sick?"

Slight nod.

"I wasn't really sick. I kept . . . disappearing. I was trying to stay here but I kept getting knocked back to my bedroom in two thousand twelve. See, that's how it works. When I try to push the limits of what I can do, I get sent back where I belong. It's like time's way of saying that I'm not where I'm supposed to be. It's the only time I don't have control. And then it hurts. Sometimes a lot. I finally . . . trained myself, I guess, to stay here."

Maggie brings her hand to her mouth but still keeps her back to me.

"I was only here because I lost my sister, Brooke. She wanted to go to this concert in Chicago in nineteen ninety-four. Neither one of us thought I'd be able to do it or anything, but it worked. We made it. But a couple of minutes later, *I* was knocked back to my present and Brooke wasn't. She was stuck back in nineteen ninety-four. So I came here, to your house, here in nineteen ninety-five, trying to get as close to her as I could."

It's silent for a minute or so. "Did you find her?" I'm relieved to hear the sound of Maggie's voice, low and calm. She's taking in facts and I figure that's a good sign.

"Yeah. She got knocked back home after a few months. And I think that's why I couldn't come back here. Once she was home I couldn't really go anywhere for a while." I picture myself returning to the same day, over and over again, to watch Anna at the track. I start to tell Maggie, but decide that might be more information than she needs to know.

I pour myself a glass of water, not because I'm dehydrated, but because I'm eager to have something to do with my hands.

I fill another glass and slide it across the table to Maggie. She picks it up right away.

"Do your parents know?" she asks.

"I was twelve when they, sort of, found out by accident."

Now Maggie's hands are trembling. She looks at me. "Do they know you're here right now?"

I shake my head. "They knew I was here last spring, but they don't know I came back. Brooke does, but my parents . . ." I trail off, but Maggie looks at me like she's waiting for me to continue. I shake my head again. "They wouldn't understand this."

Maggie leans forward. The color seems to have returned to her cheeks. "Where do they think you are right now?"

"Rock climbing and camping with my friend Sam."

"Sam?"

"Yeah, Sam."

"So you're not . . . *in* . . . two thousand twelve San Francisco right now?"

"No, when I leave I'm gone. I disappear from there and come here. This time, I've been gone since Friday night." I rest my arms on the table, and tell her how it works. She listens intently but doesn't ask any more questions. "If I wanted to, I could return to San Francisco right now and arrive back on Friday, just five minutes after I left. And even though I'd been gone for two days, my parents would never even know it. But then they'd be doing those two days all over again and that seems like a pretty horrible thing to do to them. So I just, you know . . . say I'm camping."

Maggie looks confused. "Yeah, I guess that's probably best then." She takes another sip of her water. "Or you could . . . tell them you're coming here?"

I laugh. "I don't think that would go over so well." I push my plate to the middle of the table. "Mom wants a normal seventeen-year-old kid who skateboards and takes tests and applies to college, and *doesn't* rock climb in Thailand or travel to see his grandmother back in nineteen ninety-five whenever he wants to."

That finally gets a smile. "And your dad?"

"Dad wants me to do more with my 'gift,' as he calls it. He thinks I'm special and that I should be righting wrongs, fixing things, being heroic or something." I pick up my glass and swirl the water inside, thinking about the fire back in San Francisco and what Anna and I did in Paris and how, over the last few days, I've been starting to think he could be right. "I don't know. Until recently, I've pretty much used this thing I can do for my own benefit." I don't tell her that it's also been for hers. She doesn't need to know what Brooke and I will do for her years from now, when the Alzheimer's sets in and starts taking control of her mind and her life.

Maggie looks more relaxed now. She shifts in her chair and reaches for the glass of water. "That sounds like your dad."

"Really?"

She nods. "He's always been a bit intense. Far more so than your mom is." Maggie looks past me, over my shoulder, and when I turn my head to follow her gaze, I see that she's staring at the stained glass image that hangs in her kitchen window above the sink—the one my mom made when she was a kid. "But he's a good man, I think. She definitely loves him." She looks back at me again, and leans in closer. "And you . . . my goodness. I was only there for a short time, but from what I could tell, their whole world revolves around you and your sister."

"That might be true now, but everything will change once she discovers that she doesn't have a *normal* kid who keeps her busy with Little League games or school plays." I stop short of telling Maggie what I'm really thinking. Her daughter's stuck with me, a freak show who sneaks around behind her back and lies to her, all to keep doing the one thing she so desperately wants him to stop.

Maggie lets out a sigh and shakes her head. "I bet she thinks you're pretty remarkable." I have no idea how to respond to that, and it's quiet for a long time. Finally, she looks at me wearing a huge smile as she reaches across the table. She covers my hand with hers. "I'll go back after all. I'll see what I can do. Now that I know who you are, maybe I can use my trips to San Francisco to help your mom understand you a little bit better."

My stomach sinks as I think about the photo of the three of us at the zoo, and how Maggie would never have come that weekend if Anna hadn't told her to. I don't know what happened before that visit, but I know what happened afterward—Maggie never came back.

"I'm afraid you can't do that," I say. She doesn't seem to grasp Anna's involvement in the whole thing and I don't want to ruin the one memory she has by telling her that it never should have happened. "You came to visit us once, and that was it."

"Once?" She pulls her hand away from mine, and I watch her face fall as the information sinks in. She doesn't say anything, but she doesn't need to. Her expression says everything. *That can't be possible.*

I feel compelled to tell her everything, but I can't. And now I have to choose my words wisely and use them sparingly, because the more she knows about the future, the greater the risk of her inadvertently changing it. Who knows what could happen if she does.

"The two of you didn't speak for a long time. I don't know why, my mom never talks about it, but Brooke and I never knew you." I trip on the last two words and immediately wish I could pull them back in, but it's too late. Maggie heard me. *Knew.* Past tense.

She stares at me like she wants to ask the question but doesn't know how to voice it or if she should. I answer it silently. *You died without knowing us.*

I remember those weeks far too vividly. I'd never seen Mom cry before, but the day she found out that her mother had passed away—all alone in this great big house—she became hysterical. Brooke and I didn't know what to do, so we hid in her room, wrapped in each other's arms and crying together without really understanding why. The next day, Mom and Dad got on a plane, but they couldn't afford to bring Brooke and me along. Besides, they'd said, we were too young for funerals. I was eight. I didn't know what I could do back then; if I had, things might have been different.

Maggie looks away from me and her gaze wanders around the room before it settles on the table. "Are we both that hard-headed?" she asks herself, and I hear the disbelief in her voice. She slowly raises her head and looks at me. "But now that I know, I can change it. I can be the one who makes the effort, makes it better. Right?"

I press my lips tightly together and shake my head. "You can't change it, Maggie. You weren't part of our lives the first time, so you can't be part of them now. Who knows what might happen if you were?"

She gives me a stubborn stare, like she's considering doing it anyway.

"You have to promise me you won't go back there again."

She takes a deep breath and her eyes lock on mine. "I don't know if I can make that promise, Bennett."

I don't have a choice but to give her an ultimatum. "Then I'll go back in time, right after you came into my room tonight. That Bennett—the one who's thirty minutes *younger* than me—will dissapper the instant I come back, and I'll take his place. I'll come downstairs, and you and I will have a nice chat and eat this delicious dinner. And then I'll get up from the table, help you with the dishes, and this whole conversation we're having right now," I gesture back and forth between the two of us, "will never happen."

She rests her elbows on the table and buries her face in her hands. The two of us sit like that for a long time, Maggie thinking about the future and me feeling horrible and helpless because we're all stuck with it.

"Fine," she says, her voice cracking. "I won't go back." Suddenly she sits back in her chair and crosses her arms. "You said earlier that it hurt when you traveled. What did you mean by that?" I'm surprised by the question but grateful for the subject change.

"It doesn't hurt when I travel *to* another destination—like when I come here from home—but when I return, I get hit with these terrible migraines and I'm completely dehydrated. I drink coffee because the caffeine helps the headache and I down a bunch of water for the dehydration, and after a half hour or so, it goes away."

"So did you have a headache when you returned earlier . . . from wherever you went?"

I shake my head no. "I really only get the major side effects when I . . . leave the timeline, if you will. Earlier, I just went upstairs, counted to ten, and came back. I used to get a little headache when I returned after doing those short hops, too, but that doesn't happen so much anymore."

Maggie nods and it looks like she's following me. But then she leans in closer and her forehead wrinkles up with confusion and concern. "I don't understand. If it hurts, why do you do it?"

At first, I think about all the places I've been—all the things I never would have seen and experiences I never would have had if I'd let twenty or thirty minutes of pain stop me from traveling. But then I look at her, and I don't think that's what she means. I think she wants to know why I come back here.

My eyes scan Maggie's kitchen until they stop on that same stained glass oranament my mom made. I think of the photos of my family that line the walls of the living room and the hallways, and how happy we all look. I remember how I opened the front door last Friday, stepped inside, and felt this invisible weight lift from my shoulders.

"I feel at home here," I say. I watch Maggie's eyes well up.

The phone rings and she stands, leaving me alone at the table, and I'm relieved to have a few seconds to catch my breath. After she answers it, she glances over at me. "Yes, he's right here."

She returns to the table and hands me the cordless phone.

"Hello?" I say.

"It's me." The second I hear Anna's voice my whole body seems to relax.

"Hey, you." I can hear her smiling on the other end of the line.

"It's nice to talk to you on the phone," she whispers. "I don't think I ever have."

"How do I sound?"

It's quiet for a second or two, and then she says, "Close."

I smile but don't say anything.

"So," she says. "Emma and I are going to a movie. We thought you and Justin might want to come along?"

I look over at Maggie and find her buzzing around,

gathering up pots, filling the sink with hot water. "Hold on," I say before I cover the receiver with my hand. "Do you mind if I go to the movies?"

"Of course not." Even though we were in the middle of a pretty big discussion here, Maggie looks like she means it.

I return to Anna. "Sure. What's the movie?" I ask. Not that it matters.

"Emma wants to go to some sneak preview of *Empire Records*," she says. "I haven't even heard of it. Have you?"

The words "cult classic" start to leave my mouth but I stop them. "Yeah," I say instead. "I hear it's good."

"Great. We'll pick you up in twenty."

I press the end call button and return the phone to its home on the wall. When I reach for my plate to clear it from the table, Maggie swats my hand away. "Stop it. I've got the dishes. You go have fun."

"You sure?" I ask. Her hands still look a little shaky.

"Positive." She turns her back on me and continues collecting the rest of the dishes in the sink. She turns the water on, and I'm about to leave the room, when I hear it stop. "Bennett?"

I look back as she wipes her hand on a dish towel.

Then she crosses the room and surprises me when she pulls me into a hug. "Thank you. I'm glad you told me," she says. I close my eyes as I wrap my arms around her. She feels small in my arms, and when she rubs my back, I squeeze her even tighter. I've spent all these years sneaking around, helping her secretly and always from a distance, and I'm filled with relief that I don't have to do that anymore. She knows who I am. And it suddenly hits me that I'm hugging my grandmother for the first time. I squeeze her even tighter and she does the same.

"I'm glad I get to know you now," she says.

I choke out the words "Me too."

She takes a deep breath and gives me a hard pat on the back. "Okay, scoot. You have a date." Then she takes two steps away from me and stops. "Bennett?" The tone of her voice is careful and questioning, the wrinkles on her forehead more pronounced as she asks, "How long has Anna known?"

I close my eyes, thinking back to the day I stood in Anna's kitchen and showed her what I could do. Then I let my memory take me back even further, to the day she handed me that letter in the park.

I open my eyes, feeling this overwhelming sense of relief as a smile slowly spreads across my face. "Anna's known from the beginning."

19

Anna and I spend most of Sunday hanging out in my room, listening to music and talking about the next time I'll be back: three weeks from now. Homecoming. Anna tells me that I'll finally get to see her in the dress she bought for the auction party last May and reminds me to get here in time to pick up a tux.

The room is getting darker, and when I glance over at the clock and tell her I should be getting back, I feel a pit form deep in my gut. It's followed by a rush of guilt for feeling that way about my own home.

"I have something for you." Anna says as she crosses the room and flips on the light. She pulls something out of her bag and hides it behind her back. "Pick a hand."

I point to her right side and she opens her hand, shows me it's empty, and pulls it behind her back again. She must switch hands, because when I point to her left side and she opens her other hand, it's empty too. She looks up at me with a mischievous grin, so, on impulse, I grab her wrists and kiss her while she twists in my arms, laughing and trying to keep whatever she has behind her back out of my grasp.

"Fine!" she says, cracking up as she squirms away and holds me at arm's length. "Here." She hands me a three-by-five-inch album with geometric designs and the word PHOTOS in block letters across the front.

I turn it over in my hands and Anna gives me a proud grin as she opens the cover for me. The first picture is the two of us, standing at the top of the Eiffel Tower. Her arms are wrapped tight around my waist, the inky black Parisian sky in the background, and we're beaming at the camera like there's no place in the world either one of us would rather be.

I flip page after page, looking at the photos we took as we walked around Paris that night and the following day. Me standing in front of the Fontaine du Cirque. Anna in front of the wrought iron gates that led to the park, holding a baguette like a baseball bat. Me at the base of *The Thinker*, mimicking the pose. Her on the bridge, standing next to our lock. God, was that only yesterday? I look through the pictures, feeling grateful for a talent that allows me to take her to Paris at the drop of a hat. I feel equally grateful that it allows me to buy a whole extra day with her.

"This is incredible," I say as I flip through the plastic pages.

And then I get to the last one. It's not from our Paris trip yesterday, but I remember the night we took it in vivid detail. She'd just come back from La Paz. We were sprawled out on her rug in her bedroom and she held her arm high in the air, balancing her brand-new camera in one hand. She'd planted a kiss on my cheek as the shutter snapped. I study the expression on my face. I look happy.

"I love it." I stare at the picture, and then look over at her again. I think I'm supposed to tell her how nice it will be to have something to look at when I'm home and missing her, because I'm pretty sure that's what she wants to hear right now, but the truth is, when I'm seventeen years away from her and wishing I weren't, subjecting myself to these photos will be the last thing I'll want to do. Still, I'll probably do it anyway.

"See." She taps on the cover of the book. "And now you have something to show your family." Her smile looks sweet and hopeful, but it's her words that snap me back to reality. "I figured since I'll never be able to go home with you and meet them, at least you could show them these pictures." She lets out a laugh. "You know, so they don't think I'm a figment of your imagination or anything." My stomach knots up into a tight fist.

She waits for my reply, and when nothing comes she continues talking.

"I made a photo album for myself, too, but of course I have to keep mine hidden from *my* parents. I've convinced them that the pins in my map are just wishful thinking, but I'm not sure how I'd explain photos of you and me on the top of the Eiffel Tower."

I look down at the pictures in my hands, thinking back on our weekend. Talking with her under a canopy of trees during Emma's birthday party. The look of anticipation on her face when I took her hands in mine and told her to close her eyes, and the sheer awe I saw when she opened them. Falling asleep with her in Paris. Waking up to her in Paris.

I shove the photo album into my backpack, avoiding her eyes. "Good idea." I wonder if she hears the guilt in my voice. I wish she hadn't brought this up now, when I'm minutes away from leaving and I won't see her again for three more weeks. "Speaking of my parents, I'd better get going." I zip my pack closed and feed my arms through the straps, and Anna looks down at the carpet.

I step closer to her and rub her arms. "Are you going to be okay?"

She nods without looking at me. I take her chin and tip her head up. "Go downstairs and talk to Maggie." Anna closes her eyes, presses her lips tightly together, and nods.

I muster a valiant smile, but inside, I'm thinking how I'd give anything to stay here another day, another week . . . another three months. This whole being strong for someone else thing is a lot harder than I expected it to be. I can tell she's trying to keep it together for my sake as well. "I'll be back before you know it," I say, and clench my jaw the minute the words leave my mouth.

"I know." She takes a gulp of air and lets it out in a sigh. "That was the most incredible weekend." She buries her face in my chest and wraps her arms around me. We stand like that for a long time, listening to the music in the background, trying to ignore the inevitable.

Out of nowhere, it hits me: this is how it's going to be for the next year. Every few weeks, *this* is how it will feel to say good-bye to her. What's worse, every few weeks for as long as we're together, this is how it's going to feel. Will we ever get used to this?

I block out the thoughts as I plant kisses in her hair and on her cheeks, which are now wet and salty. I kiss her forehead and then her lips. It takes everything I have to let go of her and step backward, but I do.

I close my eyes and fade away.

september 2012

20

san francisco, california

My forehead slams against something hard, and I struggle to open my eyes. When I do, I can make out the Jeep logo on the steering wheel. Everything's blurry, the interior of the car is spinning, and my arms feel heavy, like I've got weights attached to my wrists. It takes all of my energy to bring my hands to the wheel, but when I feel the leather, I grip it hard and push, throwing myself back against the headrest.

I let out a groan.

My eyes fall shut on their own, and I sit there in the dark, smelly garage, breathing in, breathing out, and trying not to think about the fact that this hurts more than usual. That's when I feel the tickle, something warm sliding down onto my upper lip. I lick it, and my mouth fills with the unmistakable taste of blood, metallic and sticky-feeling. I wipe my nose with the back of my hand and it comes back with a streak of red.

I tilt the rearview mirror toward my face. What the hell?

The box of supplies proves to be worthless for this situation, but it's not like I could have anticipated a need for Kleenex. I've never had a bloody nose in my life. I use the bottom of my shirt to pinch my nose together, and a few minutes later the bleeding has stopped.

There's a tiny patch of evening sun peeking in through the sides of the garage door. I down my Doubleshot without stopping and chase it with a warm Red Bull and two bottles of water. I sit there for a long time, eyes closed, willing the pain to stop. I look in the rearview mirror. My face is red and patchy, my eyes bloodshot. Then I look at the clock on the dashboard. I've been back for almost an hour.

Finally, when my head is no longer throbbing, I push the button on the remote control and the door lifts slowly and rattles into place above me. I twist the key in the ignition and pull out of the garage.

Before I close the door, I twist in my seat. Looking back inside, I can't help but laugh. If I'd ever allowed myself to think that my ability made me some kind of superhero, this would certainly put things into perspective. My secret hide-out isn't a subterranean cave or a cool arctic ice structure. It's a garage. A dark, smelly garage that an average-size car and average-size me can barely occupy at the same time. And exactly like I hoped it would be, it's perfect.

Luckily, the house is quiet and I sneak inside, through the kitchen and into my bedroom, hoping to get there before

Mom notices the bloodstains on the bottom of my T-shirt. I undress, hiding my dirty clothes deep in the bottom of the hamper in my closet, and throw on a clean pair of sweats. In the bathroom, I wash my face hard with a washcloth.

Back in my room, I unzip my backpack and remove the photo album Anna made for me. I hold it in my hands, examining the colorful patterns on the cover. I start to open it, but I just can't bring myself to do it. Not yet.

I open my desk drawer, and down near the bottom I see my red notebook. I stuff the photo album inside with everything else and shut the drawer.

I'm halfway down the stairs when I look over the banister and see Mom and Dad by the front door. He pulls his suit jacket over his shoulders, looks into the hallway mirror, and adjusts his glasses. He grabs my mom's purse off the table and hands it to her. She thanks him as she throws it over her shoulder.

"Hey," I say. They both look up at the same time. Mom's face breaks into a wide grin.

"Oh, good. You're back. I didn't even hear you come in." She meets me at the bottom of the staircase. "How was your climbing trip?" she asks as she kisses me on the cheek. "Did you and your friends have fun?"

I ignore her question and change the subject by stating the obvious. "I take it you guys are going out?"

"We realized that we haven't been to a nice dinner together in weeks," Dad says. He stands behind my mom, rubbing her arms lightly.

"Do you want to join us?" Mom asks. "With all your homework, we've barely seen you since school started." Her expression is sincere, but Dad's standing there, looking at her like he can't imagine why she'd invite me to join them on their "nice dinner." From behind her shoulder, he stares at me wide-eyed and gives me a small shake of his head, just in case I didn't know how to answer.

I look at the two of them, maybe for the first time, through a different lens. I think about Maggie's comments last night, and how Dad was always more intense than Mom but she loved him. How their worlds revolved around Brooke and me. More than anything, I wish I could talk to Mom about Maggie. Every time I've tried to tell her about those three months I spent living there, Mom stopped me short and said she didn't want to hear it. I'm guessing that it's not because she doesn't want to know; it's because she can't handle the guilt.

"Want to come?" Mom repeats.

"No, thanks," I say, and Dad gives me a grateful nod. "You two have a nice date."

As Dad grabs my mom's hand and leads her outside onto the front porch, he says something under his breath. She's laughing as the door closes behind them.

After they're gone, I stand at the bottom of the stairs for a long time, looking across the room at the huge picture window that overlooks the bay and wondering what to do with myself. I drum my fingers against the banister and think about the week ahead of me. There's a physics test tomorrow and I have an interview with the tutoring organization Sam works for on Tuesday. I should start studying.

I make it back to my room, but just as I'm about to turn on the music and hit the books, I have a different idea. I open the largest drawer of my desk and dig down to the bottom. When I find the photo album, I return it to my backpack and head downstairs for my board.

The sun is just starting to set when I arrive at the park, and I'm relieved to find it relatively empty. It's still warm outside, and I look over the horizon at the San Francisco Bay, bright blue and full of sailboats. I sit down on the bench, remove the photo album from my backpack, and flip through the pages. This time, Anna's here with me.

october 2012

21

san francisco, california

I scroll through the calendar on my phone, looking at all the days that have passed since my last trip. I picture Anna doing something similar, adding one more x in today's square on her wall calendar before she heads off to school. We're getting closer and closer to the one marked with the word "homecoming." Three more open squares. Three more days to go.

I'm supposed to be writing an essay on the Zhou Dynasty for AP World Civ, but instead I'm staring at the tabs at the top of the browser: ZHOU DYNASTY—WIKIPEDIA, WORLD CIVILIZATION/ONLINE STUDENT RESOURCES, PANDORA.

I click on Pandora and change the station a few times before I settle on "90s Alternative." Without even thinking about it, I open a new browser window and a news page pops open. I scan the stories about the upcoming presidential election and watch today's most popular YouTube video.

I click on the Local News button and scroll through, reading the headlines: VICTIMS OF A SMALL PLANE CRASH IDENTIFIED. MAN ARRESTED FOR ARSON. WOMAN SHOT OUTSIDE MARKET. SIXTEEN-YEAR-OLD RUNAWAY FOUND DEAD ON LOCAL BEACH. The list of tragedies and near-tragedies that occurred in the greater Bay Area over the past twenty-four hours goes on and on.

I'm just about to close the window and return to my essay when a story farther down the page catches my attention: FATHER AND DAUGHTER KILLED BY TEEN DRIVER.

I click on the link and it opens to a picture of a light-blue bike, twisted and lying in the gutter. I read the story:

> *7:34 P.M.—A seventeen-year-old male driver struck a family riding bicycles shortly after 3:30 P.M. today. The teen's truck lost control and collided with a fire hydrant before hitting a man and his two daughters, killing the man and one girl and injuring the other. The driver was released from the hospital with minor injuries and was immediately arrested on suspicion of involuntary manslaughter.*

I tell myself to close the window, but instead, I scroll down and continue reading.

Identities have not yet been released, but according to police, the cyclists were a man, his nine-year-old daughter, and her twelve-year-old sister. Both the man and nine-year-old girl were pronounced dead at the scene. The twelve-year-old was taken to the hospital with minor injuries. The father met his two daughters at school every day to ride home with them, to make sure they got home safely.

The words make me sick, but it's the pictures that do me in. In addition to the one of the light-blue bike, there's a photo of the building that eventually stopped the car. Its stucco is scattered and stacked in piles on the ground, its framing exposed.

I stare at the screen, thinking about the driver, and how such a small mistake—something that happened in a fraction of a second—just changed his entire life. He's only seventeen, but his whole future came to a screeching halt today. Even if the jail time is minimal, how could he ever be the same knowing that a girl and her mother are now without a sister and daughter, and a father and husband. I picture him, sitting in an orange jumpsuit down at county, wishing he could do it all over again, wishing for a second chance. And two keystrokes later, the printer whirs to life. I grab the paper while it's still warm and head downstairs.

Dad's office door is ajar, but I knock before I push it open anyway. He's behind his desk, working at his computer, and he looks up and watches me with a curious expression as I cross the room. I don't say a word as I set the news story on the desk in front of him.

"What is this?"

"Read it."

He scans it quickly and looks up at me.

"Tell me it's a really bad idea," I say.

He's quiet for a long time, reading the article, then he grins. "It's a really bad idea."

"I know, right?"

He stares at me.

"Want to come along?"

～⌒

I find Dad's old backpack on the shelf in the garage reserved for our family's neglected camping gear, and I shake off the thin layer of dust that's collected over the years. When I was little, I saw this pack nearly every weekend. I remember how big it used to look as I trailed behind Dad on Cub Scout hikes through the wilderness.

Now I work quickly to ready it for a completely different kind of adventure, filling it with two room-temperature bottles of water from a flat lying on the floor next to the refrigerator. I'm about to head back inside when I spot my skateboard leaning up against the far wall, and it gives me an idea. I jam it into my pack, one end sticking out through the gap in the zipper.

Back in my room, I add the rest of the essentials—large wads of cash stuffed into the front pockets of both packs and a clean T-shirt balled up in the main pocket of mine, just in case. As I pass the bathroom, I grab a big handful of Kleenex from the box on the counter.

Dad's pacing his office and cleaning his glasses with the hem of his shirt. I hand him his backpack and shut the door behind me.

"What's that?" he asks, pointing to my pack.

I turn around to look at it. "That's a skateboard, Dad."

"Thanks, Bennett." He shakes his head at me. "Why are you bringing a skateboard?"

"I'm sticking to my rules. I still don't believe I should change things deliberately, but I've been sort of . . . experimenting with altering little things: you know, small, insignificant details that could have a huge effect on the outcome." I give him a mischievous grin and gesture toward the board. "This is a diversion."

Dad seems relatively comfortable with the small amount of information I'm giving him, so I hold out my hands. He looks wary as he glances down at them. "It's been a while. Do you still remember how this works?"

He nods once. When he takes them, his grip is strong and his hands feel rough and large in mine, nothing like Anna's or Brooke's. For a moment, I feel like I'm ten again; small, fragile, and not at all like the person with the power.

"You ready?" I ask.

Dad doesn't say anything as he closes his eyes.

I close mine and lock in the time. I visualize the nondescript alley I found online, a half a block away from the intersection where everything just changed for four people. I muster a silent plea that I'll be able to fix it for all of them.

⁓

"Open your eyes."

Dad opens them and looks around. I can tell he's trying not to panic. "Where are we?"

I gesture toward the far end of the alley. Cars are zooming

past, and I start off walking in that direction and tell Dad to follow me. When we arrive, I peer around the corner and take in the surroundings. Halfway between the alley and the busy intersection, I see a wide cement stairway that leads to an office building. I didn't see that on the map, but it makes this spot even more perfect.

I point into the distance, across the intersection, and Dad stands next to me, following my gaze. "See that red fire hydrant on the next block?"

He squints. "Yes."

I tell him everything I know from the news story online. "The car went out of control and slammed into that hydrant, and a few seconds later, hit the bikers. But all of them passed through this intersection first, at different times, before any of that happened. We have about ten minutes before the bikes arrive at this spot, so here's our plan." Dad stares at me with wide eyes as I describe what I have in mind, and when I get to the part where I tell him his role in the whole thing, he lets out a series of "okays" and "got its." He might be a bit shell-shocked, but as far as I can tell, he's taking it all in.

"That's the plan?" he asks.

"Yeah." I brace myself for criticism or, at the very least, additions. Dad smiles and says, "That's really good."

I smile back. "Thanks. I kind of thought so too." He has a funny look on his face, like he's about to say something important, but instead, he looks over his shoulder and down the street. A bike courier zooms past us.

"You'd better get going," he says, pointing toward the

intersection. He heads off in the opposite direction.

In one swift string of moves, I pull my skateboard out of the backpack, start into a run as I throw it on the ground, and swing the pack over my shoulders as I skate away. I push with my back foot and glide, weaving back and forth to find my balance. A minute later, I'm at the bottom of the steps. I pop my board into my hand and race up to the top. It's perfect—the ground is smooth and there's no one here.

I'm floating around the empty courtyard, feeling the board under my feet and gathering my nerve, when I spot a short cement divider at the far end. I build up speed, heading straight for it. I'm feeling confident as I pop an ollie at the base. I clear it easily and land clean on the other side.

I turn around and skate back toward the steps. I leave my board at the top and race halfway down so I can check the scene. There are other bikers on the road, but I think I spot the three of them on the next block. They're riding slowly in a single-file line, and when the light turns, they stop. So far, so good.

At the top of the steps I grab my board, jump onto the ledge, do a 50-50 grind to the bottom, and land perfectly. Now I see Dad clearly as he rounds the corner, just in front of the bikers, all of them moving quickly. I run back up to the top of the stairs and skate deep into the courtyard so I can generate enough momentum.

Then I'm off, skating fast toward the steps, the wind pushing my hair off my face. I speed toward them, focused on nothing but the cement ledge that separates the steps from a cluster of trees. I ollie onto it, balance the trucks on the edge, and slide down—fast, but completely in control. And I land, bending my knees to absorb the shock and forcing the board into a quick turn to keep from going into the street. And that's when I fake my crash.

I let my board slip out from under my feet, sending me tumbling hard toward the ground. I fall onto my shoulder and roll it out like I've done hundreds of times, but I imagine the whole thing looks far more dramatic to a nonskater. In case it doesn't, I add a little flourish, taking the whole display up a notch or two.

Gripping my leg to my chest I lie on the ground, yelling loudly and writhing in pain. And that's when Dad arrives at my side, wearing his suit and looking like a concerned pedestrian. "Are you okay?" he keeps asking, while I respond with more yelling. And writhing.

He reaches for his cell phone and I have to turn away to conceal the grin on my face. I never thought I'd turn a do-over into a heroic act, and I sure as hell never thought I'd make Dad my sidekick.

Now the man has stopped and is straddling his bike and balancing his weight on the curb. His two daughters are stopped too, waiting curiously behind him and staring at me. I let out a high-pitched groan and return to thrashing on the ground.

Dad has to yell to be heard above the hum of the passing traffic. "My cell phone is dead and this boy needs some help. Can you call nine-one-one?"

I can't hear what the man says in reply, but he appears to be digging around in the pocket of his jeans.

This brilliant street performance should probably be my sole focus, but I can't stand not knowing what's going on. I look past the girls and into the street, and see the truck. Dad's watching it too, and I'm sure neither one of us is breathing as it shifts into the lane closest to us.

I sit up to get a better view, no longer caring if I've broken my cover. In a fraction of a second, no one will be looking at me anyway.

The truck speeds up to make the light and travels through the intersection, and a few seconds later, it veers off the road and up onto the curb. It sideswipes the fire hydrant, sending water shooting into the air. It doesn't stop moving until it slams into the side of the building. Stucco goes flying in every direction and smoke starts shooting up from the open hood.

I know how this scene will look a few hours from now—I clearly remember the "after" photo of the building: windows shattered, framing exposed, stucco piled on the sidewalk— but when I look at the little girl in front of me, I remember the other picture that ran with the news story. She's still standing astride her light blue, *un*twisted bike, and craning her neck to see what happened on the next block. Suddenly, she catches me staring at her. She hops off and hits the kickstand with her foot, and walks over to me.

She crouches down low. "Is your leg okay?" she asks.

"Yeah. I think it's okay." I'm sure I look ridiculous, sitting in the middle of the sidewalk, wearing this goofy smile.

Then my dad is by my side, his voice loud and direct. "Stay here. We're going to go check on the driver." The little girl and I watch as our fathers take off running toward the scene of the accident.

"I hope he's okay," she says.

"Don't worry," I say in a tone of voice that's probably far too enthusiastic for this situation. "I have a feeling he's fine."

22

Dad opens his eyes and looks around at his office, like he's seeing the bookshelves and paintings for the first time. "Did we do it?" He drops my hands and starts pacing back and forth in front of me. "How do we know if we changed it or not?"

I look at the clock above the door. It's only a quarter to four.

He crosses the room in three long strides and stands behind his desk, shuffling papers. "Where is it? Where's the story you brought in here?"

I keep my voice calm to offset the anxiety I hear in his. "It's okay, Dad. That hasn't happened yet." I point up at the analog clock above his desk. "I came down here and showed you that story around seven thirty. That's four hours from now."

His eyes follow my finger but he only gives it a quick glance before he returns to digging through the stacks on his desk. "Dad. Stop." I rest my hand on one of his. "We'll check the news tonight, but now there probably won't *be* a story. Or, I guess, there *will* be a story but it will be a completely different one. Are you okay? You look pale."

He gropes around for his chair, sits down hard, and rolls it toward the desk so he can rest his head in his hands. I can see his shoulders rise and fall with each slow, deliberate breath, but aside from the panic attack, he doesn't seem to be showing any post-travel reactions.

Which makes me realize I feel pretty good too. My heart is racing and my stomach feels light and I just want to . . . move. I want to go outside, hop on my skateboard again, and power down the hill, feeling the wind prickle my skin and lift my hair off my forehead. I feel incredible—no nosebleed, no migraine—just buzzy, like my whole body is vibrating, surging with adrenaline.

Dad's head springs up and he starts typing on his keyboard. I come around to his side of the desk and watch as he types in every possible combination of words that could lead us to today's events: "bicycle" and "accident" and "intersection" and "manslaughter."

He's not getting it.

"Dad, you're not going to find anything yet. The accident just happened. It won't show up for a while. Dad . . ." I lead his hands away from the keyboard. "We'll check later tonight, okay, but trust me, it won't be there. It worked. Everyone's fine, except the kid driving the truck, who's a bit banged up but probably being arrested right now for reckless driving and not vehicular manslaughter."

Before I can comprehend what's happening, Dad stands up

and pulls me to him and hugs me so hard I can't breathe. Eventually, he releases me, but he still keeps my arm in his grip. He stares at me like he's trying to decide what to say, and finally settles on "They were really nice people, weren't they?"

I let out a nervous laugh. "Yeah, Dad, they were really nice." I picture that little girl, worried about the condition of the driver who—in a version of a timeline that no longer exists— left her family fatherless and cut her life short at age nine.

"I'd better get back to my homework," I say, gesturing toward my bedroom. "I have an essay I need to start all over again."

Dad pats my arms hard and chuckles. "Sorry. That sucks," he says.

"That's okay. So did the essay."

My backpack is a lot lighter without the skateboard. As I throw it over my shoulders and readjust the straps, I steal one last glance at the clock on my nightstand. I'm not supposed to be in Evanston until homecoming this weekend, but I can't help it. I have to see Anna right now. I have to tell her what I just did.

I grab my car keys off my desk and speed out to the Jeep, and a half hour later, I'm backing it into the garage on the other side of town. I switch off the ignition, lower the door, and close my eyes.

I open them on the cross-country course that sits adjacent

to the Westlake track. I've arrived exactly where I intended, in a quiet spot off the trail behind a cluster of trees and a fat shrub that conceals me from sight. Resting my backpack on the ground, I feel around inside until I find what I'm looking for. Then I sneak out toward the trail, listening for their footfalls. I can't hear a thing.

It doesn't take me any time to find the perfect spot. Smack in the middle of the trail I spot a log, large and intentionally placed to be hurdled, and I jiggle the postcard into a crevice so it's standing up straight. Then I duck back out of sight.

The adrenaline is still surging through me, and even though I know I should stay silent and still, I can't stop pacing across the dirt. I'm waiting and listening and ready to burst out of my skin. Finally, a few minutes later, I hear the rhythmic sound of feet padding against the dirt, followed by heavy breathing and the occasional grunt. I force myself to relax, pressing my back firmly against the tree bark.

Then the footsteps stop.

"This was just sticking out of the log," someone says.

"What is it?" asks another.

"A postcard. From *Paris*." I still don't recognize the speaker, but I laugh under my breath when I hear the fascination in her voice as she says the word "Paris."

"That's weird."

More footsteps.

"What's up?" Ah, there's Anna's voice. I stand still, listening.

"It's nothing. Come on, we're losing time," another voice says, and I hear footsteps on the trail again.

"Here, check it out. This was wedged into the log."

"Huh . . ." I picture Anna taking it from her teammate, flipping the postcard around in her hands. "Weird. Come on, Stacy's right, we should go."

They run off and everything's quiet until I hear footsteps on the trail again, this time coming from the opposite direction. Leaves crunch and twigs snap, and Anna's face comes into view as she clears the short incline and peeks around a bush.

"What are you doing here?" she asks, clearly surprised to see me. "I'm in the middle of practice." She's taking long strides, beaming as she walks toward me. I wrap my arms around her waist and lift her off the ground. "*Ew*, what are you doing? Put me down!" She laughs and smacks me with her hand. "I'm all sweaty."

"I don't care." I tighten my hold on her and plant a kiss in her hair. I'd been hyperaware of the adrenaline surge, but now I don't notice it as much. I feel a headache coming on but I ignore it.

"Is everything okay? You're shaking."

"Yeah. Everything's fine. I have to tell you something." I comb my hands through my hair. "You're not going to believe what I just did—"

Suddenly, I don't know where to start. Anna stares at me, looking confused and curious and waiting for me to continue. Every detail of *everything* that happened over the last forty-five minutes is swirling around in my head, flying around too quickly for me to grasp on to just one. Did all of it actually happen? The bikes. The crash. The girl.

"You're not supposed to be here until Friday."

"I know, but—" A faint ringing in my ear makes me stop in midsentence, and before I can say another word it completely changes pitch—high and piercing and constant—and I grab the sides of my head and crouch down on the ground in front of her.

I hear Anna say my name, but her voice sounds far away. I try to take my hands off my head so I can steady myself on the ground, but I can't move. I feel my whole body grow weak, like my muscles are atrophying as I sit here. I feel my knees buckle and my cheek hit the dirt.

My eyes are open so wide they're stinging and watering, and I feel pebbles and mud collecting under my fingernails as I claw my way back to sitting. I fall into the ground again and my head hits something that feels like a rock. Without my ability to control them, my eyes shut tightly. And suddenly, the piercing sound is gone and everything falls silent.

23

The pain hits me all at once, so hard and so unexpected I don't even have time to grab on to anything for support. My head falls forward and my face slams against the ground, and when I open my eyes, I see the blood, pooling under my head. I stare down at the pattern that unmistakably places me in Dad's office.

No bushes, no trees, no Anna. And no garage, no Jeep.

I crawl over to the end table next to Dad's leather chair. Using it for support, I try to push myself to standing, but my knees can't hold me and I fall sideways, collapsing into the side of the ottoman. I feel it slide out from underneath me, and I try to keep my grip, but it's useless. I'm back on the floor in a crumpled heap within seconds.

The front of my shirt is drenched with blood, and it's only getting worse. I can feel it trickling down my upper lip, warm and thick, sneaking into my mouth so I taste it too, metallic, disgusting. Using a clean corner of my shirt, I bring my hand to my nose, pinching hard. I sit up again and I let my head fall backward, feeling the edge of the end table dig uncomfortably into the back of my neck.

Every time I blink, my eyes feel like they're on fire, and I can feel the sweat beading up on my forehead. My head is pounding and my mouth feels like it's full of cotton balls.

Everything goes dark.

⁓

"Bennett!" The voice is far away and muffled, unrecognizable. I try to open my eyes but nothing happens. "Bennett. Wake up. Drink this."

"Anna?" I can't see anything, and when I speak the words "Where am I?" I hear them come out slurred and unrecognizable. I try again to open my eyes and finally see a sliver of light. I feel the ground beneath me for clues. It's soft. Like a rug. "Anna?" I ask again.

"Bennett." There's a hand on my shoulder. My head wobbles and I send all my energy to my neck in a desperate attempt to keep it in one place.

"Where am I?" I try again. This time my voice sounds clearer, but still, there's no reply.

The hand squeezes my shoulder hard. "Drink this, son."

I feel something cold and smooth at my lips, and before I can even process what's happening, I feel the liquid, ice-cold on my tongue but searing my throat as it slides down. I cringe and push the glass away.

"Keep going," he says, and the glass is back at my lips. I take small sips at first, but the water feels so good, so wet, that I lean into it, suddenly desperate for more. The glass tips up and I take huge gulps until it's empty.

"Good. That's better." I open my eyes. Dad's face is full of worry as his hand settles on my shoulder again. I hear him set the glass on the table next to me. "Do you think you can sit up?" I give him a weak nod and use all my energy to push myself up from the floor.

This bloody nose is nothing like the last one. This time my T-shirt is soaked in blood. I remember the feeling, the taste, and it makes me slump down again, feeling nauseous. Dad grabs me by both shoulders this time and props me up again.

"I'm going to get you some more water. I'll be right back." I want to ask him to make it room temperature, but the door clicks shut behind him before I can get the words out. I stare at the ceiling and fix my gaze on a small crack in the plaster. I won't close my eyes, even though they're watering and burning and begging me to shut them.

A few minutes later, Dad's back at my side, pressing a glass of water into my hand and a cold washcloth against my forehead. He opens my other hand, palm up, and sets three pills in it. I give him a weak shake of my head. "They're just Advil," he says. "Take them. They'll help."

I start to tell him that the headache is normal. That it always passes on its own, and all I need is water, coffee, and twenty minutes to rest. But it occurs to me that this particular headache is different from others, and that what I know about what "always" happens most likely doesn't apply in this situation. I throw the pills into my mouth and chase them down while Dad watches me. I drain the water in a few gulps.

My hands are still shaking so I clench them into tight fists by my sides. "I'll go get you a clean shirt," he says as he heads toward the door.

"Dad." I stare at the crack in the ceiling again, but in my peripheral vision I can see him stop.

"Would you stay here? Please?" I ask, and before I know it, he's back by my side, sitting on the ottoman, watching me. We sit like that for a long time, neither one of us speaking.

"Are you ready to tell me where you've been?" he asks.

I rub my temples hard with my knuckles, and look across the room at the clock on the wall behind his desk. My eyes narrow as I strain to read it, but the hands keep coming in and out of focus. "Where I've been?" I ask, forcing myself to walk through everything that just happened. We were waiting to see the news story about the accident, to see if it was different from the first one I printed out for him. Then I went to see Anna, everything went dark, and when I opened my eyes, I was a bloody mess on the floor and Dad was here with water. "What time is it?" My voice still sounds weak, scratchy. I rub my throat.

Even though the clock is in plain sight, Dad looks down at his watch. "It's a few minutes after two. Bennett, I need to know where you've been."

"After two?" I repeat, ignoring his question entirely. I rub my temples even harder. That doesn't match at all. It had to be four o'clock when I left to see Anna.

Suddenly, everything falls into place and I start to realize what's happening. I was knocked back. Hard.

My heart speeds up as I piece it together in my head. The news story I printed and brought downstairs to show Dad said the accident occurred around three thirty. We haven't done it over.

Now I'm fully conscious, eyes wide as my head spins in Dad's direction. My sudden movement startles him and he recoils, but I don't even try to keep the fear from my voice. "Please tell me we stopped it. We stopped it, right?"

He looks confused. "Stopped what?" Dad asks, and my hands immediately start shaking. "Bennett, I want to know where you've been."

"The *bikes*?" It comes out like a question. My hands clench by my sides again.

"The bikes?" I can hear the confusion in his voice. He doesn't know what I'm talking about. We didn't stop it. I got knocked back and we didn't stop it after all. I cover my face with my hands.

"Dad," I say without looking up. "There was an accident with these bicyclists and we went back . . . I brought my skateboard and caused a distraction and you helped. This little girl—" I choke on the last word.

"I know," he says, as if he's now concerned about my mental state in addition to my physical one. "She's okay. They're all okay. Just like you said they would be."

I pull my hands away from my face and stare at him. "What? Are you sure?"

"Absolutely. I was waiting for you to get home so I could show you the article." He sounds pretty certain but I keep staring at him anyway, as if I'm waiting for him to change his mind. "The news story read exactly the way you thought it would. A kid crashed his truck into a building. There wasn't a single word about a family of bicyclists."

He remembers. If he remembers, it happened. I didn't wipe it out. None of it makes sense, but a huge smile spreads across my face anyway, and as it does, my face feels tight, like it's cracking. I scratch at my skin and pull my fingernail away. It's caked with dried blood, but I don't care. I let out a laugh.

"Bennett, that was yesterday."

I stop in midlaugh and the smile disappears. "What?"

Dad nods. He's still looking at me like I've lost my mind.

"Yesterday? No . . . that can't be right." I was just in my room. I was just with Anna.

"Bennett, it's Thursday afternoon." He scoots the ottoman a little closer to me, and he seems to be choosing his words carefully. "Your mother and I have been worried sick. You left my office, said you were going upstairs to work on an essay, and when your mom tried to find you for dinner, you were gone. You didn't come home all night. An hour ago, I found you here on the floor."

I think about the day. I can't even bring myself to say it out loud. *Thursday?*

"Son." Dad draws out the word, nice and slow, like I need more time than usual to process what he's about to say. "The accident happened yesterday. Do you remember what happened when we got home?"

I try to. I remember returning from the do-over and leaving his office. I walked upstairs, grabbed a postcard from my desk drawer, and stuffed it into my backpack. I closed my eyes and went to the cross country track at Westlake. I hid off the trail, listening to Anna and her teammates speculate about the mysterious postcard. She found me right after that, and we talked. I felt great until the piercing sound brought me facedown into the dirt. And then I was back here in Dad's office. It all happened fifteen minutes ago, twenty tops.

But it wasn't twenty minutes ago. It was yesterday.

"I need to know where you've been, Bennett. You need to tell me the truth. Why didn't you come home all night?"

The truth. I look away from him and shake my head. I can't tell him where I've been because I have no idea.

I look right into his eyes. "Dad, I honestly don't know."

He looks at me like he isn't buying it, and lets out a long sigh to make it even clearer. "Don't lie to me, Bennett. How could you not know where you've been for the last twenty-two hours?"

Twenty-two hours? My mouth drops open and I stare at him wide-eyed, shaking my head. I don't know. I really, truly, in all honesty have no clue where I've been.

Dad must be able to tell by the look on my face that I'm

telling the truth this time. "You seriously don't know, do you?"

I shake my head even harder, bring my legs to my chest, and bury my face in my knees. This can't be happening.

"What happened while I was gone?" I ask without looking up.

He hesitates before speaking, as if he's weighing his words carefully. "I told your mom everything," he says quietly, and my head snaps up. "When you hadn't come back by midnight . . ." He trails off. I let my head fall into my knees again.

"What's the last thing you remember?"

I lie. "Sitting in my room, working on my report."

"And then?"

I think about it for a minute, and decide to keep lying. "And then I was trying to peel myself off your carpet."

I need to get back to Anna and tell her that everything's okay. I left her standing in the woods, watching me fade away. I promised her I wouldn't leave like that again. And then it occurs to me. What if I haven't left at all? What if I've been there for the last twenty-two hours and just don't remember it?

"Look, you did a great thing the other day. You should be proud of yourself."

"But?" I ask.

"But this is dangerous." He points down at the bloodstains soaking into the rug. "Bennett, you're a smart kid and you already know this, but I feel like I have to say it anyway. This is it." He scoots the ottoman even closer to me. "Whatever is happening to you right now is because of the traveling. You know that, right?"

I stare at him blankly.

"Your mom was right all along. This is too dangerous."

I inhale slowly, processing his words. Mom's not the one who was right . . . I was. I knew all along that I shouldn't change things. There's no such thing as second chances, even when they're deserved.

It felt good after Emma. Even after the fire. There was the nosebleed after I returned from Evanston last time, but I didn't even think it was connected. Now I can't account for twenty-two hours of my life and I'm covered in blood; it's pretty obvious that it is, in fact, *all* connected. I can use this gift of mine for good, but not without a cost.

"Where's Mom?" I ask.

"Sleeping. She was up all night. I finally convinced her to get some rest. She'll be happy to see you home safe." Dad stands up and brushes some imaginary dust from his pants. "She's pretty angry at me right now. She thinks I made you do it."

"Why does she think that?"

He shrugs. "Because I told her I did. Besides, it *is* my fault. This might have been your idea but I'm the one who pushed you to do it."

"No you didn't," I say, but it doesn't help. He stares off across the room looking completely deflated.

"Dad?" He looks at me again. I think about my 50-50 grind

down the side of the staircase and how I faked my fall at the bottom. I picture the look on that little girl's face. I remember how hard Dad hugged me when it was all over. "It was really fun."

"It was pretty incredible wasn't it?" And there it is: the look I saw on his face when we first returned. He looks triumphant and proud, and I feel emptiness deep in my gut when I wonder if it's the last time I'll see this expression. "Actually, I was kind of excited to do it again, but . . . oh, well." He shakes his head and rests his hand on my knee. "Thanks for taking me along." He gives my leg a comforting little shake, and then, for something to do with himself, he reaches past me and grabs the glass off the table. "I'll go get you some more water. I'll be right back."

As soon as he's out of the room, I stand up. My legs still feel wobbly and weak, and I grab on to the side of the chair to steady myself. Just as I'm heading for the door, the glow of the monitor gets my attention, and I feel the urge to see that news story for myself.

I hobble over to the desk, sit down in the leather chair, and reach for the mouse. I start to open a new browser window, but I don't need to because there's already one on the screen. It's a news story from this morning, about a local boy who was last seen at his bus stop but never arrived at school.

Dad wasn't exaggerating when he said he was looking forward to our next do-over.

He'd already found it.

24

I'm halfway up the stairs when Mom sees me from the top landing. She starts racing down the stairs and I grab the railing. "You're home. . . . What happened to you?" She blinks fast, like she's trying hard to focus.

"I'm fine."

"You're *not* fine, Bennett!" Her eyes travel from my face to my jeans and back up again.

"It was just a bloody nose." I stare blankly at my shirt.

"*That's* a bloody nose?" She presses her lips together and her chin trembles. "Where have you been all night? Please, just tell me what happened to you."

She looks at me with this glassy stare, and I can see how hurt she is. There are so many things I'd love to tell her, but I'm in so deep now I don't even know where to start. When my eyes meet hers, I feel like a five-year-old who just fell off the play structure and needs comfort and reassurance. If I told her everything, I bet she'd give me that.

"Where have you been?" she repeats softly.

"I don't know, Mom." My voice cracks when I say it, and I suck in a breath. I can tell from the look on her face that she believes me. But I can also tell that it's not enough. If I ever want to make it to the top of these stairs, I need to come up with something better.

Mom rests her hand on mine, encouraging me to say more. "I woke up in Dad's office like this." I pull my T-shirt away from my body and shake my head. Then I look down at the banister, hesitant to go on, choosing my next words carefully. I've never really talked with my mom about what I can do. We always just, sort of, dance around it. But now there's no other approach than a direct one. "Dad told you what we did, right?" Mom nods. "I must have blacked out afterward."

She crosses her arms. From the neck down, she looks angry, but her face gives her away. "This whole time?" she asks, and she shakes her head as if she can't believe she's asking such a ridiculous question.

I shrug, trying to look cool, like it's no big deal. But I feel my face contort, blowing my cover. I look straight into her eyes. "I honestly don't know where I've been."

Mom's expression turns into this odd mix of sympathy and alarm.

The fight-or-flight instinct kicks in, making me tighten my grip on the handrail and pull my shirt away from my body again. "Can we please talk about this later? I'd like to clean up." Without waiting for her to respond, I plant a kiss on her cheek and squeeze past her.

"Do you need anything?" she calls from behind me.

Yes. I need to be able to be in two places at once. I need to not miss anyone and I need for no one to miss me. "No, thanks," I say as I turn the corner.

In the bathroom, I work quickly to wash the blood from my face with soap and hot water. I run a comb through my hair, but even when I'm done, it still looks greasy and stringy. I pull my shirt off over my head and toss it into the garbage can. It's one of my favorites but now I hope I never see it again.

I close my bedroom door and lock it behind me. My eyelids are heavy, and even though I feel the gravitational pull coming from my bed, I ignore it. After all that's happened, I realize it's the stupidest thing I could do and that the number of things that could go wrong are practically infinite. But I have to go back and see Anna. Just for a few minutes. Just long enough to tell her that I'm okay and to find out if my version of what happened on the cross-country course matches hers. Then I can sleep.

My jeans feel like they're glued to my skin. I peel them off and toss them into the hamper and dig through my drawers until I find my favorite sweats and a Cal Bears hoodie. I change my socks and slip my feet into my shoes. My eyes burn and start to water, but I wipe them with the back of my hand.

My backpack's loaded and I'm almost ready to go. I head to the mini fridge in the closet and grab a Red Bull and reach under the bed for a couple of room-temperature bottles of water, then set everything on the nightstand so they'll be in easy reach when I return.

I'm standing in the center of my room, about to close my eyes, when there's a knock at the door. I swear under my breath and chuck my backpack into the corner. "Come in," I say, once I'm lying on my bed as if I'm about to doze off. The knob turns and clicks a few times.

"It's locked," Mom calls out from the other side, and my legs feel heavy as I make my way across the room to open the door. "Can I come in?"

No. I'm about to leave. I *need* to leave. But I take a few steps backward and open the door for her. She walks in and heads for the turret window over in the corner that overlooks the bay. She runs her fingers along the molding, then crosses her arms, keeping her back to me.

"I remember the day we moved into this house."

"Mom," I say. "I'm really tired." I cover my eyes with my hand. Do we have to do this now?

She continues as if I hadn't spoken. "You and your dad were on your way over in the moving truck and I walked around, room to room, trying to figure out which ones you and Brooke were going to choose. I was standing right here, admiring this view, when Brooke walked in and said this was the one she wanted. But I talked her into taking the other one."

"Why?" I ask.

"This one was the nicer of the two. It had this view and I thought it should be yours. You're the one who got us this house, after all." She turns around and looks at me. "I gave your father a lot of grief about what the two of you did . . ."

"We just bought some stocks." It was more than that, but I don't feel like getting into it with her right now. I've been down this path before, arguing over the nuances of manipulating the market and buying stock based on information neither one of us should have had or been able to use. But last time I checked, insider-trading laws didn't mention anything about time travel.

"I'm not going to ask you to justify what you did, Bennett. Even though I thought it was wrong, I understand why you did it."

I don't say anything.

"You did it to make us happy. To give our family a better life."

"Yeah."

"And probably to get your dad off your back." She smiles.

I smile back. "Yeah, maybe that too."

She gives me this meaningful look and steels herself, like she's preparing to say something important. "I'll always appreciate what you did for our family, Bennett, but I want you to know something." She takes a few steps closer to me but stays just out of my reach. "You didn't have to do this." She holds her arms out to her sides and glances around the room.

I shoot her a skeptical look and she shakes her head. "Don't get me wrong. I appreciate all of this . . . I admit, I'm a bit of a sucker for the finer things in life, and life has been a lot easier with, well, everything we have. But I don't need it."

She looks resolute, but I can't help raising an eyebrow.

"I mean it. Your dad didn't like his job, and I didn't like living in that tiny apartment in an unsafe neighborhood. And yes, money was tight and we fought about it a lot. But you know what?"

I shake my head.

"Your dad and I love each other, and we love you and Brooke more than you two will ever know. This family would have been fine without all of this." She must see a trace of disbelief in my eyes because she adds the word "Really," and gives me a stern look to demonstrate her conviction.

I still must seem doubtful. I've seen the way she cherishes her car and her designer clothes. "You'd give this all away?" I ask, pointing to her pearls.

"Absolutely. In fact, it would be nice to be rid of the guilt."

I look in my mom's eyes and see that she means it.

"Dad told me what the two of you did for that family yesterday. And he told me about the fire . . ." She trails off. Then she takes three steps forward and wraps her arms around me. "I hope he didn't talk you into—"

I cut her off in midsentence. "He didn't talk me into anything, Mom. I swear. It was completely my idea." I feel my face getting hotter. "If you would just stop worrying and see that I have this under control."

"Do you?" Mom shoots me a sideways glare. She's right and she knows it. Two days ago I could say those words and mean them, but today . . . yeah . . . not so much.

"Look . . . I love what you did for those kids, Bennett, I

really do. But you're *my* kid, and I know it's selfish, but I don't want to trade your safety for *anyone* else's."

I shake my head at her. "Come on . . . This isn't about my safety."

"Yes, it is. I've spent far too many nights wondering where my kids are, Bennett. It is about you being here, in this place, living like a normal person."

I knew the word "normal" would pop out of her mouth eventually. Without even thinking about it, I hear myself say, "Mom. I'm still going back to visit Maggie."

Her jaw drops. I reach over to the desk and pick up the photo of my grandmother and me. "I told you this picture was taken when I was living with her a few months ago, in nineteen ninety-five, but that wasn't true. She didn't look like this in nineteen ninety-five. This was taken in two thousand and three, just before she died."

Her hands are trembling as she takes the frame from me.

"I've been going back there for years. I take care of her."

Mom looks for something to hold on to but there's nothing in sight, so she takes two steps back and sits on the edge of the bed. "You go back?" Her lip quivers when she asks, and when I nod, she covers her mouth with her hand.

"All the time," I say.

Mom sits on my bed staring at the photo, and as I watch her, I realize that now would be the perfect time to tell her about Anna too. All I have to do is grab the album from the bottom of the drawer, say something simple like *I also go back to see her. This is Anna,* and start turning pages. Then she'd get it. She'd have to.

But before I can move, Mom looks at me, her eyes welling up, and pats the mattress next to her. "Tell me about her." she says, referring to my grandmother, not my girlfriend.

And instead of going over to my desk, I sit down next to my mom and tell her everything, from the flowers Brooke planted in Maggie's garden and the bills we paid right down to the details of the room I've been staying in when I visit. The tears spill down her cheeks, but she hasn't even heard everything yet.

I ask her to tell me what happened between the two of them.

"Our fights were about such unimportant things, and I honestly don't know why I let it go on so long," she says, her whole body trembling as the tears fall even faster. "I let a few stupid disagreements keep me away from my mother and keep her from knowing my kids . . ." She takes a deep breath. "And she was all alone when—" She can't finish her sentence, but she doesn't have to.

I scoot in closer and fill the gap between us. "She wasn't alone," I say quietly and mom looks up at me. I tell her how Brooke and I went back to the day Maggie died, and how we held her hand as we watched her slip away. Brooke called 911 and we disappeared as soon as help arrived.

She hugs me hard and I relax in her arms, relieved to finally have everything out. I try to think of a way to tell her about Anna too, because it would be nice to come clean completely, but this doesn't feel like the right time. "Thank you," she says as she rubs my back.

Then Mom leans back and stands up. She brushes her hands on her pants and adjusts her shirt, looking around the room like the walls are closing in and she needs to escape. She gives me a peck on the cheek, tells me she loves me, and looks me right in the eye. "Please do me a favor," she says, her voice a bit steadier. "Don't travel for a while. I need to think about all of this, okay? For now, I just need to know you're here and safe. Will you do that, please?"

Without waiting for an answer, she says, "I should let you rest." She's about to leave when she stops and turns around. "Oh, and call Brooke, please." She glances over at my desk, like she's expecting to find my cell phone where it usually is. "She's worried." The latch clicks shut behind her.

I look at the door, thinking about my mother's request and wishing I could respect it. I look at my bed, wishing I could lie down and sleep for the next ten hours or so. I look out the window, hoping the Jeep is still in the garage and that my phone is still in the glove compartment, and wishing I could call Brooke and tell her everything. The risks are huge. But the pull to see Anna—to tell her I'm okay and let her help me piece together what happened yesterday—is stronger than all the others.

Once my backpack is out from under the bed and in place again, I stand in the center of my room and let my eyes fall shut. I'm tempted to picture the cross-country track and arrive there again, just a minute or two after I estimate I was knocked back, but I'm still worried about wiping out the bike accident. So instead, I lock my mind on yesterday, a little before midnight. I picture Anna's room. I visualize the clock on her nightstand. I let myself go. A few seconds later, I open them.

I'm expecting to take in her familiar shelves lined with trophies and CDs, but instead, my eyes open to a view of my boring white room. I close my eyes and try again. When I open them, I'm right where I started.

This can't be happening.

It's just like last time, when Anna got knocked back from my bedroom and I was stuck, unable to leave this room. Maybe my brain is simply too exhausted. Maybe it just needs some extra help. I stand in place, spinning a three-sixty, looking for anything that will help me visualize where I want to go.

The photo album is still buried deep in the bottom of the drawer, but I dig it out and flip to the very last photo—the one of Anna and me, lying on her rug in her bedroom. Her arm is extended in the air and we're both smiling. I bring my fingertip to the plastic and close my eyes. This is where I need to be.

I close my eyes. I open them. Again and again.

After six more attempts, I slump down on the floor next to my bed, feeling sick and utterly spent. The next thing I know, I'm waking up and the morning sun is streaming in above me.

25

I have no idea what's happening back where Anna is. All I know is what's happening here. The days keep beginning and ending and I've spent four of them trying desperately to get back to the day I left Anna in the woods. I'm closing my eyes, opening them, repeating the same actions over and over again, and hoping for a different result. I think Einstein was the one who called that the definition of insanity.

It's been three weeks and four days since Emma's birthday party, which means that homecoming weekend has come and gone. Even worse, I've left Anna exactly the way I did last time: alone, without any warning. Just like I swore I wouldn't do again.

Mom lets me skip school on Friday and again on Monday, but by Tuesday, she insists that I look just fine and completely capable of a day full of learning. So I drag myself from the parking lot and head straight for AP World Civ. I'm not the first one in the room but at least I'm not the last.

I pull my notebook and a pen from my backpack and start doodling while I wait for the bell to ring.

"Hey, stranger." I look to my left and find Megan taking her seat. "Welcome back."

"Thanks." I smile at her and go back to my drawing.

A minute or so later, she leans over across the aisle. "You missed the midterm yesterday. It covered all the material so far." I stop drawing and look over at her. "It was pretty hard, but . . ." She shrugs. "I think I did okay. Anyway, if you want to borrow my notes . . ."

Mrs. McGibney walks in, her briefcase swinging by her side, and looks right at me. "Mr. Cooper," she says flatly. She drops the case next to her desk and it lands with a thud. She starts writing the day's agenda on the whiteboard, but I can tell she's still talking to me when she says, "You missed an exam yesterday. You can come in at lunch and take it."

I sneak a peek at Megan as she grimaces.

"Today?" I ask.

"Yes, sir. Today would be perfect." She takes her eyes off the board to look over her shoulder at me. "Don't worry, you can bring your lunch." She returns to writing.

"I was kind of hoping for a couple of days to brush up."

"I announced this test last Wednesday, Mr. Cooper. According to my records, you were here last Wednesday. Judging from the scores, everyone in this class spent the last few days 'brushing up.' If you didn't, that is not my problem."

"But I was sick."

More writing. "I'm offering the test today at lunch. Otherwise, it won't be fair to the rest of the class." She finishes the agenda and brings the dry-erase marker to the board, punctuating the last line with a loud period. "Sound good?" She turns around and stares at me.

It doesn't matter. Today, next week, the grade I get on this test will likely be the same either way. I nod.

"Great. I'll see you then."

I spend the next forty-five minutes cramming. Every time McGibney turns her back, I thumb through my notebook, desperately trying to recall all the things I've learned about world civilizations since school started. The notes are fairly detailed in some places, but I honestly don't remember writing many of them. In other places, I find page after page with nothing but doodles. Apparently, a few weeks ago, I spent an entire class trying to figure out what to name my garage.

The bell rings and everyone rises from their seats and heads for the door. As I turn into the hall toward my next class, I spot Megan leaning up against the locker bank, smiling and clearly waiting for me. "Man, that was harsh," she says when I'm within earshot.

"Remind me not to get sick again."

She smiles. "Here." She reaches into her messenger bag and hands me a black-and-white composition notebook. The cover is bent and the pages are frayed, and as I turn it over in my hands I notice that it looks a lot more battered than mine does, as if she's actually been using it to take notes in class and then refer to them later on.

"Really?"

"Sure." She closes her bag and readjusts the strap on her shoulder. "Maybe you could skip your next three classes and go study in the library."

Under normal circumstances, that's exactly what I would do. And after I was finished cramming, I'd go back to the beginning of the day to do it over. The second time around, I'd be ready for both the test and for McGibney's question. When Megan wasn't looking, I'd slip her notebook back into her pack before she even realized it was missing. This conversation would never happen, and Megan would never know that there was a version of events that I wiped out, where she stood in the hallway and offered to let me borrow her notes.

But these aren't normal circumstances. I don't know if I could go back four hours even if I wanted to. If I had the ability to travel again, I certainly wouldn't be here at school, worrying about a test. I'd be with Anna.

"Thanks," I say. I shove the notebook into my pack and start thinking of excuses for missing my next three classes. "That's really cool of you."

"No problem." She stands there, looking at me like she has more to say. "Well, I'd better get to class. Good luck." Before I can respond, she turns on her heel and walks away. I turn on mine and head for the library.

~⁓

I've been sitting in the same carrel, staring at the same page and trying *not* to stare out the same window, for more than an hour now. Megan's notes are clear and detailed, but the words seem to leave my brain faster than I can bring them in.

I twist my pencil back and forth between my fingers, thinking about Anna and the last words I heard her say: *You're not supposed to be here until Friday.*

But I can't get to Friday. And I can't get to Wednesday and I can't get to Thursday either. Every time I try, I open my eyes in the exact place I closed them. And suddenly it dawns on me. I've been trying to get back before homecoming so I don't let Anna down. But what if I'm trying too hard to go back to a precise moment, when I should just be trying to get *back*?

I grab my phone but leave the rest of my stuff at the carrel, and head for a computer kiosk. I look up a 1995 calendar and find the month of October. I open up the calendar on my phone to today's date and hold it up next to the screen. The calendars are nearly identical, only a day off. In 2012, it's Tuesday. In 1995, it's a Monday.

I head straight for the men's room and lock myself in a stall. I leave my phone on the back of the toilet and close my eyes. I think back to the layout of Westlake Academy, trying to remember the quiet spots I found to hide in every time I felt like I was about to be knocked back to San Francisco.

Right outside our Spanish building, there was a rarely used path obscured by overgrown plants and shrubs. I brought Anna there once, the day we cut class and I told her the last part of my secret.

I have no idea if this will work, but I close my eyes, mutter the word "please," and picture the location.

My skin prickles from the extreme drop in temperature and I breathe in fresh air that couldn't possibly exist in a men's room. As soon as I open my eyes, they dart around the empty field and I let out a gasp. I'm actually here.

I bring my hands to the sides of my face and peek through the glass doors. It's quiet, and even though I landed *where* I intended to, I'm still not sure if I landed *when* I intended to. I pull the door handle and it opens. At least it's a school day.

The hallway is empty. I look around for a clock and find one just above the next locker bank. I've timed it perfectly. I'm only a few feet away from where I need to be and I make it there with a minute to spare. I'm leaning against the lockers, trying to look like I belong here, when the bell rings. That's when I realize that I'm the only one who's not wearing a uniform.

Up and down the corridor, classroom doors begin opening and people start spilling out into the hall wearing the traditional Westlake black-and-white plaid. The girls are in skirts and white blouses. The guys are in slacks and dress shirts. I spot the occasional tie or V-neck sweater.

The rules are clear in this circular hallway dubbed The Donut, and because everyone's required to walk clockwise between classes, they all head in my direction at once. A few people notice me standing here, looking out of place in my street clothes, and shoot me a questioning look as they pass.

I'm combing the crowd for Anna, but I don't see her anywhere, and as the activity level dies down, I'm starting to question myself. Maybe I was wrong about her class schedule?

But then I see her come around the bend, talking with Alex, and my heart starts pounding hard.

When she's within a few feet of the classroom door, she finally spots me. She stops cold and covers her mouth with her hand. Her expression is impossible to read, and as she takes long strides in my direction, I can't tell if she's relieved to see me or furious that I didn't show up when I was supposed to. I brace myself for the worst, but as soon as she's close enough, she throws her arms over my shoulders and squeezes me tight. I've never been so happy to see her. "I'm so sorry," I whisper in her ear.

Alex walks past us into the classroom, and mutters the word "asshole" under his breath.

"Ignore him," she says as she buries her face in my neck.

I try to release her so I can see her face, but she tightens her grip. "I'm so sorry I missed homecoming."

"I don't care. You're here now."

The Donut empties out and I can tell the bell's about to ring. I take a step back and rest my hands on her shoulders. "I need to talk to you." I point with my chin toward the double doors that lead outside, and I can tell by the look on her face that she knows exactly what I mean. "I can't bring you back this time though. You're going to have to miss Spanish, for real. Is that okay?"

"Yeah." She says it with a little laugh, as if it's the only possible answer.

We follow the path up the slope until it ends at the big tree at the top of the ridge. We sit down next to each other, exactly the way we did last year when I told her the third and final part of my secret, and she became the fourth person in the world to know everything there was to know about me. But now, there's nothing but pain and worry on her face, and I can't help but wonder if I made the right decision that day.

"I didn't know what to do." Her voice is shaking and so are her hands, and I reach for them and scoot in even closer to her. "You were just standing there in the woods that day, all excited about something, and then out of nowhere you just collapsed. What happened? Why couldn't you come back?"

I shake my head. "I don't know. There's some stuff . . . missing. Was that the last time you saw me?" She nods but she's clearly confused as to why I'm asking when this is information I should already know.

She's breathing faster now and I can hear the panic in her voice. "Yeah. You got knocked back home."

Not home. Not right away at least. If I wasn't here and I wasn't there, where was I, passed out in the garage for twenty-two hours?

Over the next fifteen minutes, I talk nonstop, telling Anna about everything that happened last week—the news story and me on my skateboard, the two little girls and my dad on sidekick duty—and that I have no idea where I was for nearly a full day, and how I've spent the last five days trying to get back to her. Her face contorts when I tell her how painful the returns have become, and how they got progressively worse and a hell of a lot bloodier.

"It'll be fine now." I put on my best smile and hope I sound reassuring. "I'll just go back to doing what I've always done. Apparently, as long as I use this ridiculous thing I can do for my own selfish purposes, I'm free to come and go as I please," I say.

Anna takes my face in her hands and makes me look her in the eye. "You have to promise me. No more do-overs, okay? Never."

I nod. "Yeah, I'm pretty sure that's the message I'm supposed to be getting here." I let out a laugh, but Anna doesn't join in.

"Promise," she says.

"Yeah. I promise." As I say the words, I wonder why it's so easy to make this promise to her when I can't make it to my own parents.

I sigh. "Well, at least my mom and dad can now agree on one thing. They've both made it crystal clear that I'm not to travel ever again."

"Not even to see me?" she asks, and I stop laughing.

"No . . . well. Yes. Not exactly."

Anna drops her hands and leans away from me. "What does that mean, 'not exactly'? Did they tell you that you couldn't come back here anymore?"

I look down at the dirt. "Actually, they did. But that was five months ago."

She waits for me to explain, but I have no idea what to say next. This conversation was inevitable, and there have been plenty of times I walked through it in my head, but having it today was the farthest thing from my mind.

"My parents don't . . . exactly . . . know about you." I suck in a deep breath and wait while she stares at me for a painfully long time.

"They don't know about me?" I can't tell if she wants to cry or punch me. I shake my head no and Anna's eyes narrow in disbelief. "What about your sister?"

"Brooke knows," I whisper.

"Brooke?" Anna's voice cracks as she says her name, and there's a questioning tone at the end, like she can't believe that there's only one person in my world who knows she exists.

"Listen, please. My parents wouldn't understand. And I can't tell my friends . . . I mean, what am I supposed to tell them?"

"Tell them that I live in Illinois. Just like my friends think you're a normal guy from San Francisco." She scoots away from me, looking both confused and disgusted at the same time. "You don't have to tell them I live in nineteen ninety-five." She says that last part so quietly that I have to strain to hear her. But then she finds her voice again. "Look, I know you have a thing for secrets, but I thought we were done with that."

"We are. I don't have any secrets from you."

"No, just that I *am* one." She lets out a sarcastic-sounding breath.

She looks down at the dining hall windows, and this time, I'm sure she's wondering why she ever entertained the idea of letting complicated me into her rather uncomplicated life.

"Look," I say, "last June, when I was stuck in San Francisco and couldn't get back here, I thought I'd never see you again. I didn't know what to say to my parents or my friends."

Anna gives me a hard look and shakes her head. "Everyone in *my* life knows about you, even though they don't know your big secret." She says the last part sarcastically, wiggling her fingers in front of her face for emphasis. "Nobody here gets it. None of them understand why I'm in a relationship with a guy who lives two thousand miles away—and they don't even know the half of it." She huffs. "But they know about *you*.

"I could never keep you to myself." She says the last part quietly, but loud enough for me to hear.

I rub my forehead with my fingertips as I try to find the right words. "I didn't want to hurt you. And, I swear, I was going to tell them eventually, but it was just . . . easier not to."

Her head snaps up and there's that look again. "Easier?" she asks. Now I'm pretty sure she's about to punch me.

"Not more *convenient. Easier.*" I bring my hand to my chest. "On *me*. Look, you seem to enjoy torturing yourself with photo albums and things that remind you of the two of us, but I don't. That only makes it worse. It's *easier* for me to pretend you're not real when we're not together."

A tear slides down her cheek and she quickly brushes it away.

I reach for her hands, and I'm a little surprised when she lets me take them. "Do you have any idea how much I hate being there without you? When I'm supposed to be doing homework, I go for drives instead. I take the top down on the Jeep and turn up the music and cruise around the city I've always loved, and all I want to do is show it to you. I want to bring you to my favorite café in North Beach, where they serve lattes in bowls instead of mugs. I want to show you this wave organ that's built into a bunch of rocks and has an insane view of Alcatraz. I want to bring you to my school and introduce you to Sam and the rest of my friends, so you'll know them the same way I know Emma and Danielle and Justin. But I can't *ever* do that." She squeezes my hand. "We've already tried and it was a disaster. I guess I figured, the less I had to be reminded that you couldn't be there, the easier it would be."

Anna releases my hands so she can wipe the tears from her cheeks.

"Look," I say. "All I want is a normal relationship with you, and when I'm here, it feels like I have it. But when I'm there . . . I just miss you. All the time."

She grabs one of my hands in both of hers and squeezes it tight.

"I'll tell them about you, okay? I'll show my mom and dad your photo album, and I'll tell them everything. And I'll explain that I'm done with do-overs—that they're the only reason I've lost control—but that I need to keep coming back here to see you. Okay? I promise."

The bell rings but neither one of us move. Eventually the dining hall below starts filling with people, and I spot everyone taking their usual places and their usual tables and starting in on their usual conversations.

"Great," Anna mutters, watching the scene below.

"What?"

"Ten bucks says Alex has already told everyone about seeing you here." She stands up and brushes the dirt off her jeans. "This should make for a delightful lunch."

"Do you want me to stick around?" I ask.

Anna offers her hand to help me up and I take it. Then she looks at me and lets out a heavy sigh. "It's okay. I've got it." We start walking down the hill and she threads her arm through mine. "But I'll tell you, next time you're in town you better bring me a giant bouquet of flowers or something. If you show up empty-handed my parents might come up with something more painful than being knocked back to San Francisco."

"That bad?"

"Yup."

"I didn't get to see you in the dress."

She lifts two fingers into the air. "Twice now."

I wince. "Were you actually wearing it this time?"

She raises her eyebrows and nods slowly.

"God, I *am* an asshole."

"Yeah." She gives me a sad smile and bumps my hip with hers. "But not on purpose."

⁓

Exactly fifty-five minutes after I left, I open my eyes in the men's room stall. I push through the door just as the migraine hits. My eyes are burning as I stumble over to the sink, feeling my way with the help of the walls.

I find the spigot, turn it on, and stick my mouth under the stream. I drink as fast and as much as I can before cupping my hands and splashing cold water on my face. The fluorescent lights make it impossible to open my eyes, and my head is pounding, but at least it all feels familiar.

I push my hands into the countertop and keep my head down, breathing and concentrating, willing the pain to disappear. Twenty minutes later, the pounding subsides to a dull ache in my temples.

And it feels like everything is back to normal. Well, *my* normal, at least.

november 2012

san francisco, california

The sound of my phone chirping wakes me from a deep sleep, and I roll over, pulling the comforter over my head to block out the sunlight. I'm starting to slip back into sleep again when there's another chirp. I feel around on the nightstand for my phone and open my eyes to back-to-back texts from Brooke:

> Good morning!

> Hey, what r u doing tonight?

My eyes are still adjusting when another message appears.

> Party at our apartment. Come!

I stare at the screen as I consider it. Aside from a some-what loose plan to meet up with the guys and loiter around

Lafayette Park later, I really don't have anything else to do this weekend. But social conflicts aren't the real reason I think I should stay away. I only have one more week before I can go see Anna again and I'm not about to do anything to jeopardize it. Another message:

> I want my roommates to meet you!

A groan escapes my mouth as I fall back into the pillow. I lift the phone above my head and text her back.

> I think I'd better stay put.

I toss the phone onto the comforter and close my eyes. It hasn't even been five minutes when my phone chirps again. I'm expecting to see another overly enthusiastic message from Brooke, but this one's from Sam.

> Sup?

I type back:

> Sleeping.

Then I clarify:

> Was.

Sleep might be impossible at this point, but I let my hand fall to my side and the phone lands on the bed again. I'm lost in a restful daze when another text arrives, followed by another. I sigh and reach for the phone.

> Wake up.
> We're climbing.
> Outside.
> On real rocks.

> Pick me up in 20.

The sun's peeking in between the curtains. I haven't been climbing outdoors since last summer. Pretty soon the rain will start falling and Sam and I won't have any other option but the climbing gym. And it sounds so . . . normal. I could use a day of normal.

I throw off the covers and force myself into the shower, and ten minutes later, I'm feeling like this was the right call. I pour coffee into a travel mug, load my stuff into the Jeep, and pull into Sam's driveway right on time.

I have no idea where we're going, but he has our destination all figured out, and before I can even back out of the driveway, he's programming it into the GPS. The route starts with a short drive to the Golden Gate Bridge and ends at the base of a mountain three hours away.

"We're climbing Donner?" I ask as I pull up to a stop sign and consider the map.

Sam gives me an exaggerated shrug and gestures out the front window. "Have you seen this day?" He gives me a hard stare like he can't believe I'd suggest anything else.

I crane my neck to get a better view. It's one of those near-winter days: deep blue sky, bright sun, crisp wind. I hit the gas pedal with my foot and roll down the window, and as we cruise down the hill toward the bay, the car floods with cold air.

At the next stop sign, I turn left onto a residential street and pull over to the side. Sam looks at me sideways as I climb out, but it doesn't take him long to figure out what I'm doing, and when he does, he hops out and starts helping me unbuckle the Jeep's soft top. We pull it back and secure it in place. And then we're off again.

"Now it's a road trip." Sam crosses his arms behind his head and reclines the passenger seat. As he searches on my iPhone for music, we make small talk about the tutoring job I'm starting on Monday. He tells me about the kids, and how he'll point out the troublemakers, as well as the ones who seem to really care about being there.

I was great in the interview. The head of the organization offered me the job on the spot. Now I've pushed my start date back twice, like I'm avoiding it, and the more Sam says, the more I start to realize that I don't want to hear about it. There's something offputting about the whole thing.

The Jeep creeps forward until we finally arrive at the entrance to the Golden Gate Bridge. Out of nowhere, I remember the organization I stumbled upon when I was first researching community service projects. The one in the Tenderloin, down the street from the apartment that burned down but didn't take the lives of two kids.

I've don't even give it another thought, and I hear the words just slip out. "I'm going to pass on the job, Sam."

"What? You can't pass on it. You already took it."

I keep my eyes on the traffic in front of me. "I know. I'm going to un-take it."

I can feel him looking at me. "You need to do something for your transcripts," he says, and I assure him that I plan to. As we drive onto the bridge, I tell him everything I learned from the online video that day, and with every word, I'm more and more excited about getting home tonight and filling out the application.

"Whatever you want." Sam falls back into the headrest and stares through the open roof. "Check it out," he says as we pass under the dark orange gates that span the bridge. "Ah, best part . . ."

Without looking away, he tosses my phone into the console. "It's not too early for Jack White, is it?"

"It's never too early for Jack White." I hear the first song on the playlist I made a few months ago. It's a solid mix of the White Stripes, the Raconteurs, the Dead Weather, and White's solo stuff. The four electric guitar notes kick off "Sixteen Saltines."

Saltines. I smile as I picture Anna nibbling on the corner of one and I turn up the music as loud as it will go.

Over the next three hours we make our way to Donner,

listening to a lot of music, talking very little, and stopping only once along the way for lunch at In-N-Out. We down our shakes and stuff french fries into our mouths, but leave our burgers wrapped so we can eat them at the summit.

After we arrive at the parking area off the freeway, we grab our gear and walk thirty minutes to the base of the first route. Neither one of us has been here before and Sam's giddy, rattling off everything he learned during his Internet research last night. Clean granite. Lots of routes. Incredible views from the summits.

At the base of the first rock, I ready myself. I tie my shoes, clip my chalk bag to the loop on my pants, and stuff my sweatshirt into my backpack. I open one of the granola bars I grabbed out of the pantry this morning before I left and eat it in three bites. At the bottom of my pack, I feel for the six-pack of lukewarm Gatorades and I open one and drink it without stopping.

I look around. Sam and I are the only people out here. I point my head at the sky and let out a loud yell, and Sam jumps and scolds me for scaring the crap out of him. He returns to tightening the Velcro on his shoes. The air is clean and this place is amazing and I can't wait to see the view from the top. I had no idea how much I needed this.

"You want me to lead?" I ask as I start clipping the cams onto my harness.

Sam looks up at the rock. "Actually, this is a popular one to free solo. What do you think? You up for it?"

I consider it. It's not that vertical, and the holds look relatively easy to spot, even from here. "Sure," I say as I drop the gear back into my pack.

"You have the burgers?" Sam coils the rope and throws it over his shoulder, then clips his chalk bag to his belt loop.

"Yep." I pat the smaller backpack I brought along and feed my arms through the straps. I'm not hungry at all. Just euphoric and full of energy.

Sam checks his watch. "We made good time. It's only twelve thirty."

The climb is easy at first, and I have no trouble finding hand- and footholds. I pull myself up, slide to the left, and pull up again. The granite is cold and dry beneath my fingertips. I'm moving quickly through the route.

About a quarter of the way up, I see a good spot to take a break, and I wedge my hand into a large crack and find an equally large space for my toe. I let my arms slacken a bit.

I look for Sam. He's ahead of me, and he seems to be maneuvering the rock well. I see his fingers grip the edge and watch him pull himself onto a ledge to rest. He's only about ten feet higher, and I can see the sweat glistening on his forehead and dripping down his cheeks. He wedges himself into a position where he can free one hand, and he lifts the edge of his T-shirt and wipes his face dry.

It's time to move, so I chalk up my hands again and reach up for a hold. It's barely enough to grip on to, and within a few seconds, my knuckles are turning white and my forearms are burning. I see a better grip only inches away and swing my body around so I can grab on to it, rising to a ledge that's wide enough to stand on. I stop and catch my breath.

The summit is farther away than I expected it to be, and it'll be slow going from here. I don't know what I was thinking. It's been months since I climbed outside, and even though this was supposed to be an easy route, I'm starting to think the free solo climb was a bad idea. When I chalk my hands, my arms are shaking with fatigue.

I start back up the rock, and a little while later I see Sam reach the summit. I stop and consider my last few moves while he stands there, doubled over and beaming down at me.

"Dude, my mom climbs faster than you do."

I tighten my fingers around the hold with one hand, freeing the other one to flip him off. Sam lets out a loud laugh, and returns to sweating and panting. I'm waiting to feel the euphoria I usually experience at this point of the climb, but each move feels harder than it should be. I'm going to be insanely sore tomorrow.

I'm almost there. In just one or two more strategic, well-thought moves, I'll be at the top. I take one more deep breath and lock my eyes on my next hold. I make my move, then the next, and suddenly I'm gripping the shelf.

I breathe. My fingertips dig into the granite.

"Jesus, it's about time." Sam takes a swig of Gatorade and checks the time on his phone. "It's already one o'clock. Get up here, would you? I'm starving."

As I pull myself up, I feel the edge break in my hands. Dust and bits of rock tumble down into my eyes, and I grope blindly, reaching up for anything to hold on to. My right hand falls away and I grab the rock harder with my left, but it just slips off.

Sam reacts immediately, dropping his Gatorade and falling to his stomach. His hand juts out over the edge, but by then I'm nowhere near it.

My cheek skids against the surface and my hip hits something sharp. My shoulder slams against a boulder and that slows my momentum, but only temporarily. My already-raw fingers burn and sting as they claw at the granite.

I hear Sam yell from the summit.

I'm waiting for my body to shut down so I don't have to endure the pain of the crash. Suddenly, I feel my hip connect with something hard and I stop fast. I'm lying in a crumpled heap on the ledge I'd been standing on earlier, and it's wide enough to keep me secure, but I scramble to find something to hold on to anyway.

"Stay there," Sam says, and I laugh. He disappears from the edge and I keep laughing, but I'm not sure why. Maybe because it keeps me from thinking about how fast my heart is racing and that my legs feel rubbery.

A couple of minutes later he returns to the shelf, flattens his chest against the rock, and slaps a coil of blue rope by his side. He feeds it over the edge and I watch it fall, dancing and squirming its way toward me. When I look up, I see Sam.

His face is drawn, his eyes are full of panic, and his hands are shaking violently as he guides the rope down.

I tie the rope to my harness. Sam yells, "Hold on," and then he's gone for a full minute. I picture him tying the rope to the anchors at the top and feel the slack disappear. He returns and looks over the edge. "Okay. You're on belay. I've got you!" He gives me a thumbs-up and drops to the ground again. He's trying to sound stoic, but I can hear the worry in his voice.

I start climbing again, taking my moves a lot more slowly, thinking through each one more than I usually do. I try not to think about falling again. I don't look up, but I can feel Sam working to keep the rope taut.

I'm only a few feet from the top when Sam drops to the ground again, and when I'm close enough, he lowers his hand. This time, I grab it and let him pull me to the surface.

Neither one of us says a word as we collapse back on the sun-warmed rock and stare straight up at the sky. I don't even remove the rope from my waist. I just lie there. Eventually, I bring my hand to my face. My cheek is throbbing and my arms are covered in deep scratches. My right hip hurts when I try to sit up, there's a small gash on my shoulder, and my fingers are caked with blood.

"You okay?" Sam asks and I nod. I don't look at him, but his voice still sounds a little shaky. "Give me your pack." He holds out his hand and I slide it off, but the strap grazes the cut on my arm. I cringe. He rifles through my stuff, and when I look up a minute later he's dumping Gatorade onto an In-N-Out napkin. "All the water's at the bottom," he says as he hands it to me. "This will have to do."

I wash the dirt off my face and clean up my arm. Without saying a word, I hold my hand out to Sam and he tosses me the rest of the Gatorade. I dump a little more on a clean corner of the napkin, take a big gulp, swish it around in my mouth, and spit out a mouthful of dirt.

"Well at least you crushed your face and not the burgers," Sam says with a laugh. He reaches into the bag and pulls out his Double-Double, then tosses the bag to me.

I down another Gatorade, Sam takes a big bite of his burger, and neither one of us speaks as we stare out at the view. I take a few bites, but when I start thinking about what might have happened, I feel my stomach tighten up and my appetite disappears.

What if I had fallen to the bottom? I didn't think about doing it over—it all happened too quickly—but I could have. What if I'd locked in on a time before we started up that rock, closed my eyes, and brought myself back? What would have happened if I'd saved my own life? Could I even *do* that? If I had, Sam would have seen everything.

Out of nowhere, I think about something I once said to Anna. As I was envying her deep roots in Evanston and a normal life she couldn't wait to leave, I told her that, aside from my parents and my sister, everyone I knew back home was somehow temporary. Now I feel guilty for saying that. I watch Sam mowing his burger and wiping sauce from his face, and I can't stop picturing how he dropped to the ground and reached over the edge for me.

Sam's not temporary. He never was. And it occurs to me that, while I can't tell him my biggest secret, perhaps I shouldn't keep so many of them from my best friend.

We finish our burgers and I toss my backpack—now much lighter, since it's filled with nothing but trash—over the edge. I use the top rope to rappel down to the bottom, and Sam follows me.

We pack up and head down the path to the next rock. It turns out to be a lot more technical, and when Sam offers to lead, I accept immediately. We climb two different routes. At dusk, we start the half-hour hike back to the Jeep.

We're walking single file and almost at the end of the trail. "Sam," I say to his back.

He lets out a "huh" that's barely audible.

"There's something I've been wanting to tell you."

He keeps walking and doesn't turn around.

I take a deep breath. "I wasn't backpacking in Europe last spring."

He flips his head around and gives me a quick nod. Then he turns back to the path.

"I was in Illinois."

"Oh . . ."

"Living with my grandmother."

The fact that I can't see his face makes this easier.

"And while I was there, I sort of . . . met this girl."

He stops cold and I almost run into his backpack. He turns

around, his eyes wide with surprise. "Why were you staying with your grandmother?"

I stare at him. I wasn't expecting him to go there and don't have a great answer for this. "I was just . . . dealing with some family stuff. It was complicated. I just needed to get away." It's not the whole story, but so far, I'm not lying.

His eyebrows knit together. "Coop," he says. "We all know you were in rehab." Then he stops cold and stares at me. "Wait, did you meet a girl in *rehab*?"

"In rehab? Why would I be in rehab?" My mom swore she didn't tell that ridiculous story to anyone outside the school administration. And Sam has never seen me drink or smoke or pop a pill. Even if he'd heard that, how could he actually believe it? How can he just be telling me this now?

"Come on, why else would you take off suddenly in the middle of the school year, not come back for three months, and when you do, tell everyone you were traveling in Europe." He rolls his eyes. He's got a point. "Besides, your mom told Cameron's mom that you were away 'dealing with some issues.' What else would we think?"

Great.

I step in front of him and start walking down the trail toward the car. I didn't want to start some kind of major confrontation about where I was last spring; I just wanted to tell him about Anna. I'm tired. I could have died on that rock today. And now my brain isn't working fast enough to feed me new lies and help me keep up my cover. All this lying is exhausting, so I decide to give up, play it straight.

"Look," I say without turning around, "You don't have to believe me, but I wasn't in rehab. I was living with my grandmother in Illinois for three months and then I came back. Now I go visit her. And Anna." It feels good to say her name aloud.

I can hear Sam's footsteps behind me, but he doesn't say anything and neither do I. Once we reach the car, we silently load up our packs and get inside. I turn the key in the ignition and crank up the heat, and then I reach for my iPhone, looking for music.

Sam buckles his seat belt. "Is that why you stayed there for the rest of the semester?" he asks.

I don't look up but I nod.

"Because of Anna."

I inhale sharply when I hear Sam say her name, and I turn to look at him. "Yeah, because of Anna."

"Who lives in Illinois."

"Unfortunately, yeah."

He gives me this *let's hear it* gesture with his hand, and as I back out of the lot and turn onto the two-lane road that heads to the bottom of the mountain, the words just start pouring out.

Omitting details about the decade I visit, I tell him everything there is to know about Evanston, Illinois, and what I do when I'm there. I even give him the history, going all the way back to last March, when I first arrived at my grandmother's house and enrolled at Westlake. A half hour later, he not only knows all about Anna, he knows about Emma and Justin, Maggie, and the Greenes, too. Anna was right. My shoulders are lighter right now than they've been in months.

When we reach the bottom of the mountain, Sam points out a diner that serves twenty-four-hour breakfast, and I pull in and park. I'm just about to get out when my phone chirps. I pick it up and read:

> Miss you here.
> Come next weekend? There's someone
> I want you to meet. :)

"You want to get us a table?" I ask Sam. "I've got to reply to this message."

"From Anna?" he says, like he's enjoying being in the know. If he only knew how impossible that is.

"It's from Brooke. Give me a sec. I'll be right in."

Sam shuts the car door and heads inside. It occurs to me that, as much as I miss Brooke, and as much as I'd love to tell her what happened today, I'm glad I'm not in Boulder right now. I can't remember the last time I wanted to be exactly where I was.

I type the words:

> Miss you too,
> but can't do next weekend (Anna).

A minute later, her reply arrives:

Bummer.

I'm just about to shove my phone in my pocket and join Sam when I have an idea. Anna told me I'd better bring flowers next time, but I can do a hell of a lot better than that. I start typing.

There's someone I want you to meet too.

Wanna come along?

november 1995

27

evanston, illinois

"God, it's freezing out there!" Brooke pulls her leg inside and slams the car door shut again. She tightens her jacket around her body and shivers.

"Actually, I was going to ask you to wait in the car. Do you mind?"

"Are you kidding? We just drove three hours, the last of it in an electrical storm, and now it's, like, twenty degrees out there." It's actually closer to ten but I decide not to tell her that. "I am *more* than happy to wait in the car." Brooke holds out her hand, palm flat. "Keys?"

"What?"

"Keys. Heat. Music." She points at the ignition. "Keys?"

I hand her the car keys and reach behind me to grab the huge bouquet of flowers I bought on the way here. "I'll be over there." I point at the crowd of people gathered in the field surrounded by white pop-up tents. "See the guy in the blue parka? That's her dad. As soon as you see Anna join us, give me ten minutes and then come over. Got it?"

"Got it." She turns the key backward in the ignition, cranks the heat up to ninety, and starts spinning the radio dial, looking for a station. She stops in midspin and shoos me away. "Go. I'm fine."

As I close the door, I hear the gunshot off in the distance and I follow the signs to the starting line. Anna's dad is still huddled up with the other parents, each of them clutching a matching Styrofoam coffee cup in one hand and checking a stopwatch in the other.

I stand in the empty space next to him. "Hi, Mr. Greene," I say quietly, and he turns to face me. I keep the flowers low at my side, but visible.

He studies my face and says, "You're here." Then he looks back at the course and takes a big sip of his coffee.

I shift in place. "Yes, sir. I'm here."

"Anna told me you would be, but I didn't believe her." He looks down at the flowers and brings his cup to his mouth again, tips his head back, and drains it.

"I wanted to tell you personally how sorry I was about homecoming. I would have been there if there was any way, but . . . I . . ." I trail off because I can't find any words that wouldn't be lies.

He stares at me. "Why didn't you call?"

I shift nervously. I'm searching for a way to explain this and still tell the truth, but I'm coming up blank.

"Did you know that she stood there for an hour, in that

dress, waiting for you? And you didn't even *call*. How could you do that to her?" He's not yelling, but I almost wish he would. That would be easier to take than his calm demeanor and the way his voice is dripping with disgust and disappointment. It's almost too much to take. It's almost enough for me to tell him everything, all my secrets, right now, so he can understand why I keep disappearing on his daughter when that's the last thing in the world I want to do.

"I can't possibly explain how sorry I am. I know I . . . let her down." He must hear the genuine remorse in my voice, because his eyes soften, but only for a second or two. He walks away without saying anything else, and I think that's the end of it. But then he drops his empty cup in a trash can and heads back toward me.

The hard stare has returned. "My problem, Bennett," he finally says, "is that you *keep* letting her down. And for some reason her mother and I can't comprehend, she keeps letting you do it." I feel my face contort. I didn't think I could feel more horrible than I did after I told Anna she was a secret.

The crowd starts moving into formation, standing on opposite sides of the bright yellow tape and making a path between the edge of the forest and the finish line. Mr. Greene checks his watch and says, "She should be here in a few minutes."

I think he's going to follow the other parents, but instead he takes a deep breath and turns to look at me. "Look, I'm not going to pretend to understand this thing between you two. She doesn't seem to care that you live two thousand miles away from each other, or that she only gets to see you every few weeks, but I do. It was fine when you lived in the same town, but this is ridiculous. Do you really think you can keep this up?"

I grip the flowers a little tighter.

He gestures toward the finish line. "Here they come," he says, and he walks away from me and squeezes in among the other parents. He's clapping and yelling in a deep, booming voice, even though there are no runners in sight yet. When Anna comes into view, he takes it to a completely different level. I step in to get a better view but keep a safe distance from him.

Three runners emerge at the same time, Anna in third, but tight on the heels of the girl in second. She passes her easily and then kicks it up a notch. Her feet are spinning so fast they're a blur, her arms are pumping hard by her sides, and she has this look of determination on her face that I've never seen before.

"Go, Annie!" Mr. Greene shouts. "Come on! Punch it! Let's go!"

I can see her eyes now, fixed on that yellow tape. She's gaining on the leader, but she's running out of time to close the gap. She's right on her heels, and the other runner speeds up again. Anna barely overtakes her at the very end. She breaks through the tape first and throws her arms in the air.

Mr. Greene is still hollering, but he suddenly stops and presses a few buttons on his watch. "Yes!" he yells. Anna's across the field, doubled over, hands on her knees, until she stands up and starts walking in circles, working hard to catch her breath. She stops next to the girl who almost beat her and reaches out to shake her hand.

Her teammates gather around her, bouncing up and down, blocking her from view. But a few minutes later, she emerges from the pack and I see her looking around, presumably for her dad. He spots her right away, and gives her an enthusiastic wave.

She starts running toward us and I watch him, pacing back and forth, as if it's all he can do to keep from running over to her and picking her up like she was six and not sixteen.

"Did you see that?" she asks. Her dad holds up his hand and she gives him a high five. "Man, I had to turn it on at the end there!" Her shoes are completely covered in mud, and as she gets closer, I can see that everything from her calves on up is speckled with it too.

"That's my girl!" I hear her dad say as he pulls her into a tight hug. She pecks him on the cheek and he squeezes her again, even tighter, and that's when she opens her eyes and sees me standing there. She pulls away from him.

"Hi," she says.

"Hi." I hold out the flowers and her eyes light up. Then she covers her face with her hands and says, "I was totally kidding about the flowers."

Mr. Greene clears his throat and Anna looks over at him and nods once, like she's dismissing him, but he doesn't budge. "Dad."

"Fine. I'll go verify your time," he says, and he leaves the two of us alone.

"Man, your dad's pissed at me," I say as I watch him walk away. My pulse is racing and my hands are still shaking as I hand her the flowers. "I'm afraid these didn't help much."

"Thank you anyway. I love them." She takes the bouquet with one hand and rests the other on my right cheek. "What happened to your face?"

"I scraped it rock climbing." I cover her hand with mine and kiss her palm. "I brought you something else, too."

"Oh, yeah?" She looks over my shoulder, like she's trying to get a glimpse of what's behind my back. "Where is it?"

"In the car. I was hoping I could drive you back home." Anna looks confused, so I keep talking. "I've been thinking about what you said last time I was here, and you were right. You should know my family. And I want them to know you." Her forehead crinkles up and she stares at me. "I'm starting with Brooke."

"Brooke?"

"Yeah. She's in the car." I gesture behind me, toward the parking lot. My face breaks into a huge smile, and I expect hers to do the same, but instead she looks horrified.

"In the *car*? I can't meet Brooke *now*. I'm not . . . I mean . . ." Her shirt is drenched in sweat and her cheeks are dotted with mud. She pulls her hair out of the ponytail, brushes it back off her face again, and puts it back exactly the way it was, but then her eyes grow wide as she stares over my shoulder.

"What's the matter?"

"Hi!" I hear Brooke's voice behind me. I'd forgotten that I told her to wait ten minutes before she got out of the car. I should have told her to wait there until I got her. I should have given Anna more time to get used to this idea. Surprising her with this suddenly feels selfish.

"Hi." Anna looks down at her clothes and shakes her head. "Wow . . . I was kind of hoping to meet you when I was . . . cleaner."

Brooke flicks her wrist in the air, like she's swatting Anna's comment away. "No worries," she says. But then she stands there awkwardly, crossing and uncrossing her arms, while she tries to think of something else to say. "I'm so excited about this road trip. I lived in Chicago for a few months, but I never saw the rest of Illinois."

"There's a good reason for that," Anna says. She lets out a nervous laugh and goes back to staring at Brooke like she's still trying to wrap her head around the fact that she's standing in front of her.

Then Anna's dad returns and I introduce the two of them.

Brooke is bouncing in place as she holds out her hand. "It's so nice to finally meet you, Mr. Greene. Bennett's told me so much about your family," she says. She's still shaking his hand, and Anna's dad looks down, as if he's wondering if she's planning to let it go anytime soon.

"It's nice to meet you," he says, stealing a quick glance at me. "We've heard a lot about you, too. I'm glad to see you in such good health." Brooke's whole face contorts and she starts to say something, but then she looks over at me and I stare back at her with this *Just go with it* look.

She nods and says, "Thanks," and drops his hand. When he looks away, Brooke shoots me a glare.

"There's a local reporter interviewing the team," Anna's dad says to her. He points off in the distance to a white tent with a sign that bears the Illinois High School Association logo. I recognize her coach and a few of her teammates. "You should probably join them." His eyes dart in my direction and then back at Anna. Everything, from the expression on his face to the way his arms are crossed, makes it clear that he doesn't want me here.

"I'll be right back," she says to us, and then to her dad, "I'm going to ride back with them, okay? I'll just go back to the hotel with you so I can shower first."

"What about the store?" He's talking to Anna, but he's staring at me, red-faced and expressionless. I can practically see his blood boiling. He finally looks away and I take a deep breath. "I only need you for an hour," he says to her. "I can't close in the middle of the day."

Then she and her dad exchange a meaningful look, and I have a feeling I've been a subject of a number of tense discussions in the Greene house over the last few weeks. After a few more uncomfortable seconds, he looks back at me, his arms still crossed, his forehead still tight. "She needs to be at the bookstore by three o'clock."

"She will be," I say.

He returns his attention to Anna, pointing at the flowers in her hand. "Do you want me to bring those back with me and get them in water?" His face relaxes and she gives him a grateful smile as she hands them to him.

When they head off to the tent for her interview, Brooke punches me hard in the arm.

"Ow." I grimace. "What was that for?"

"Nothing. Just proving that I'm in good health."

I laugh and rub my arm where she hit me. "Yeah, I'd probably better fill you in on that."

Brooke and I wait out in the car in front of the hotel, and we finally see Anna walk through the double doors. She climbs into the open passenger seat. Her hair is still damp and she smells likes soap.

"All the places we could go in the world, and you want to drive three hours from Peoria to Evanston."

"It'll be fun."

"Fun?"

"Yes, fun. In fact, Brooke and I have designed a trip that will have all three of us in completely new territory for the next three hours. We're taking the scenic route."

"There's nothing scenic between here and Lake Michigan. Trust me."

"Now, that's not true. We're going to pass eighteen lakes in the next hour."

"Really?"

I nod proudly. "I bet you've never even been to Oglesby." Anna raises her eyebrows at me. "No, right? How about Starved Rock State Park?" She's trying not to smile. "Did you even know that rocks could be starved?" I shake my head like it's an impossible idea.

"How do you even know about these places?"

I can't tell her that I've spent the last week researching this trip online, so I joke instead. *"Lonely Planet: Illinois.* What, you haven't heard of that either?"

She just stares at me. "Maybe you should start driving," she says, and I take off for Route 29.

Anna folds her leg underneath her and twists around to face Brooke in the backseat. "So . . . tell me everything about you," she says. For the next hour, they talk nonstop, and I don't even try to get a word in edgewise.

⟨────⟩

I spot a diner that overlooks Fox Lake, and the three of us get out and stretch our legs. Inside, the hostess seats us in a booth with a view of the water, and Anna and I take one side while Brooke settles in across from us.

"Coffee?" our waitress asks as she hands each of us our menus. After a round of "Yes, pleases" she returns with three steaming coffee mugs. Brooke and Anna reach for the milk at the same time and I laugh to myself.

We consult our menus and the waitress returns to take our orders.

"I'll have the special, please," Anna says. I quickly find it on the menu: eggs, hash browns, bacon, toast. "Eggs scrambled, please."

"I'll have the same," I say.

Brooke lets out a heavy sigh when the waitress asks her what she'd like. "I'll have the veggie omelet, but can you make it with egg whites only, please. And no bacon or sausage on the side. Just whole wheat toast. No butter, please."

The waitress stares at her. "Egg whites only?" she asks tentatively, and Brooke nods. "No yolks?" She squints and cocks her head to one side.

"That's right."

The waitress shakes her head and writes it down. "I'll see what the cook can do." As she walks away, Brooke looks at me and throws her hands up. "It's like she's never heard of an egg white omelet."

"You're in nineteen ninety-five," I remind her.

"You're in the middle of Illinois," Anna adds.

I put my arm around Anna's shoulders and she kisses me on the cheek. Our eyes lock on each other's for a moment, and I try to read her expression. "You okay?" I ask.

She thinks about it for a second. Then she nods. "Definitely."

"Good." I give her a small kiss.

"You guys are going to stop that when the food gets here, right?" Brooke says. I reach across the table for a packet of sugar and chuck it at her.

Brooke grabs it in midair and returns it to the container.

"So juvenile," she says, shaking her head. But then she lets out a laugh and presses her palms into the tabletop. "Okay, I can't stand it anymore. I have news."

Anna and I look at each other, and then at her.

"I met someone. His name is Logan and he's from Australia. He has the most adorable accent." She looks especially proud of that last part.

Anna looks at me sideways and leans forward on the table. "Where did you meet him?" she asks, and Brooke's whole face brightens again. She bounces in her seat and leans forward, mirroring Anna's pose. "We met at the Train concert."

I clear my throat. "Watch yourself . . ." I say, and Brooke throws her hands in the air and says, "What? They've been around forever!"

My eyebrows shoot up. "Not as long as you might think."

She sighs. "Got it." She starts again, choosing her words more carefully. "We met at this concert at Red Rocks." Brooke looks at me for confirmation and I give her an affirmative nod. "He's there with a bunch of guys and I'm with my roommates, Shona and Caroline. Shona recognizes one of his friends from a class, and so the two of them start talking, and pretty soon we're all hanging out together, waiting for the show to start. Then one of them asks if we want to sit with them." She stops to take a breath and a sip of coffee.

"Logan sits next to me and we start chatting." She beams. "He loves music too." She leans over toward me. "I was dying to tell him that I'd been to Sydney to see a Maroon 5 concert in two thousand eight."

"Again," I remind her.

"Oh, right." She leans closer to Anna and winks. "The lead singer is *hot*."

I kick her under the table and she laughs.

"So we talk off and on throughout the show, and in the middle of the second set, he leans into me and asks—in this totally cute, kind of shy way—if I have a boyfriend. To which I, of course, say that I do not. And I can tell he wants to kiss me, right? But he doesn't. We keep dancing and brushing up against each other and stuff, but he doesn't make a move."

The waitress arrives and slides our plates across the table. Brooke looks down at her omelet, which looks like a totally normal three-egg omelet, and then looks up at the waitress. "Thank you," she says. She grabs her fork and starts picking all the vegetables out.

"At the end of the night we exchange numbers and say good-bye, and everyone starts walking their separate ways across the parking lot, but then I hear him call my name behind me." She beams. "So I turn around and he's standing there, and he asks if he can kiss me good night. Isn't that sweet?"

She leans on the table and Anna does the same. "He's an unbelievable kisser." I steal a glimpse at Anna. She's wearing a shy smile and the flush is already creeping up her chest again. She reaches for a strip of bacon and takes a bite.

"We went out the next night and get this . . . he lives a block away from me. Can you believe that? We've been inseparable ever since. We ride our bikes to campus together and meet for lunch and we're ridiculously cute." Brooke stops for a breath and takes a bite of her toast. Then she lets out a sigh. "I miss him already."

I look at Brooke and I feel a wave of jealousy. Anna and I will never know what it's like to live a block away from each other. We'll never plan our class schedules so we can ride to school together, and we'll never run into each other on campus and feel giddy when we unexpectedly spot the other one heading our way. It hasn't even been a full day since Brooke last saw this guy; she has no idea what it's like to miss someone.

But if Anna's thinking the same thing, she never lets on. "He sounds great." Then she picks up her fork and says, "I'm starving," as she starts in on her breakfast.

28

The three of us spend the next few hours on the road. We stop at Starved Rock State Park and wander around the trails, looking at the rock formations and waterfalls. Anna doesn't say anything, but she looks exhausted, and it hits me that this probably isn't the ideal time for a hike. After forty-five minutes of sightseeing, I suggest we head back to Evanston and she looks relieved.

When we arrive at the bookstore, it's only two-thirty, and the downtown area is busy. I don't find a parking spot until I reach the next block.

"This is perfect," Anna says as I pull the SUV into a tight space across from the park. "We can stop in the coffeehouse and grab a latte."

We pile out of the car and I feed some quarters into the meter. Inside, we head over to our couch in the corner and Anna and Brooke plop down facing each other. Anna starts telling Brooke about the bands that play here on Sunday nights while I order drinks from the barista.

The three of us sit together for a little while, and I can tell that Anna's stalling. She keeps checking her watch, and finally, when she can't hold off any longer, she says good-bye to Brooke. The two of them hug and exchange a few more words, and Brooke makes me promise to bring her back here again soon.

After Anna's gone, Brooke and I sit a little longer, sipping our coffees and talking about the day. "Mom and Dad would like her," Brooke says.

"Yeah." I let out a huff. "As soon as they get past the part where she lives down the street from our grandmother." I roll my eyes. "And that she goes to the high school our mother graduated from. And that she and Maggie have become close friends. But yeah, as soon as they get past all of that, I bet they'd love her." I set my coffee on the table, lean back against the couch, and fix my eyes on the ceiling. "I have to tell them when I get home tomorrow." My head falls to the side and I look at Brooke. "They're going to kill me."

"No, they won't. They might not get it completely, but what are they going to do? Besides, think about how nice it will be not to have to sneak around." I try, but I've been doing it so long I can't even imagine it.

Brooke tips her head back and takes another gulp, and then sets her cup on the table next to mine. Neither one of us say anything, but we both know it's time for her to go.

She follows me past the barista and down the long hallway

that leads to the bathrooms, and I check the men's room while she stands outside waiting. Once I've confirmed that it's empty, I open the door a crack and wave her inside.

I lock the door and without even saying a word, she reaches for my hands. She shakes her arms out hard like she always does and then kisses me on the cheek. "Thank you so much."

"Any time," I tell her, which isn't entirely true but sounds like the right thing to say.

She shuts her eyes and I do the same. When I open them, we're standing in Brooke's bedroom, right where I picked her up this morning. "I still want you to meet everyone," she says, and I tell her I'll try. Then I close my eyes. When I open them again, I'm standing in the bathroom alone.

I'm not sure what to do with myself for the next hour while Anna's at work. I head outside and start walking in the general direction of the record store when an ambulance turns the corner and flies past me, siren blaring, lights spinning. I'm just about to cross the street when I see it pull to a stop directly in front of the bookstore.

I take off running.

When I reach the entrance, the EMTs are wheeling a stretcher through the door, parting the crowd that's already started gathering outside. I follow behind them.

"Anna!" I call out once I'm inside, but I don't see her anywhere.

I keep following the stretcher as it turns down the Cooking aisle.

And that's where I find her. She's sitting on the ground,

her hands wrapped around her father, who's slumped down against the bookcases, his legs bent at an awkward angle. One of the EMTs reaches out to pull Anna away, but she looks at him with terror in her eyes and refuses to budge. "What's wrong with him?" she cries.

"I don't know," I hear him say. "I need you to move away so we can figure it out, okay? Please."

I can't get to her side fast enough.

When she sees me, she grips her dad's arm even tighter, but I kneel down next to her and pull her toward me. "Come here," I say. My hands are shaking as I reach for hers. "Let them help your dad."

I look over at Mr. Greene. His eyes are wide open, staring straight ahead. But then his head falls slowly to one side and he looks right at me and blinks in slow motion.

Anna's head spins toward me, then back to her dad, and back to me again. Finally she releases his arm and lets me leads her a few feet away. The paramedics lower Mr. Greene to the floor and start working to bring him back from wherever he is right now.

"What happened?" I ask her.

"I don't know. When I got to the store, I didn't think he was here." Her voice is trembling, and she's breathing so hard the words are coming out all choppy. "I walked around for a few minutes and finally found him." She gestures toward her dad. "I don't know how long he's been like this, Bennett. I don't know what's wrong."

Justin must have heard the sirens from the record store

because he bursts through the door, looking rattled as he scans the room. He's clearly relieved to see Anna, but his expression changes again when he spots the paramedic team that's gathered around her dad.

"What happened?" he asks us, but neither one of us knows what to say. "I just found him like this," Anna says. She's crying now, and I keep telling her it's going to be okay, even though I have no idea if that's true.

One of the EMTs stands up and walks over to us. He looks directly at Anna. "We're taking him to Northwestern Memorial."

"My mom works there," Anna says quietly. "She's a nurse." Then she looks at me. "We need to find her," she whispers, and before I can say a word, Justin says, "I'm on it," and takes off toward the phone in the back room.

The EMT pulls out a clipboard and dislodges a pen from the plastic holder. "Were you with him earlier today?" Behind him, the other two paramedics are strapping machines to Mr. Greene's chest and moving him onto a stretcher.

"This morning," Anna says, her voice quiet and weak. "He was fine."

He writes it down. "What time did you see him last?"

Anna speaks louder this time. "About ten o'clock." She looks away, and I don't know if she's thinking the same thing, but I have to ask.

"What would have happened if we'd found him earlier?"

The EMT shakes his head. "We don't know anything yet. I really can't say."

"What would have happened?" I repeat.

"I don't know. You may have seen signs that something was wrong." He looks straight at me. "Look, let us get him to the hospital first and find out what happened, okay?"

The other two paramedics give him a sign, and he snaps the notebook shut and starts moving toward the door. "You can ride to the hospital with us," he says to Anna. To me, he says, "Sorry, family only."

He looks at Anna again and says, "Follow me."

Anna starts to move but I tighten my hold on her. "Ride with me. We'll be right behind him."

The EMT's eyes narrow as he addresses Anna. "You're going to let your father ride alone?"

"We'll be right behind you," I say. The other paramedics pass us wheeling the stretcher to the ambulance, and he gives me a disgusted shake of his head before he follows them.

I push a few gawkers out the door, and the little bundle of bells rings hard as I slam it closed. I snap the deadbolt into place.

As the sirens blare away and the spinning red lights disappear from view, I grab Anna's hand and lead her to the other side of the bookstore. We walk by the front desk, and I spot the flowers I bought her this morning. They're in a vase. In water. Exactly as promised. I take a deep breath.

"We're going back to this morning." Justin's in the back room but I keep my voice low anyway. "Listen to me, okay? We have to go all the way back to this morning—back to the hotel. That's the only time we weren't moving or in plain sight today. I can't time it right otherwise."

Anna doesn't move or say a word.

"We're going back to ten fifteen, right before you left your dad at the hotel. You're going to ride home with him instead and that'll give you three hours to watch him for . . . whatever . . . some kind of sign that something's wrong."

She blinks a few times. "What if we get all the way back and nothing's happened?"

"I don't know, then tell him something's wrong with *you*. Tell him you're having trouble breathing, or come up with an excuse to stop by the hospital and see your mom. Do whatever you have to do to be sure he goes straight to a hospital."

Anna nods.

"Do you remember where he parked the car?" She thinks about it for a minute. "Yeah," she whispers.

She's ghost-white and trembling. "You have to pull yourself together now, okay? Don't worry. We'll fix it." A vision of my battered self, lying in a puddle of blood, stuck who knows where or when, flashes in my mind. I push it away. The side effects don't matter. All that matters is getting Anna back to this morning.

I rest my forehead against hers. I don't even have to tell her to close her eyes. Before I close mine, I think back to this morning and try to lock in a mental image of the hotel and a precise moment I can let the other "me" disappear without disruption. I picture the circular driveway leading up to the hotel where Brooke and I picked Anna up this morning and—

"Brooke." I didn't mean to say it aloud, but I must have, because I open my eyes to find Anna staring at me. I drop her hands and rub my temples with my fingertips. "What will happen to Brooke?" I hear myself say.

She was with me the entire time. If Anna and I go back without her, what happens? Does Brooke disappear too? If she's in the car when I get back, what do I do with her? If she's not in the car, where has she gone?

I have to go back even earlier. I have to go back to this morning, before I picked Brooke up. I take Anna's hands again, but this time, it's not because we have a destination. Without thinking, I start voicing everything that's going through my head aloud. "I'm not sure how to do this. It's not clean, like the others were. It just . . . messes with so many things." I barely have time to get the words out when Justin peeks around the corner and flies down the aisle toward us.

"There you are. I found your mom," he says to Anna. "She's still at the hospital. I'm supposed to take you." Anna untangles her fingers from mine and follows Justin out the door. As he puts his arm over her shoulders, she stops and turns around. I'm still standing exactly where she left me.

"Aren't you coming with us?" she asks.

"Yeah." I stuff my hands in my pockets and follow them, still thinking through the morning in my mind, desperately looking for a loophole.

Justin's car is parked across the street, around the corner from the record store. He opens the door for Anna and she climbs in while I slump down in back. I've never felt so powerless.

When we pull up to a stoplight, Anna points out the window as she looks at Justin. "Would you pull over, please?" Justin drives through the intersection and stops on the next block, and Anna gets out of the car, pulls the bucket seat forward, and climbs in back next to me. She rests her head on my shoulder and whispers in my ear, "I can't let you go back."

I look up at the rearview mirror and my eyes meet Justin's. He stares at me for a moment, and then hits the gas.

29

Mrs. Greene spots us the second we round the corner and step into the ICU waiting room, and all three of us freeze in place as she bolts from her chair and speeds across the room toward us. She's still wearing her uniform.

She hugs Anna hard and then leads her away from us, returning to the chairs in the corner, where she fires questions at her. Anna sounds calm as she fills her mom in on everything that happened, from the moment she and her dad left the house the night before to the series of events that led to her finding him on the bookstore floor.

Justin gives me a look and I give him one back, silently confirming that neither one of us knows what to do with ourselves. He glances awkwardly around the room and I point at a couple of chairs a polite distance away. We spend the next twenty minutes in silence.

Then Justin's parents burst through the door, and that sends the energy level soaring again. "Where is she?" Mrs. Reilly asks as she heads straight for us. Justin hugs her and then points over toward the corner. I wish I didn't have to overhear Anna's mom repeat the same horrible details, but I'm close enough to pick up every word she says and every gasp that leaves Mrs. Reilly's mouth.

I lean over, resting my elbows on my knees so I can cover my ears and at least muffle the sound. I'm just about to go outside and get some fresh air when I hear Anna's voice.

"Do you have a quarter?" she asks as she collapses into the chair next to me. She kicks her legs out straight and lets her head fall back against the wall while Justin and I dig around in our pockets.

"Here," Justin says.

Anna reaches across me to take it and stands up. "I'm going to find a pay phone and call Emma. I'll be right back."

Anna's gone for a full ten minutes, and Justin and I return to our silent state. But then the doctor enters the waiting room and calls out, looking for Mrs. Greene. She stands up and crosses the room. The two of them speak in hushed tones for a moment.

Her mom's head spins in my direction. "Bennett, would you go find Anna?"

I move quickly, out of the waiting room and into the sterile halls, but I don't have the slightest idea where she is. I turn down corridors and double back when they look like dead ends, and I finally spot her at the far end of a hallway, leaning against the wall and playing with the steel phone cord as she fills her best friend in on what happened.

She sees me coming.

Doctor, I mouth, and Anna says something I can't hear before she slams the phone down hard. The two of us speed back to the waiting room.

As soon as she's within arm's reach, Anna's mom takes her by the shoulders and pulls her closer, then waves the rest of us over to her. "Go ahead."

The six of us stand in a semicircle while the doctor explains far too matter-of-factly that Mr. Greene has had a stroke. She goes into detail about the battery of tests they're running to determine exactly what time it occurred and the extent of the damage.

She looks right at Anna's mom, addressing her more like a peer than the wife of a patient. "Strokes are tricky at first, as you probably know. Everything hinges on how long he was out before your daughter found him. When the medical team arrived on the scene, they administered medication that dissolved the clot, but . . ." The doctor trails off and Anna starts twirling her hair around her finger. "Until we can pinpoint exactly *where* in the brain the stroke occurred and how long ago it happened, we won't know about his chances for recovery."

Anna takes a few steps back, as if that's too much for her to take, and I ask her mom if I can take her outside to get some air.

We take the elevator down to the first floor and I steer her toward the entrance. The wind outside blows our hair back, but we huddle close to each other on a cement bench next to a tall ashtray. It smells like fresh rain and stale cigarettes.

"I want to go back." I don't wait for her to answer; I just start running her through the plan I've been concocting since we left the bookstore. "I'll go back to this morning. I'll get Brooke and bring her to your meet, and then I'll tell you what's going to happen with your dad, okay? It'll be fine."

Anna shakes her head. "What about the side effects? Last time you ended up with twenty-two hours you could never account for. What if you try, and instead, we all get knocked back somewhere? Or what if we lose those hours and I don't find my dad when I did? You can't mess with this one, Bennett."

I hear her, but that doesn't stop me from running through the easier scenarios again. If we went back to the bookstore, I don't know what would happen to Anna. If we went back to this morning at the race, I don't know what would happen to Brooke.

"Stop," she says, as if she can tell that I'm still trying to figure out a way to make it work. "Listen. You promised me you'd tell me if you ever lost control. But apparently I need to be the one to tell you." Anna locks her eyes on mine. "You're not in control. You cannot fix this."

My stomach sinks. God, if she only knew how much I want to. That I'd do anything to fix it. But she's right. I can't. There's too much at stake this time. I'm not in control anymore. Not unless I stick to the rules.

Anna presses her lips tightly together and runs her thumb along my cheek. "You aren't supposed to change things, remember?" Then she rests her head on my shoulder. The two of us sit like that for a long time, listening to the sound of the automatic doors sliding open and snapping shut as people pass us on their way in and out of the building.

I tell her I'm sorry a few more times, and she tells me not to be. But I don't tell her what I'm really thinking: If I hadn't come here today, she would have driven home with her dad instead of Brooke and me. She would have had three hours in the car with him. Three hours to notice that something was wrong.

Those three hours should have been his, and I took them away.

Today, after we found her dad in the bookstore, we both went straight to one question: *What if we could do it over?* We never once thought: *What if we hadn't changed anything in the first place?*

⁓

As Justin and I leave the hospital, the wind slaps us hard in the face. We pull our coats tighter around us as we march, heads down, plowing toward the car. He climbs in first and unlocks my door for me.

"You okay to drive in this?"

His shoots me a look and turns the key in the ignition. "Yeah."

And that's the last thing he says for the next twenty miles.

Every time I look over at him, he has this strange look on his face and his fingers are white-knuckled from gripping the steering wheel so hard. We're traveling down Lake Shore Drive, at or just under the speed limit, but the wind packs a wallop. Each time it slams into the side of the car it feels like it's about to wrap its fingers around this lightweight Honda Civic and hurl it straight into Lake Michigan.

I try to make small talk. "I didn't know you had a car."

"I got it over the summer." He turns onto a side street. "It's nice, but it's light. When it starts snowing, I'm going to have to load the trunk with sandbags so I don't skid."

Now that we're off Lake Shore and heading into the wind, the car feels a little less squirrelly. I see Justin's shoulders relax slightly and his fingers uncurl. He takes one hand off the wheel and squeezes the back of his neck.

"I've known him since I was a little kid," Justin says, his voice deeper than usual. "Our parents have played bridge together every other Saturday night for as long as I can remember." He takes a deep breath. "He's so *healthy*, you know? Healthier than my parents. God, he's been trying to get my dad to go running with him for years."

"I know," I say. Of course, I don't know. I've never heard any of this. But I have no idea what to tell him right now.

"This whole thing is just so weird . . ." Justin trails off as he takes another turn, and I resist the urge to say that I'm sure Mr. Greene will be okay, because I have no way of knowing this, and he may not be. The air in the car is thick with tension, and Justin keeps looking at me like it's my turn to talk.

I haven't known Mr. Greene very long. I don't have years of collected stories that substantiate his impact on my life or anything. I just know that I like him, that he's a nice person and a good dad, and that he doesn't deserve to be hooked up to machines right now.

Justin blows a mouthful of air at the windshield. "They say he could be totally fine, and make a full recovery, but I can't help but wonder." When he pulls up to the stoplight, he turns to me. "I mean, I don't know anything about strokes, but it seems pretty far-fetched that there wouldn't be any damage to his brain. He had to have been out for at least . . . what did the doctor think? Twenty . . . twenty-five minutes?"

This is the part I can't think about, let alone talk about. Anna and I were just down the street during those twenty minutes. What if there had been a parking space in front of the bookstore? What if we hadn't stopped for coffee? What if I hadn't come here today?

"I guess we'll know more tomorrow when the test results are back."

"I guess. But man, doesn't it make you wish you had future sight or something? I mean, if we could just *know*, right?"

As the light turns green, he looks away from me, shaking his head as if it's a ridiculous thought.

~

The deadbolt clicks open with a loud *thunk*. I tiptoe inside and shut the door behind me, grateful to find the house is silent and dark, save for the glow of the light that Maggie always keeps on over the desk.

My feet drag across the hardwood floor and it takes far too much effort to lug myself up the stairs. My brain is working overtime, but my body can't wait to fall into bed.

I head straight for the bathroom, where I splash cold water on my face and check out my reflection. My skin is pale and my eyes are bloodshot, lids half closed despite the cold jolt I just gave them. I flick off the light and head back to my room.

I should have insisted on staying with Anna at the hospital, even though the look on her mom's face made it pretty clear that she didn't want me there. For the hundredth time tonight, I picture Anna's expression when she told me I couldn't go back, and I wonder if I'm doing the right thing by not even trying. Especially when I remember how Mr. Greene blinked at me.

But of all the things that happened tonight—of all the things that were said—Justin's words are the ones haunting me and keeping me awake.

He said he wished he could see into the future, with absolutely no idea that *I* can.

I can't fight it anymore, so against my better judgment, I dig my heavy boots out from the back of the closet and step into them, and then I zip myself into my black parka and pull my wool cap low to my brow. I fill my backpack with bottled water and a wad of cash.

I'm not changing anything. I'm not manipulating the clock,

and I'm not doing anything over. I'm observing, just like I've always done. This time, I'm not breaking the rules, and when it's over, no one ever has to know what I did.

The doctor said it would take time and patience; that even if he made a full recovery, it would probably take a year or two. With her words in mind, I stand in the center of my room and close my eyes.

I visualize the yellow paint that's chipping and peeling on the side of the Greenes' house, and clear my head of everything but today's date: November 15.

I pick a time I know he'll be home: six thirty A.M.

And I choose a year in my past, but in Anna's future: 1997.

30

I arrive on the side of Anna's house, exactly where I planned to, and slowly peer around the corner. It must have snowed last night, but not hard. I can still see tiny tips of grass poking up through the thin layer of ice covering the lawn. I feel overdressed in my heavy winter gear.

Peering in the window, I find that the kitchen looks exactly the same—same appliances, same bar stools. I can see the coffeepot perfectly, in the same spot it's always been. I look around, waiting for someone to appear and preparing to duck down fast when they do.

By now, Anna must be away at college, but this is a good time to catch Mr. Greene making the morning coffee.

I hear the front door open and peek around the corner just as footsteps land on the porch. The feet look like they belong to a man, but the door is blocking my view and I can't be sure.

The newspaper disappears and the door closes again. I race back to my spot at the window.

Mr. Greene steps into the kitchen and walks straight for the counter. He unfolds the newspaper, removes a section, and tosses the bulk of it onto the kitchen table.

As he steps away from the counter, I notice the slight limp on his right side. Over at the coffeepot, he treats his right hand like it's cumbersome and in his way, and when he tries to use it to open the bag of coffee he quickly gives up and uses his left hand and his teeth instead.

As the coffee brews, he reaches up into the high cabinet above him and pulls down two mugs. He shuffles over to the refrigerator and returns with a carton of milk.

He's about to bring it back where it belongs when Anna comes around the corner. She rests one hand on his shoulder, takes the carton from him, and puts it away. Then she gives him a quick peck on the cheek, and heads over to the counter for her mug.

Her hair is shorter, hanging loose and just brushing her shoulders. She's wearing jeans and a sweatshirt. It takes me a minute to realize that it reads NORTHWESTERN CROSS COUNTRY and to put the pieces together. Anna still lives here.

Mr. Greene starts off for the pile of newspaper again, and Anna speeds past him and grabs it first. She hands him a section and he folds it in half and uses it to smack her on the arm. She laughs, but I can hear him through the glass as he tells her to stop helping him.

A few minutes later, the doorbell rings, and I look around the corner and find Justin standing on the porch. He's wearing a baseball cap and his backpack is slung over one shoulder. The door opens and Anna yells, "Bye, Dad," before stepping out and shutting it behind her. The two of them head down the walkway toward campus.

I've seen all I needed to see. I close my eyes and bring myself back to my room at Maggie's.

My temples are throbbing. I sit down on the floor next to my bed and reach into my backpack for the water. I down both bottles without stopping, and reach for a room-temperature Frappuccino. When the bottle is empty, I let my head fall back onto the bed and I wait to recover.

I'm in pain, but the symptoms feel more like what I'm used to—a fierce headache and a dry mouth—but no nosebleeds, no piercing sounds, and most important, no losing control of my place on the timeline. I've managed to stay in 1995, successfully go to 1997, and return to 1995 unscathed.

I lie there, picturing Mr. Greene moving around the kitchen, the way Anna helped him, and the way he scolded her for doing so. He's okay. He's not back to normal, but he's alive, capable, and obviously in good hands. And while I know that part of him is relieved that Anna's still living at home, I'm sure that a larger part feels guilty, knowing that Northwestern was never her first choice.

My eyelids are heavy and I can't wait to let them close and drift off to sleep. But just as I start to doze off, something the doctor said tonight jolts me awake again. She said it would be a slow recovery. That it might take years. Her comment makes me wonder what I might have seen if I'd gone forward even farther. Maybe I'd have more solid news for Anna tomorrow.

I stand up and return to the center of the room. I stomp hard until the last of the snow has fallen from my boots. I close my eyes and picture a date in the future when I know Anna will no longer live at home, but will certainly be visiting: Christmas Eve, 2005.

31

I'm at the wrong house.

The driveway is in the right spot. The kitchen window is where it's supposed to be. I walk around to the front of the house and look up toward Anna's window. I'm in the right place, but the house is no longer covered in yellow, peeling paint. It's now painted deep gray with white trim. It looks nice.

It must have been snowing just hours ago because my feet are buried deep in this light, white powder that doesn't look or feel at all like the snow I remember. It covers my jeans, up to my shins, and I can feel my toes turn cold inside my winter boots.

I look through the window. The kitchen looks different too, with fresh paint and new cabinets, new granite countertops and a bunch of new appliances. It could be the work of new owners. But then I notice that the bar stools are exactly the same, and I smile when I think back to the first time I came to Anna's house and perched myself there, carefully studying her for signs of fear as I disappeared before her eyes.

Anna's mom walks in and I duck back down under the windowsill and count to five. Then I peek inside again, studying her as she reaches into the oven and removes a roasting pan. She scurries around the kitchen, stirring pots on the stove and putting rolls in the oven.

I'm starting to get concerned about Anna's dad, when he breezes into the room and sticks his finger into one of the pots. Mrs. Greene slaps his hand with the wooden spoon she just took out of the gravy, and I can practically hear her chide him from here. I can't hear his response, but it makes her throw her head back and laugh.

I watch him walk through the kitchen and into the dining room and notice a slight limp. When he returns he's carrying a silver platter, and he rests it on the countertop. It's hard to see from this vantage point, but his hands appear to be working like they're supposed to.

Then I hear tires slowly crunching their way through the snow. Lights reflect off the snow on the front yard, and I stand still and watch as a car pulls into the driveway. I come out from behind the house and hide behind the large oak tree so I can get a better look. I'm just in time to see Anna step out.

The driver's-side door opens, and someone else comes around the front of the car. The house lights are illuminating Anna's face perfectly, and I'm close enough to see every detail, but he's in shadow, and all I can see is the back of his head.

He casually grabs her hand, like he's done it a million times before. Then he kisses her. He says something that makes her smile at him. My chest constricts and I suck in a breath.

It's a smile I know well. I thought it was the one she reserved for me, but here in 2005, it seems to belong to him.

The two of them walk toward the porch, holding hands. Before they've even hit the first step, Mr. Greene flings the door open wide and scoops Anna up in his arms. She laughs and says, "Hi, Daddy," as she regains her footing.

Mr. Greene turns to the guy and says something I can't hear from this distance. He pulls him in for a fatherly hug, patting him on the back. He releases him but keeps one arm over his shoulder, leading the two of them into the house. The door closes behind them.

I head across the lawn, over to the driveway, and look inside the car for anything that will tell me who he is and where they came from, but the interior is completely clean. I walk around the back of the car and look at the license plate, and spot a sticker from the rental car company in the corner. They flew in from someplace. Or at least he did.

I retrace my footsteps until I've returned to my position under the kitchen window. I must be a glutton for punishment because once I pull myself up into the corner and peek inside, I find myself stuck there. I want to stop watching them, but I can't.

The guy is nowhere to be seen, but I have a perfect view of Anna as she stands in the center of the kitchen, her parents buzzing happily around her. God, she looks incredible. Her hair is long again, and tonight it's pulled back in a clip at the nape of her neck. I can't stop staring.

She's fluttering around the kitchen like she used to, breaking off pieces of bread and dipping her finger into sauces and closing her eyes as the tastes fill her mouth. She turns and says something to her dad, and he starts cracking up.

Suddenly, Anna pivots toward the window and looks right at me. I duck down quickly, out of sight, and everything's quiet for a moment except the sound of my heartbeat, which I'm pretty sure they can hear from inside. I wait for a full minute to pass before I look through the corner of the window again.

Anna's now sitting on the bar stool with her back to me. Mrs. Greene sets a drink on the counter in front of her and I watch Anna bring the glass to her lips.

He's back. The guy she brought home with her returns to the kitchen and walks straight to the refrigerator. Anna's blocking my view of him and I adjust my position, trying to get a better look, but I accidentally tap the windowpane. Anna spins in her seat and I flatten my back against the side of the house.

"I saw it again, Dad." She's far away and muffled, but I can make out her words, and her voice grows louder, clearer, as she cups her hand to the window and speaks. "There's something out there, I swear."

My heart is pounding hard against my rib cage and it takes every ounce of control to remain silent and motionless. She's right there. I want to say something. I want to stand up and look at her face and see how she reacts. There must be something I can say that will make her come outside, put her hands in mine, and let me take her away to a warmer place so we can sit in sand and talk. I need to know who this guy is and what he's doing in her house and why she's looking at him like that. I need to know what happened to us and how we stop it.

I hear her dad's voice, low and clear. "What is it?"

"I don't know, but I swear, I keep seeing something move out there."

"I'm sure it's nothing," he says. "Stay here. I'll go outside and check it out."

I spin in place looking for somewhere to hide, but there's nowhere to go. I hear the front door open and slam closed, followed by soft footsteps on the wooden porch.

I panic and close my eyes.

When I open them, I'm back in my room at Maggie's. I'm sitting on my bed with my head pounding and my stomach sinking, knowing that Mr. Greene found all my footprints, and wondering what happened when he did.

32

The hospital is busier today. I step out of the elevator and into the waiting room, and it takes a full minute for me to spot Anna. I finally see her, sitting in a chair against the far wall, her mom on one side and Justin on the other, holding her hand. Emma is sitting next to him, arms folded across her chest and staring up at the ceiling.

There isn't anywhere for me to sit, but I walk over to them anyway. As soon as I arrive, Justin stands up. "Hey." He gestures toward the seat. "Take mine. I was just leaving anyway." Anna stands up next to him and wraps her arms around his shoulders, and Justin hugs her tightly, eyes closed as he rubs her back. "Call me later, okay? Or even better, come by the store. I'll be there late."

Anna kisses him on the cheek.

"Mrs. Greene?" I hear the voice behind me, and when I turn around I find the doctor from yesterday standing there.

"You and your daughter can see him, but let's keep this visit short."

Anna grabs my hand as she walks past and gives it a squeeze. She and her mom follow the doctor out of the room and I flop down next to Emma. I let my head fall back against the wall. "How's he doing today?"

"Better, it seems. He regained consciousness in the middle of the night. The test results are promising, but he doesn't have any function on his right side." I picture Mr. Greene using his teeth to open a bag of coffee beans. Emma rubs her forehead with her fingertips. "But they think he'll make a full recovery, eventually."

This is good news, but Emma's lower lips quivers and I can tell she's fighting back tears. "Are you okay?" I ask her.

"Me?" She takes a deep breath and brushes her fingers across her cheeks. "I should be asking you that question, Shaggy. You look like hell."

I thought I looked pretty good considering everything I've been through in the last fifteen hours, but then I bring my hands to my face and feel the thick stubble and realize I'm still wearing the same clothes I was wearing yesterday. "I'm okay," I lie.

She takes a deep breath and sits up straight in her chair, looking around the crowded waiting room like she's taking in the ugly furniture and the stacks of magazines piled up on the end tables for the first time. "This is so weird. I've never been in a hospital before. Have you?"

I picture Anna and me sitting in a different waiting room

in a different hospital—one closer to Chicago and the scene of Emma and Justin's car accident—but similarly ugly and equally devoid of anything even remotely cheerful. "Yeah, I've been in a few."

"It's so strange . . . I have this feeling, you know, like I *must* have been inside a hospital at least once, aside from being born in one, but I don't think I ever have. No one in my family has ever been sick and I've never broken a bone or anything . . . Knock wood," she says, bringing her knuckles to the chair's wooden arm. Then she shudders. "This place gives me the creeps."

I never saw Emma after the accident, but Anna told me everything. It's impossible to look at her right now without picturing her in that sterile hospital room, scratched up and stitched together on the outside, broken and still bleeding out on the inside. Emma will never know what I did for her and I'll never want her to.

Emma's eyes dart around the room again and she leans in close. "Can I ask you something?"

"Sure."

She comes in even closer, resting her forearms on my chair. "Do you think Justin has a thing for Anna?"

"Anna?" I don't mean it to come out in such a "*my* Anna" tone of voice, but I think it does. "No. I mean, they're friends. They've known each other all their lives. Anna thinks of him like a brother."

"Oh, yeah . . . of course. I'm not talking about Anna's feelings for *him*—it's all *you* in that department—I'm just referring to his feelings for *her*." She looks around the waiting room. "Never mind. I shouldn't have even mentioned anything. I've just been curious about your opinion and we're here, just the two of us, stuck in this crappy hospital." She taps her bright pink painted fingernails on her jeans. "It was just the way he hugged her a few minutes ago looked a little bit 'more than friends.'" She says the last part with air quotes. "That, you know, combined with the whole near-kiss thing . . ."

My head falls to the side and I look at her. "What 'near-kiss thing'?"

Her eyebrows furrow as she chooses her words more carefully now. "You know. After you left town last spring." She must be able to tell from the look on my face that I'm hearing this for the first time, because she covers her mouth with her hand and pulls away from me fast. "Anna told me you knew. She made it seem like it was no big deal."

She never told me. And it might not have been a big deal. If this conversation were happening yesterday, I might have just laughed it off, but coming in on the heels of what I saw last night, I might be feeling a little too raw for this.

"Justin got a little bit drunk at my birthday party, and I might have been taking advantage of the situation, because I finally decided to come right out and ask him how he felt about her, you know? Just to see what he'd say." I'm not sure I want to hear this, but she keeps talking and I don't stop her. "At first he swore they were just friends, but then he told me that after you left last spring, they were hanging out at the record store together one day and they almost kissed." She shrugs, as if that will make it seem like she isn't bothered by the whole incident, but I can tell by the look on her face that she is.

"But don't get mad. It wasn't Anna *at all*. Justin tried to kiss her—he made that part crystal clear. I mean, if you weren't in the picture, who knows, but . . ."

I flash back on what I saw last night when I went to 1997. How Justin met Anna at her house, and the two of them walked to school together. And then I think about the guy I saw her with eight years later. The guy she kissed in her driveway. I hadn't even considered the possibility that it could have been Justin, but now I can't get the idea out of my mind. I don't think the guy had red hair, but I never got a very good look either. I remember how Mr. Greene wrapped him up in a fatherly hug and led him into the house.

"The whole thing is totally one-sided . . ." She stops and lets out a cynical laugh. "Which should have been my first clue, right?" She matches my posture, her head against the wall, her legs kicked out in front of her. "I'm not quite sure why I'm waiting around as if I'm perfectly content with being his consolation prize."

She starts to say more. I wish she wouldn't. I don't have the energy to think about any of this right now and I have much bigger things on my mind. Before Emma can speak again, Anna and her mom return to the waiting room and sit down in the chairs across from us.

"Nothing new, I'm afraid," Anna's mom says as she twists her hair around her finger and lets out a heavy breath. Then, without prompting, she launches into a story about a stroke patient she worked with a few years ago. I pretend to listen before I shoot Anna a look and thankfully, she understands.

"We'll be right back, Mom," she says, and she grabs my hand and leads me down the hall toward the vending machines. She digs around in her jeans pocket for change. "Want to split a bag of Doritos?"

She's about to slip a quarter into the slot but I stop her. "Wait. There's a coffee shop across the street."

"Yeah?" She covers her mouth as she yawns. "Actually, that sounds good." She tells me to wait by the elevator while she tells her mom where she's going, and she comes back holding her coat. I help her into it.

The coffeehouse is nothing like the one we're used to, far more institutional than cozy, with metal tables and matching chairs. Anna finds a spot in the corner window while I go to the counter to order. A few minutes later, I return with a bowl of soup, a chunk of bread, and a latte.

Anna picks up the bread and turns it over in her hands. "This reminds me of Paris," she says. She gives me a tired smile before she takes a bite. "Sadly, this tastes nothing like *that* baguette." She stares down at the bread, looking disappointed. "I'm convinced I'll never taste anything that delicious again."

I don't respond. In fact, I hardly say a word as she finishes off her soup. But as she's balling her napkin up and stuffing it into the empty soup container, I can't hold it in any longer.

"I have to tell you something," I practically blurt out, and she looks up at me. I probably should have planned out what I was going to say, but I didn't. Now I'm just making it up as I go along and hoping it will make sense. "Remember last night, when we were sitting outside and you told me I couldn't fix this?"

"Yeah."

"Well, I thought of something else I could do."

She takes a sip of her coffee and waits for me.

"I went forward."

She yawns again. Then she says, "I don't know what you mean."

"I went forward . . . into your future. To see what happens to him."

Her head springs up and she goes to set her coffee cup on the table but she loses her grip and it crashes to the table. Some of the coffee splashes over the side, and Anna reaches for her napkin to wipe up the mess. She suddenly stops and stares at me.

"I don't want to know, do I?"

I nod my head. "You do. It's good news. He's going to be okay."

She lets the napkin drop as she puts her elbows on the table and buries her face in her hands. I can't tell if she's crying or laughing or so overwhelmed, she's doing a combination of the two.

"It will take a while. In a couple of years, he'll still walk with a limp and he won't have full use of his right hand, but eventually, he'll be fine."

"Eventually when?"

I look at her. "I'm sorry, Anna. I wish I could tell you that, but I can't."

"No, of course you can't. Okay." She shakes her head hard, like she's scolding herself for asking in the first place. She comes in even closer. "I still can't believe you did this," she says excitedly. "What else will you tell me?"

She takes a big sip of coffee and licks the froth from her lips and I take a deep breath. "I saw enough to know that my coming here is a mistake." There. I've said it. "I'm not supposed to be here, Anna. It's changing your whole life."

She presses her palms into the table to steady herself. "For the better."

"I'm not so sure anymore."

She looks out the window and doesn't say anything. "What aren't you telling me, Bennett? What did you see?" She gives me a hard look.

"I saw you and your family with a happy future. And if I tell you any more about it, it might not happen that way." That's enough. That's all she gets to know. Anything else and I might change what I saw, and I can't do that.

"Well, it's *my* future. I want you in it." Her eyebrows pinch together. "Don't *you* want to be in it?"

I nod. "But think about it," I say, shaking my head. "If you'd been in the car with your dad yesterday you would have known something was wrong. You would have seen the signs and gotten him to a hospital faster. He might not even be here right now."

"Oh, come on . . . he had a stroke. That would have happened no matter what. You didn't do anything wrong."

"I was *here*, Anna. With you. And I shouldn't have been. If I hadn't been here you would have been with your dad."

I didn't expect to feel this way, but the more I talk to her, the more anger I feel building up inside me. I seem to be livid with everyone right now. With Emma, for telling me about Justin and Anna's near-kiss, because I didn't want to know that, especially today. With Anna, for making me think that do-overs were okay, simply because her best friend's life was at stake. With my dad, for letting me believe I was more powerful than I really am. And with myself, for going forward and opening up a view into a future I never should have seen and certainly don't want to exist.

And it's selfish, but I'm angry because it's starting to seem like every time I do something good for someone else, I'm the one who pays the price.

I take a deep breath and steady myself for my next words, the ones that have been rattling around in my head ever since I returned from her house on Christmas Eve 2005. This is it. If I'm going to guarantee the life I saw for Anna, where she's happy without me, I have say it.

"I'm not coming back anymore."

"What?"

I start to reach for her hands but before I can, she pulls them away and stands up. The metal chair tips over behind her and crashes to the floor, and she looks over her shoulder like she's considering righting it, but she doesn't. She turns on her heel and heads for the door, out into the cold.

By the time I catch up to her she's standing at the edge of the curb, waiting for a break in the traffic. "Anna. Please."

She stops and turns around, arms crossed, tears sliding down her cheeks. "You cannot do this!" she yells as the cars speed past us. "You cannot do this to me. You promised you wouldn't leave . . ." Her whole face is bright red and the tears are coming fast now. She tries to wipe her face dry but she can't keep up.

I grab her by the arm, but she pulls it away. "Go!" she yells. "If that's what you want, just go!"

I feel something in me snap.

"What *I* want?" I yell back at her. "What do you mean what *I* want? When is this ever about what I want? I don't have anything—not one single thing—that *I* want. Don't you get it?" In my mind's eye I see Anna, standing in her driveway, smiling up at this guy who isn't me, and I feel the blood coursing hot through my veins.

"See, I get to have this tiny little taste of all these incredible things but I don't get to *keep* any of them. I get to meet you and be part of your life, and I get to know your family and your friends, but I don't get to hold on to any of it. I can't stay here. This isn't my home. And every time I have go to back, it kills me. Every. Single. Time. And it always will."

"Bennett . . ." Anna steps back onto the sidewalk and pushes me away from the edge.

"No, wait. It gets even better." I let out a sarcastic laugh and bring my hand to my chest. "I finally find something that makes me feel good about this thing I can do. I figure out how to *save* people's lives. I get to give a few deserving people a second chance. And that feels really incredible for, like, twenty minutes . . . right up until the second it starts beating the shit out of me."

I let out another laugh. "Oh wait, and here's the best part. The more good things I do, the more I lose the one thing I promised you I wouldn't lose—control. It's like this infinite, totally screwed up loop," I say, spinning my finger in the air.

Anna takes a deep breath and presses her lips tightly together. She's crying even harder now, which should make me feel horrible but for some reason doesn't.

"Check it out," I say, bringing my hand to my chest. "I don't get to have what I want. Not ever. Because the one thing I want is a normal life. I don't want to be special and different, I just want to wake up and go to school and do homework and ride my skateboard in the park with my friends. I want my dad to be proud of me because I got an A on some stupid paper, not because I saved some kids' lives. I want to stare out a window and think about how cool it would be to be able to travel back in time, but I don't want to actually be able to *do* it. And I want to be in love with a girl I can see every day, not every three weeks."

I've been gesturing wildly with my hands but now that I'm done ranting, I don't know what to do with them. I run my fingers through my hair.

"I have to go. I'm sorry." I head back toward the coffee shop, but before I can reach the door, I feel Anna's grasp, tight on my arm.

"Bennett, I'm sorry . . . I didn't mean—"

"What? Didn't mean to talk me into all of this?" The words just slip out, even though I know they're not true, and I turn around in time to see her face fall. That should be enough to stop me from talking, but it isn't. "If you hadn't made me help Emma, I never would have known what I could do. I could have spent the rest of my life going to concerts and climbing rocks in exotic locations, never caring that I was being selfish with my ability, because you know what, it's *mine*. Not yours. Not my dad's. Mine." I slap my chest.

"I know that . . . I never meant . . ."

"I structured my life around a set of rules, and then I broke them for *you*. And for what? So I could be a better person?" I huff in exasperation. "How is my life better because a stranger never broke his leg and five people are alive who probably shouldn't be?"

"What you did was *really* good. And if you were a normal person, we never would have met."

"Yeah . . . well I think that's how it's supposed to be."

She pulls away and looks at me. "You don't really mean that, do you?"

As hard as it is to do, I nod.

Tears are streaming down her face and I can't look at her. I need to get away from here.

"I need to think, Anna. You need to think."

"I don't need to think."

"Well you should, because this is crazy." I remember the words Mr. Greene said to me at the meet the other day. *This is ridiculous. Do you really think you can keep this up?* "Come on, what were we thinking? We can't do this forever."

She wipes her face dry and stares at me.

"I'm going to go back to my real life for a while, okay? I'll come back at Christmas," I say, as if this will make it better. "Your dad's going to be okay," I say, as if this justifies my leaving.

She finds her voice, but it's low and quiet and I have to strain to hear her. "Please stay."

Before she can say another word, I take two steps back until I feel the corner of the building behind me, and without even caring who might be watching, I close my eyes and disappear.

december 2012

33

san francisco, california

I spent the whole drive over here psyching myself up for my performance, but once I walked through Megan's front door it all sort of clicked on its own. It could have been the loud music or the underlying buzz of conversation that carried from one packed room to the next, but whatever it was, I was grateful. I stood in the entryway, looked around, and sucked in the intoxicating scent of holiday cheer and out-of-town parents. I reminded myself that I didn't have to genuinely enjoy being at this party; I just had to play the part.

Now I'm all smiles and backslaps, quick one-liners and snappy comebacks, acting so out of character of late that when Sam sees me, he shoots me this *Who the hell* are *you right now* look. I may suck as a superhero, but as it turns out, I'm a fairly decent actor.

"You're certainly chipper tonight." Of all people, I would

have expected Brooke to see through me, but she must not, because I can hear the bitterness in her voice.

"I am," I lie. "And I'm going to stay in a good mood because it's Christmas vacation and you're home from school and I'm surrounded by good friends and I'm tired of feeling like shit." I smile and take a sip of my drink. "I'm done. From here on out, I'm living in the moment." I raise my glass in the air, toasting no one in particular.

"You were pretty upset last night." I look around at the guys to be sure no one overheard her, but I realize it's impossible. *I* can barely hear her over the music.

I lean in close. "Well then, last night marked the end of my wallowing."

Brooke looks at me and slowly shakes her head. After my parents and I picked her up from the airport last night, the two of us sat in my room talking for a long time. Then I made the mistake of showing her Anna's photo album. We got about halfway through when I had to leave the room, and while she was flipping through pages, I was in the bathroom trying not to hurl. I returned with my eyes burning and my cheeks feeling hot, took the photo book out of her grasp, and smashed it back in the drawer. She never got to see the last picture.

"No offense," Brooke says as she taps away on her phone, "but I'm not sure how much longer I can stand this high school party. Kathryn just texted me to see if I wanted to do something, but—" She looks up at me and stops talking.

"But?"

"Nothing," she says, shaking her head. "I guess I just

thought you might need me around tonight, but you seem to be doing just fine, so . . ." She trails off, looking around the room. "I'm going to go outside and call her. See what's up."

Brooke walks away and I spot Sam and Lindsey hanging out by the fireplace. I'm just about to head over there when the room goes dark.

"Merry Christmas," a voice whispers in my ear. I pull a pair of hands away from my face and turn around. Megan's standing there wearing a red dress and a big grin. She pops one hip.

"It's about time you made it to one of my parties." She holds her arms out wide, palms up, and looks around the room. "See, now aren't you sorry you didn't get to one of these earlier?"

I smile and give her an exaggerated nod. "Truly devastated. I had no idea what I was missing."

"Right?" She keeps coming in closer, shouting to be heard above the music. "And now your life is complete." She rests her hand on my arm and lets it linger there a little too long. When I instinctively take a step back, she gets the hint and lets it drop.

"So, what are you doing over vacation?"

I shrug. "People keep asking me that, but I don't think I have a very good answer."

She tilts her head to one side. "What's your answer?"

"Hanging out," I say definitively, crossing my arms like I'm proud of myself for being so aimless. Megan shakes her head as if she's actually disappointed in me and I shrug. "See what I mean? I'm not shooting very high."

"No, not so much."

I think about the only plan I have. The one I can't tell her or Sam or Brooke or anyone else about. The plan I do *not* want to think about right now.

"Bennett?" Megan is using a singsong voice, waving her hand back and forth in front of my face. "You still here?" she asks.

I blink fast. "Yeah. I'm sorry. What did you say?"

"I said that I'm just hanging out too." She looks down at the ground for a moment, and locks her eyes on mine. "I said, 'Maybe we could hang out together?'"

I don't say anything at first and Megan stares at me, eyebrows raised, expression hopeful, while I consider her suggestion. It's not like I know her that much better than I did at the end of last summer, but I think back to the words I said to Sam in the park that day and feel a little bad about my response. Megan's nice. She's pretty. And from what I've learned about her over the last few months, she's not at all vacuous. Besides, Lindsey's incredibly cool and *she* likes her. I don't know, maybe it's time for me to find a "four of us" that exists in 2012 and not in 1995.

"Maybe," I tell her.

Then we hear a crash in the distance, coming from the kitchen. "Uh-oh, that did *not* sound good. I'd better go find out what broke." She brushes my arm again and says, "See you," before she heads off, pushing past people, fighting her way out of the room.

As soon as she's gone, my stomach clenches. I don't want Megan and I don't want another *four of us*. I want Anna. Here.

Now. So I don't have to wake up tomorrow morning with my chest hurting and my mind all fuzzy, or go to sleep tonight feeling sick because I can't stop picturing that horrible look on her face the last time I saw her.

"Kathryn's on her way." I look up and see Brooke in front of me, her thumbs still tapping against the glass on her phone. "I think we're going to—" She stops cold when she sees me, hand clenched at my forehead, my face turning redder by the second. "What happened?"

I need to get out of here. I need air.

"Do you want to go?" she asks, looking me square in the eyes, and I nod quickly.

Even though it's winter, I still haven't put the soft top back on the Jeep. I've been driving around a lot this way over the last month: top down, cold wind, tunes loud, heat cranked. I maneuver out of the parking space I found a few blocks from Megan's house and drive away.

"Do you want to talk—" she begins and I cut her off with a curt, "No."

Out of the corner of my eye, I see Brooke's thumbs flying across the screen, and I can only assume she's texting Kathryn with her change of plans. I wonder if she's got a cover story or if she's texting her the truth: *Bro's a wreck. Need to stay.*

Her attention must move from texting to music, because as I crest over the next hill, she asks, "How about Coldplay on random shuffle?" It comes out like it's a question, but when Brooke's in the car, I rarely get any say in the music anyway.

Not that it matters. I couldn't care less what we listen to, as long as it keeps her from feeling like the silence is uncomfortable and it's up to her to fill the void.

"Ooh, good song," she says, cranking up the volume. She reclines the seat back and stares up at the sky. I don't know what it is. I just drive, listening to the lyrics.

Can anybody fly this thing?
Before my head explodes or my head starts to ring.

I can feel Brooke turning her head to look at me every once in a while, but I ignore it, keeping my eyes fixed on the road in front of me, tightening my grip on the steering wheel. Our house is only a block away now. It's early. I'm not at all ready to go home. And this song is right. Anna and I have been living life inside a bubble.

"Mind if I keep driving around for a bit?" I ask her.

She kicks her feet up to the dashboard and reclines back even farther. "I was hoping you would. I like this view," she says as she stares out the open roof, into the sky. Instead of taking a left turn toward our house, I take a right toward the Great Highway.

The Ocean Beach parking lot is dark and empty, and I pull into a spot facing the Pacific. I twist the key backward in the ignition, cutting the engine without killing the music. We're quiet for a long time.

Finally, Brooke speaks. "Why are you doing this, Bennett?"

I lean back against the headrest and let out a heavy exhale. "Please don't . . . Not tonight."

Brooke twists in her seat to face me. "On a completely different timeline that no longer exists, Anna came *looking* for you, remember? Because she felt so strongly that you were supposed to be in her life. Doesn't that mean anything?"

I shrug. "I thought it did, but no . . . apparently it doesn't." I haven't looked at the page in my notebook in months, but I don't need to. I've read those words from her letter so many times I've committed them to memory. *Someday soon, we will meet. And then you will leave for good. But I think I can fix it . . .*"

"You're making this far more complicated than it is, Bennett."

"It's very complicated, Brooke."

"No. You saw her with another guy and you freaked."

"I think there's a little more to it than that."

Brooke stares at me.

I fix my eyes on the sky and comb my hands through my hair. "Look, I know what I saw. She'll have a better life without me. Every time I go back there, I'm just keeping her away from the future she's supposed to have."

"But that's not the future she *wants*." Brooke tucks her hair behind her ears and leans across the console. "Besides, what's to say she won't do it all over again anyway? You saw her happy in two thousand five, but when she gets to two thousand eleven she could make the same decision she made last time—to go back and find you again."

"Why, because we're, like, *destined* to be together or something?"

"I don't know. Maybe. Yeah."

"You're just a romantic."

"Maybe. But I'm also quite logical." I let my head fall to the right and stare at her. "What you saw doesn't matter because that future isn't set in stone and you know it. Everything single decision you've made beyond that moment is changing what you saw."

"Or, it's changing nothing."

"If you're not part of her life, you'll never know." Brooke doesn't take her eyes off me. "Go talk to her."

I know she's right. I went more than a month without speaking to Anna once before, and that was excruciating. I can't believe I'm doing it by choice this time. I rest my elbows on the steering wheel and hold my head in my hands. "I will."

"Hey," she says, and I twist my neck to look at her. "Now."

"I'm not going right now."

She cranks up the heat and rubs her hands together in front of the vent. "I'll be fine here. Come back in twenty minutes or so. I'll wait."

"I'm not going right now," I repeat, this time slowly and with more emphasis on each word, because apparently she didn't hear me the first time.

"Bennett . . ." she says, almost under her breath. "Anna's *stuck* there waiting for you." She gives me this sad look, like she's upset about what happened between the two of us. But then she says, "How could—" and stops without finishing her thought. But she doesn't have to say another word. All I have to do is look at her, and even though I've never seen this expression on her face before, I know exactly what she's thinking. She's ashamed of me. And she should be. She's right. How could I have done that to Anna?

I need to go. Now. Besides, I've been missing her like crazy tonight.

Without giving myself any more time to think about it, I grab my wool coat off the backseat and pull my arms into it. Closing my eyes, I picture the one place I know I'll find Anna completely alone.

34

The sun is barely peeking over the horizon when I arrive at the Northwestern University track. Unlike all the times I was here before, there's just a light dusting of snow on the metal benches, and when I take my hand to brush it clean, it flutters into the wind, flying away in all directions.

I see Anna right away. She's down on the track, speeding around the curves, her legs reaching out in long strides, her arms pumping hard by her sides. I don't know what she's listening to on her Discman but I can see her lips moving and that makes me smile.

She comes around the bend to the long edge of the track, facing me, but her eyes are fixed on the ground like she's lost in thought. I don't move, but something must get her attention, because just as she's about to turn the next bend, she steals a glance into the bleachers.

She spots me, but it takes a few seconds for it to register.

She slows her pace to jog and stops at the base of the stairs, squinting up at me like it's totally possible that her mind is playing tricks on her. I lift my hand and wave.

Anna bolts up the stairs, taking them two at a time, but when she reaches the fourth row, she stops and doesn't come any closer. I can tell from the look on her face I should stay where I am.

"What are you doing here?" She takes her headphones off and wraps them around the back of her neck, never taking her eyes off me. "I thought you were coming for Christmas. That's still four days away." Her voice sounds wobbly and not at all like hers.

"So did I. But . . . this couldn't wait."

Anna looks around the track, then back at me. She presses her lips into a thin line. "What couldn't wait?"

"I owe you a massive apology." I brush the snow off the bench next to me. "Do you want to sit down?"

She walks toward me but stops short. Hugging her arms to her chest, she looks down at the icy bench and shakes her head no.

"I just wanted to say how sorry I am about that day . . . at the hospital . . . I was so . . . I don't know why I got so angry."

She sighs. "I wish you'd let me explain," she says quietly.

It's clear from the determined look on her face that she has something important to tell me, so even though I don't think she owes me an explanation at all, I sit quietly and let her speak.

"I didn't mean to push you so hard to do things over. I was

never trying to get you to change your rules or change . . . anything about who you are. That's the last thing I'd ever want." She plays with her fingernails as she shifts her weight from one leg to the other. "I guess I'm just . . . fascinated. Not just by what you can do, but by . . ." She looks out toward the track and covers her face with her hand. "Wow. I thought I had a few more days to get this speech down. This really isn't coming out the way I thought it would."

It feels strange to be this close and not touch her. I lean forward onto my thighs and smile at her. "I think it's coming out fine." She slides her hand down but keeps her mouth covered. Still, I can tell from her eyes that she's smiling too.

"Go on. . . . You were saying something about being fascinated." I scoot a little closer to her, but she keeps her feet planted in the snow and starts fidgeting with her headphone wires, wrapping and unwrapping the cord around her finger.

And suddenly, she stops moving and looks straight at me. "I'm in love with everything about you."

Her words make me suck in my breath, and when I look into her eyes, I see something I haven't noticed in a while—this look of pure understanding that reminds me why I told her my secret in the first place. That sense of wonder, how she looked at me like she couldn't know me well enough.

I can't take the distance any longer. I scoot over on the bench and the snow collects on my jeans. "Come here." I pull her closer, parting my legs so she can stand in between them, and she rests her forearms on my shoulders and looks down at me.

"I shouldn't have pushed you so hard to do things over again. I mean, I'm glad Emma's okay and I'll always be grateful to you for making that happen, but . . . it was wrong of me to force you to do it."

"You weren't wrong and you certainly didn't force me to do anything." My fingers settle on her hips. "I was as curious as you were, and I knew what I was doing. I *never* should have blamed you. I was just angry."

"At me?" she asks.

"No. At myself."

I grip her hips a little bit tighter and let my head fall forward until it rests against her stomach. "You know what I've been thinking lately?"

"Hmm?" Her fingers find my hair and I close my eyes. I've missed the way she touches me.

"I wish I could fly."

Her stomach rises when she laughs. "You want to fly now too?"

"No," I clarify. "Not in addition to, instead of."

"Why would you want to fly?"

I keep my eyes focused on the ground as my thumbs trace slow circles at her waist. "No one ever said, 'You really shouldn't fly' or 'Think of all the problems you could cause if you could fly,' right? You cruise around, check out the view, and come back down. Great power, none of the responsibility."

"I have a feeling you'd be bored just flying around all the time." I'm still looking down at our feet, but I can hear the smile in her voice.

"Maybe. But I also wouldn't have to worry about inadvertently changing the past. Or accidentally bumping into another *me* and sending the younger one back where he belongs."

She combs her fingers through my hair again. "You liked it, didn't you?" she asks. "The do-overs."

I pull my head away so I can see her face, and her hands settle on my shoulders again. They feel good there too. She takes another small step closer.

"Yeah . . . I did. I liked what you said about second chances. For a while there, it almost felt like I was supposed to do it, you know? It felt . . . almost . . . right." I shake my head. "I'd do it again. I'd go back for Emma and those kids. If I could have helped your dad, I would have."

Anna lifts my chin up and forces me to look at her. "You did help."

I don't say anything.

"Is he the real reason you don't think you should come back here anymore?"

I nod, even though he's only part of it. "I don't think this is right."

"For you or for me?"

"For everyone." I try to block out the vision of her in the driveway ten years from now, looking up at a guy who isn't me but makes her smile the same way I do. "But, I guess, especially for you."

She lets out a heavy sigh. "You seem to think you're somehow responsible for my future." I start to respond but she puts her finger to my lips. "Listen to me. Please, don't say anything. You are not responsible for my future, Bennett."

Sure I am. It would be totally different if I'd never come here.

"It's mine."

Yes, and you deserve a simpler one.

"And I want you in it."

You shouldn't even *know* me.

She looks over my shoulder, staring into the distance. "I don't know what you saw when you went forward, and I have a feeling you're never going to tell me. And that's fine." Now she looks right into my eyes. "Stop coming here if you think it's wrong for you, or for, I don't know, the space-time continuum or something, but don't stop because of me. From the beginning, you've made this all about how you were affecting *my* future. But I'm affecting yours, too. This time it's *your* choice. What do *you* want?"

I say the first thing that pops into my head. "You."

Her eyes light up. "I'm glad to hear that."

"But it's not that simple."

"Why not?"

"Because it's not."

She brushes my hair off my forehead and plants a kiss there. "I want you to be part of my life. When you weren't in it, I went to great lengths to get you back. So here we are." She spreads her arms out to her sides and looks around the track. "But who's to say what happens next? Maybe a year from now, we'll both be off at college and we won't want this anymore. Or after five years of this, we'll get tired of all the distance or the uncertainty . . . you'll get tired of zapping back and forth, or I'll get tired of waiting for you, or maybe the whole thing will become too much to handle. But right now, we both want to be together. Don't you think we should be?"

I stare at her. "I told you, it's not that simple."

"Sure it is." She runs her thumb across my cheek. "In fact, let's make it even simpler. I don't need a calendar. I don't care if you're here for big events or how long you stay each time. I just need to know that you're coming back."

I reach up for one of her curls and wrap it around my finger, thinking about how easy this all seemed back at the beginning of the school year. I remember that day we sat on my bed, surrounded by my new posters in a room that was starting to feel a lot like home, and built a schedule. God, how cocky I was, thinking I had it all figured out and that nothing would stand in the way of us being together as long as that's what both of us wanted.

"Will you think about it?" she asks.

I look away from her and nod.

"Don't do that," Anna says.

"What?"

"I can always tell when you're lying. You don't look at me."

I lock my eyes on hers. "I'll think about it," I say. And I will. But I know I won't change my mind.

35

Physically, I'm here in San Francisco. But all morning I've been mentally absent, my thoughts constantly wandering to Christmas 1995. Ever since I saw Anna at the track, I've been trying to bring myself to go back there, but I just couldn't. Now that it's Christmas here, the whole thing feels unavoidable.

Dad reaches under the tree and makes a big production of reading the tag on the last gift. "To Brooke from Bennett," he says, tossing it high in the air.

Brooke catches it with both hands and shakes it hard for clues. She's already grinning as she rips off the paper, but a huge smile spreads across her face when she peeks inside. "No way." She looks up at me and starts pulling out each of the ten "vintage" concert tees, one at a time. In case my parents are getting suspicious as they watch her, I describe how I found them online, but when Brooke looks at me, I shoot her a wink.

She hugs the *Incubus 2007 World Tour* T-shirt to her chest. "I love them," she says. "Thank you."

Mom tries to pass me this plate of sticky-looking pastries for the third time, and once again, I hold my hand up to block them. She tips her chin down and gives me her concerned parent look. I haven't eaten much over the last few days and Mom's starting to notice, so I grab the plainest-looking thing on the plate.

"Well, I think that's everything," Dad says, taking one last look around the base of the tree. He stands up, straightens his back, and transfers the fluffy ball on his Santa hat from one shoulder to the other like it's a mortarboard tassel. "Christmas gift exchange 2012, officially complete," he says with his hands on his hips. Brooke tosses a wrapping paper ball at him and it bounces off his forehead.

"I'm going to go buy some music," I say, holding up my new iTunes gift card as evidence, and Brooke gives me a knowing look. She's already agreed to cover for me if she needs to, but that doesn't mean she's happy about it.

I start gathering up my gifts as Mom heads for the kitchen with a handful of plates and Dad follows her carrying a trash bag filled with used wrapping paper. Out of the corner of my eye, I see Brooke staring at me from the other side of the couch. As soon as I have everything, I head for the staircase. I'm at the first step when I hear her say my name, but I shake my head and keep climbing without turning around. What's the point? She'll just try to talk me out of this again.

When I'm showered and dressed, I dig around in the back of my closet, feeling for my backpack, and do one last round of inventory. There are water bottles, coffee shots, and Red Bulls; Kleenex and a spare T-shirt, just in case; and down on the bottom, Anna's photo album. I pull it out and thumb through it, feeling sick when I think about giving it back to her. But I can't keep it here.

I stuff the album back inside and toss the pack over my shoulders. There's no reason to stall any longer, so I picture the side of Anna's house, where the yellow paint is peeling and flaking off, and I close my eyes. But before I can leave, they spring open again.

And there it is, this ridiculously stupid thought. Not only is it stupid, it's also risky and more than a little bit pathetic. But this is my last trip for who knows how long, and I haven't been able to stop wondering about the guy she was with that night. And knowing who he is might give me some peace. I could use a little peace.

I squeeze my lids tight and before I can talk myself out of it, I open them to a view of a house painted gray with white trim.

After a quick look around to be sure I'm alone, I peer through the kitchen window. Inside, Mrs. Greene is in the exact spot, wearing the exact same thing, making the same meal she was making last time I showed up here in 2005 and shouldn't have.

I'll stay five minutes. Ten tops. Just long enough to catch a glimpse of him.

I check the driveway and find it covered in a layer of snow but otherwise empty. When I return to the window, Anna's mom is still standing at the stove, and I watch as Mr. Greene sneaks up behind her and wraps his arms around her waist. He gives her a quick kiss on the cheek, and she smiles and squirms away, swatting his hand with her wooden spoon. He laughs and kisses her again. Then he walks over to the sink and looks out the window that faces the street, like he's waiting for someone to arrive.

She should be here any second now. I listen to the sounds of the neighborhood, but there's nothing. It's totally silent.

"You need something to do." Unlike last time, the window is open a crack and I can hear everything the two of them are saying. Mrs. Greene walks to the drawer by the refrigerator and removes some silverware. "Here," she says, handing it to him. "Set the table. My goodness, you're like a little kid."

"Leave me alone, I'm excited." He walks into the dining room and he's out of my sight for a good minute or two. He returns empty-handed.

"Did you get the glasses, too?" she asks.

"Not yet, but I will." He pulls four water glasses down from one of the upper cabinets, and returns for four wineglasses. "Don't you think it's fundamentally wrong to have to take a plane to visit your family?"

Anna's mom laughs loudly. "Yeah, you should have thought about that when you hung a map of the world on her wall and gave her a box of pins to mark all the places she'd go." He shrugs and carries the glasses to the table, and I watch Mrs.

Greene stir whatever she's got in the stockpot. "You should have known she'd never stay put," she says, more to herself than to him.

I picture the map that hung on Anna's wall, briefly wonder if it's still there, and before I know it I'm closing my eyes and opening them in her bedroom. Her room is dark and I have to blink a few times as my eyes adjust, but then I spin slowly in place, taking everything in.

The dimensions are the same, but nothing else is. Anna's shelves are gone, and with them, the trophies and CDs they held back in 1995. There are no more race photos or numbers, and no more travel guides peppering the surfaces of her furniture. The map is gone and so is the box of pins. All the things that mattered in Anna's sixteen-year-old life aren't important in her twenty-six-year-old one, at least not in this house.

The bed has been moved to a different wall and it's covered with a different bedspread. I slowly walk over to it and sit down, running my hand across the surface, wondering if they share this room when they visit. He probably doesn't have to sleep on the couch like I did. I bet he gets to linger here with her in the morning, not sneak out before the sun comes up. Do they unpack their clothes and hang them side by side in the closet? Does Mr. Greene pour him coffee in the morning?

Coming to this room was a bad idea.

I stand up and close my eyes, returning to my spot under the kitchen window. I wonder why it's taking so long for them to get here.

As soon as I open them, I hear tires slowly crunching their

way through the snow, so I peek around the corner and then creep over to the tree, just like I did last time.

The headlights are still a few houses away, but Mr. Greene must have heard the car too, because the front door suddenly opens and he steps out onto the porch. He heads down the front stairs and waits at the edge of the driveway, fidgeting with the buttons on his sport coat.

My pulse is racing as the front of the car comes around the hedge and two streams of light illuminate the snow-covered lawn.

～⌐

I think I yell.

I feel my stomach knot up tight and my head feels like it's going to explode. My eyes are burning, and without even thinking about it, I squeeze them shut. And when I finally peel them open, I'm standing right where I was when I left— smack in the middle of my bedroom in San Francisco.

I stumble over to the bed and sit down. I'm shaking and sweating, but when I look around and realize what just happened, I start laughing loudly and uncontrollably. It makes the headache a hell of a lot worse, but I can't seem to stop.

I'm back.

I'm shaking and sweating and laughing and . . . back.

I stand up, touching my face, my legs. I stomp the Evanston snow off my feet and watch it collect on my San Francisco carpet. I turn a three-sixty in place.

I'm back.

I was *knocked* back.

And there's only one reason that would happen.

Anna is part of my future and I'm part of hers. And that's all I needed to know, even if there are a million big and little things that could go wrong between now and then.

My backpack lands on the bed with a bounce, and I rip open the zipper, down a bottle of water as quickly as I can, and then dig to the bottom. When I find Anna's photo album, I toss it on top of my bedspread where Mom or Dad could easily find it if they happen to come in while I'm gone. There's no reason to hide it because Anna won't be a secret here anymore. I'll keep most of the promises I made to my parents—no more sneaking around, no more lies—but that "no more traveling" one isn't going to stick after all.

The Doubleshot makes me grimace as I gulp it down and I chase it with another bottle of water. I return to the center of the room and shake out my arms. My legs still feel wobbly as I close my eyes.

36

Anna's house is the color it should be in 1995.

Without giving myself time to process any more information than that, I race around the corner, fly up the front steps,
and knock hard on her front door. My mouth is still dry and
my head is a little foggy. I can feel the sweat on my brow
even though my shoes are covered with fresh snow. But when
the door swings open and I see Anna standing there, I forget
everything else.

My heart is pounding hard in my chest. "Hi," I say, combing my fingers through my hair.

"Hi." She steps onto the porch and pulls the door closed
behind her and I take a few steps back to give her room. She
stands in front of me, looking confused, like she's trying to
register the expression on my face but can't. She wraps one
arm across her body and grips her elbow.

I don't know where to start. I have absolutely no idea what

to say right now. All I can think about is that ten years from now, the two of us will be in the same car, driving back here, walking up these steps and onto this porch, together. I look at my feet because I can't look at her and piece the right words together at the same time.

"Please say something," Anna says, letting out a nervous laugh. "You're killing me here." Her voice catches.

I lock my eyes on hers. "I was wrong," I say, and tears start sliding down her cheeks, one after the other. "I was convinced that I wasn't supposed to be part of your future but I think now . . . that I am."

Her lips are pressed tightly together and she nods quickly as she brushes her hands across her face. "Of course you are," she says. And then she looks at me, tears still streaming down her cheeks, and smiles. *That* smile. My smile. It belongs to me again.

I take two steps forward and throw my arms around her neck, lacing my fingers through her curls and breathing into her hair. I feel her bury her face in my T-shirt and wrap her arms around my waist. She squeezes me so tight, pressed in as close me to me as she can get. We stand like that for a long time.

I don't know if I was wrong. I might be wrong now. But my gut feels right for the first time in over a month and apparently I'm going with it, ignoring the risks and the questions and the consequences. Again. How can I *not*?

The wind is biting and when I finally step away from Anna, I discover that her cheeks are as red as the sweater she's wearing. I kiss each one. And then I take her face in my hands.

This kiss feels completely different from all the others. It's not like the one at the track the other day, when I was trying not to give her false hope. And it's nothing like the one when I first came back to town, back when I was all euphoric and full of conviction, certain we could make this work regardless of the considerable odds stacked against us. I'm kissing her like I've just returned from a long trip and I'm deliriously happy to be back home.

I rest my forehead against hers. I can't hold back my smile.

"What made you change your mind?" she asks.

I give her the only answer I have. "You. In a bunch of different ways."

We kiss again, and this one feels a lot more familiar. I picture her room upstairs, looking like it's supposed to, and I can't wait to be alone with her there.

When Anna pulls away, she hardly leaves any distance between us. "It's freezing out here," she says, brushing her lips against mine. "Come inside." Another small kiss. "Besides, you have presents to open."

Presents. Plural. I only brought her one thing. "Presents?" I ask.

She kisses my cheek. "I got you something. My parents got you a couple things too." I pull back a bit more. Her parents? It didn't even occur to me to buy them gifts. "Don't worry," she says, reading my mind. "They don't expect you to get them anything."

Anna moves toward the front door and I trail behind her,

but when she opens it and steps inside, I stop cold.

She turns around and stares at me. God, she looks happy and relieved and beautiful and perfect as she stands there, waiting for me to follow her. I must have a stupid grin on my face or something because she suddenly smiles at me. "What?" she asks.

I shake my head. "Nothing. I was just thinking about the first time I came over here." We'd both cut school. I'd stood on her porch in this exact spot, and Anna stood inside in that exact same one. When she opened the door I'd been expecting her to be afraid of me after I'd inadvertently shown her what I could do, but instead, she was all giddy and curious, eager to hear how I performed the magic that might have saved her life the night before.

But there was something else in her expression that day. She wanted to *know* me—really know me—and I stood frozen in place, realizing that I wanted her to be the person I told all my secrets to.

I knew it wouldn't be simple. That if I walked through that front door and into her world, both of our lives would be changed forever. Still, she seemed worth the risk. Now I know that she is.

So just like I did that day, I take a deep breath and step inside. Anna closes the door behind me.

I'm not supposed to be here.

But I am.

acknowledgments

This book wouldn't have been possible without the unconditional love and support of my husband, Mike. He made sure I didn't forget to eat, knocked that super-daddy thing clear out of the park, and still found time to read this story and give me feedback. He's the love of my life and stuck with me forever; we even have a padlock on *Pont des Arts* to prove it.

I absolutely love writing, but it occasionally takes me away from my greatest love: my kids. I'm grateful to Aidan and Lauren for allowing me to be both a writer and a mom, and for understanding that it's difficult to excel at both at the exact same time. My world revolves around these two incredible human beings and I wouldn't have it any other way.

Boy, has my family turned into a bunch of vocal fans! I don't even know where to start thanking them for all their words of support and encouragement. To the many, *many* members of the Ireland, Cline/Reinwald, and Stone families: Thank you with all my heart. You've made the last year such fun.

My friends have simply blown me away with their kind words and constant support for this new endeavor of mine. Special thanks to Jennifer Fall who inspired me with her story about the love locks.

When I wrote *Time Between Us,* I got to reflect back on my days living in Evanston, Illinois. Writing *Time After Time* took me back even earlier, to living in San Francisco post-college, when six amazing women magically appeared in my life. You're sprinkled throughout these pages, Sonia Painter, Renée Austin, Shanna Draheim, Marie Bahl, Kristin Wahl, and Lynette Figueras Spievak. We were meant to be friends. San Francisco is *our* city. And yes, we are the funniest people we know.

A year ago, I was clueless about the book blogger community, but now I get it. These passionate readers make our worlds go 'round, and I am incredibly grateful for all they do to spread the word about books—not just *my* books, *all* books. Still, to those of you who consistently shout from the rooftops about my stories, I'm humbled. Thank you. I'm equally grateful to the wonderful booksellers at my local indies, Books, Inc.; A Great Good Place for Books; Book Passage; Barnes & Noble, Walnut Creek; and Orinda Books for all their support.

So many people in my life have expertise I require for my stories and don't actually possess. Huge thanks to Mark Holmstrom for continuing the rock climbing lessons, and to Dr. Martin Moran and Dr. Mike Temkin for helping me understand yet another medical condition I knew nothing about.

My agent, Caryn Wiseman, not only represents my work with passion, she patiently brainstorms with me, reads draft after draft, and keeps the encouragement coming when I need it most. Thank you, Caryn.

I'm always grateful for my brilliant editor, Lisa Yoskowitz. I'm not sure other authors get to laugh their way through revisions, but I do. Thank you for loving these characters, for caring so much about every single word, and most of all, for just being Lisa-y.

It's such an honor to be part of the Disney-Hyperion family. Huge thanks to the entire team, and special thanks to Stephanie Lurie and Suzanne Murphy for believing in these two books from the very beginning, to Whitney Manger for creating another gorgeous cover, and to my wonderful publicist Jamie Baker.